Jeannie H Grey

Tactics

Jeannie H Grey

Tactics

ISBN/EAN: 9783337105518

Printed in Europe, USA, Canada, Australia, Japan

Cover: Foto ©Andreas Hilbeck / pixelio.de

More available books at **www.hansebooks.com**

TACTICS:

Or, CUPID IN SHOULDER–STRAPS.

A WEST POINT LOVE STORY.

By HEARTON DRILLE, U. S. A.

" Essayons."

NEW YORK:

Carleton, Publisher, 413 Broadway.

M DCCC LXIII.

DEDICATION.

Beneath thy standard, flag of our great Union,
With symbols fair, — the crimson and the white —
Of purest love, and brotherly communion,
Whose stars benign, illumine our dark night,
Where rush the cohorts like a mountain torrent
From every sacred niche in our broad land —
Washing away in blood, the stain abhorrent
On fair Columbia cast, by traitor-band —
Where gather sister, sweetheart, wife, and mother,
Like the true Marys at the holy cross,
To offer father, husband, lover, brother,—
If saved their country, counting gain their loss,
Come Love and I to thy beloved altar —
Dear " Flower Flag," thy graceful folds to hail
As our Palladium, and our Gibralter —
And humbly dedicate to thee our tale.

For the appropriateness of the following beautiful extract from "John Phœnix" as a fitting prelude to this work, I appeal to my readers.

"Il frappe toute (autres) chose parfaitment froid."

"It does not depend for its success upon its plot, its theme, its school, or its master, for it has very little *if any* of *them*," but upon the forbearance of a magnanimous Public.

"With unbounded respect for everybody,"

The author remains,

HEARTON DRILLE.

ATTENTION!

T A C T I C S.

TITLE FIRST.

ARTICLE FIRST.

Formation of a Regiment.

"VIOLETTA, I have just received a letter from my niece, and look for her here on the 7 o'clock train this evening."

Mrs. Lieutenant Bobaline opened her large brown eyes uncommonly wide in reply to her husband.

There was a little fluttering in her throat, and she asked " Who ? "

" Did I not mention it to you? A letter came some months ago from my sister in San Francisco, saying her eldest daughter would like to visit us. I answered it immediately, and told her to come, and had nearly forgotten the affair, when yesterday's mail brought the news, that she will be here this evening, probably."

A pause : — rather embarrassing to the placid mind of Lieutenant Bobaline, while inditing a letter of importance, and he glanced anxiously at his beautiful wife, adding " I thought it quite providential, as I am to be away from you so long, and was sorry to leave you alone." His voice grew very tender.

Violetta smiled, and he was encouraged to proceed.

Isagone will be society for you ! " He said briskly.

" What is her name ? "

" Isagone Smith."

" Ha ! ha ! what ? " broke nervously from the lady.

" Isagone Smith ! I don't see anything so very funny in it." He said gravely.

"Oh, Adelbert! Isagone Smith not funny?" and she smothered something between a sob and a little scream, in her handkerchief.

Lieutenant Bobaline though usually invulnerable to the sly shafts of his pretty wife, now looked wounded and left the room. Mrs. Bobaline was very greatly astonished at the coolness, as she thought, of her lord's announcement of such shocking news, for she was quite unprepared for the presence of such a stranger in her family.

Mrs. Smith was the only sister of Lieutenant Bobaline, from whom he had been separated for many years. The chord so long silent, vibrated at the first touch, and he was almost childish in his desire to see his sister's daughter.

He had often spoken of this sister to his young wife, but never of his niece, because he knew nothing about her. Mrs. Smith married while very young, a restless, enterprising man ; consequently he was scarcely at home in one locality, before he bore her away to antipodal regions, till at last he left her a widow, in comfortable circumstances, in the gold country. Lieutenant Bobaline had never seen her since he was a boy. His father and mother died before he was old enough to choose a profession for himself, but he was given to the care of a maternal uncle, who brought him up in a very thorough manner, and procured him an appointment at West Point. The letter concerning Isagone was the first intelligence he had had, in many years, from his sister, and thus it came to pass, that the gay married belle at West Point, had lived, and lost the pleasure of hearing of such a funny name as Isagone Smith.

Several hours later, Mrs. Bobaline sat at the parlor window, looking out on the mist and rain, when the omnibus drove to the hotel door. A slight figure emerged from it, and the gleaming of the hall lamp revealed a lady in a travelling suit of green, and a straw hat drawn tightly down with a green veil. Lieutenant Bobaline stepped hastily forward.

"Isagone?"

"Yes, uncle!" said a low voice.

He kissed her, and drawing her arm affectionately through his, led her into the hall, and up stairs into his own rooms.

The crowded hall and parlors, quite stunned the young girl; and when she was shown into a room lighted only by a coal fire, and found herself alone, she sank on a chair in front of the grate, whose glowing coals threw the rosiest of tints over the pleasant apartment.

Nearly benumbed with cold and fatigue, she sat staring into the fire slowly pulling off her gloves, when pattering feet and a glare of light, set her heart in wild commotion, she so dreaded to see her aunt.

Lieutenant Bobaline handed his lady in, in a ceremonious manner "This is Isagone; Mrs. Bobaline. Kiss your aunt, Isagone, and be a good little girl to her, as I am ordered away immediately, and you must be her guardian angel till I return."

Miss Smith timidly touched the delicate cheek, and very gently squeezed the tiny finger tips Madam offered her.

Mrs. Bobaline looked curiously at the shrinking girl, as she unbonneted, and was secretly pleased to see only a meek little face, with a pink sea-shell complexion, quite a contrast to her own brilliant style.

Mr. Bobaline assisted his niece in a business manner, to show that she was welcome, while his wife walked the floor like an actress, or hurried about the room in an aimless way wondering what that little "angel" was sent just *now* for; she had not reckoned on being at all lonely, she was in no need of a "guardian angel," or of a spy on her every act, either. She sat down and looked appealingly at her husband. He understood her look.

"Adelbert, am I expected to stay up here all the evening and entertain this *child*?" His conjugal heart was touched, and he said "Viola dearest, order some supper up here for Isagone, as she is weary, and then she can retire when she pleases." Viola was delighted, and descended the stairs with a light step, glad to escape even for a short time from her own thoughts on this new and unwelcome responsibility.

Poor Mrs. Bobaline, the evening is gone,— and where is the parley of the soul, she had promised herself? The evening was gone,— and she had only once thought of the little intruder into her pretty boudoir, and her kind lord whom she had left so abruptly to amuse the rural maiden, as she mentally denominated Isagone — smiling to think she should certainly find no rival in her.

The saloon was a brilliant scene, there was music, and dancing, and great merriment, but Viola's eyes roved out of windows, and doors; — she had been "cracking her eye-strings," to catch a glimpse of one, who was not giving a thought to her,

> " So fondly we ourselves deceive,
> And empty hopes pursue ;
> Though false to others we believe
> They will to us prove true."

The foot-steps she listened for came not. Her fancy had taken the reins, — not nice in a dignified, high-bred wife, to allow it. She often boasted, "my husband far outshines every other officer on the post, in feature, form, and soul." Yes, but Mrs. Eve, you have been strolling out at eye-gate, and tasted the sweets of flattery,— poisonous sweets! Ah, Lieutenant Bobaline! your romantic Viola had listened to your low thrilling tones, and high thrilling sentiments, until her warm young imagination had veiled her Mars in a luminous zone, which you had dissolved by becoming a little too matter-of-fact — a little matter too soon, — when once the possession of the coveted object was " à fait accompli ! " Why not have permitted the bright tissue to screen the irregular and variable spots of La Vie by its varying brilliancy?

Mrs. Bobaline sought her own room, with a sick heart — weary with self-condemnation, and the humiliation that follows it. She stopped at her own door, and wished that Isagone was gone to her mother, safely, snugly, lodged in

her maternal arms, in San Francisco — nothing wicked in
that. Alack! there she was — incarnate! She had retired
" when she pleased " and was now sleeping — timorously
— as if conscious that unloving eyes rested on her face,
and a little double-and-twisted sigh escaped through her
parted lips, — then came a light over her face — a smiling,
speaking look, as if she were back again in the nest-full of
warm young hearts, throbbing with kindred love for her.
Alas, they were far away! and would wait her coming
for many a weary day. Mrs. Bobaline gazed long and
curiously at the fair childish face, then softly turning,
saw four or five trunks piled up in the room.

" What in the world can this child have in these
trunks? How long can she be thinking of staying,"
she queried. She quietly left the room, closed her own
door, and sat down to wonder. Wonder first. Had any
one in the world been as miserable that evening as she
thought herself? Wonder second. Where had every body
been? — to her the whole house was empty. Wonder
third. Why did Lieutenant Mera seem to be laughing at
her? Wonder fourth. What did Lieutenant Mera know
about Miss Smith? He had asked if she had arrived.
But sleep stole in and closed her wondering eyes, and
smoothed her polished brow.

ARTICLE SECOND.

Posts of Officers.

IN a room in the west tower of " Barracks," lay an officer asleep. His head was resting on his dog, a hound of great size and beauty. Under him was a white bear-skin robe thrown on the floor. His repose was the fading of a waking revery into a soft dream,—a delicious unconciousness and forgetfulness of those unpleasant intruders called compunctions, which usually gave color to his day-dreams — not always rainbow-hued. He thought he was weary — yes, he *was* weary — of a hollow-hearted world. Was he less hollow-hearted? Weary of aspirations unrealized —after Fame — the cheat! After Virtue, " one of the worshippers of whom, he was not which," a lady he would not make one sacrifice to woo — after the " *ignis fatuus*, happiness," as he growled many times a day. Yes, he was tired — of society, whose flatteries sickened him, as sweets cloy the appetite of the child. Society, false to all its promises, and stealing that which it cannot give again — peace of mind.

> " Society, that polished horde,
> Formed of two mighty tribes,
> The bores, and bored."

He was weary, weary of solitude — and — himself. Who could read this in the satirical curl on the lip of Lieutenant Saberin? In his careless indifferent morning carol —

> " To ladies' eyes a round, boys,
> We can't refuse, we can't refuse ;
> Tho' bright eyes so abound, boys,
> 'Tis hard to choose, 'tis hard to choose ! "

In his princely manner to the great world, in his gracious deferential bearing where he most despised — in his apparent self-forgetfulness, and abandon, at the nightly revels of the officers. Among these he was styled " a splendid fellow ! " The ladies flattered, and caressed him. In short all the world spoiled Lieutenant Saberin. His rooms bore witness to this. Every niche was filled with rare gifts he had graciously accepted; curiously carved camp-chest, and buffet, Bohemian glass, Dresden china, caps and slippers — quite enough for a Chinese museum. Books, papers, letters, gloves, pipes, tobacco, fresh and faded flowers, made a tout-ensemble quite irresistible to the bachelor officers.

Now, the grate was heaped with bright red coals, imparting cheerfulness to the room on this chilly May afternoon, and casting a hue, rich and golden, over the light brown hound, and dark brown head of the officer, that rested on the neck of the dog. Over the mantle-piece hung a painting of a scene in Florida, on the shelf below a pencilling of his dog, a cigar-case, a pair of spurs, a bunch of faded flowers, Weimer, his man, had held more sacred than his master — lifting and carefully replacing them every time he dusted — where more than a month ago, they were thrown, after a party, without one thought to the giver, though so humbly begged for with vows to keep them always; and they were kept longer than most flowers are under like circumstances.

The sleeper was aroused by a fierce growl from his dog. " Be quiet Burns ! " came in just as fierce a growl from the round white throat, that could utter such touchingly tender tones.

The door was opened.

" Hallo ! Did I awaken you, Saberin? I declare, I can always tell when you are asleep, by the growling of Burns, twice as fierce as usual, which is quite superfluous ! "

The speaker, a short, dark-eyed, and dark-hued, person,

with a most dignified air, took a slow march across the
room to the fire, turned, and surveyed Saberin.

"Not a bad picture, old fellow! Why don't you be
done in that style? The Professor could turn you to
some account then! Call it Fidelity and Infidelity.
Would not Madame B. send to Florida to "papa" for a
cool thousand to secure the gem? Ha! ha!"

Saberin stretched himself—patted Burns, and arose.
After lighting his pipe, he seated himself, elevated his heels
on the table, " On the same line, as near each other, as
the conformation of the man would permit, feet turned out
equally, and forming with each other something less than
a right angle."

" Take a cigar, Mera; and tell one if you think there
is a possibility of getting a few days' leave? I am con-
foundedly tired of this place, and everything in it — except Burns," and he pulled the ears of the affectionate
creature, who was fawning on him.

" The deuce! Saberin blue? that's a rich joke! I
did not know you thought the worlds, 'and all that in
them is,' of enough consequence, to induce you to shorten,
or prolong, one of those lovely whiffs! Is Miss Kilman-
segg unkind? Never mind, let's sing, " Ach, Gretchen,
mein taubchen," and only light up one taper at a time.

Lieutenant Saberin sat with closed eyes like one in a
trance. Lieutenant Mera resumed,

" Mrs. Captain Morton, gives a party next week, what
would she do without you? She would certainly postpone
it indefinitely; and Miss Dora McFlimsey stands ready to
dance her feet off, if you will only encourage her: and —
and — 'oh no we'll never mention her!' I'll just toast
the bright-eyed one, in some of your 1776." And he
rose and went to the buffet, poured out some brandy —
raised it to his lips, and said, " here's to ———— "

He stopped — " Jack was embarrassed, never hero more,
and, as he knew not what to say, he swore."

It might have been the lack of a ready toast, or was
it only the Indian hue of the rich southern blood that

coursed in his veins? Very dark he looked, as the dark words fell from his compressed lips. So Lieutenant Sabeine thought, — (not said) — as he rose. "I am going to get my leave to-night, if I can, and I will go to-morrow to the city. Will you walk round to the Colonel's with me?" and he regarded Lieutenant Mera as if he thought him drunk, or crazy.

"Certainly, certainly, Saberin —— but t'were better not to go, man! Bobaline expects his niece to-night, he told me, and we can happen into the parlor, and play a game of Boston, and see what she is like."

Lieutenant Saberin drew his brows together to make Lieutenant Mera out. He had never seen him excited as he seemed to-night. Lieutenant Mera usually so placid! What had come over the man! His loss of toast and temper — could he be jealous of him about Mrs. Bobaline? He sneered at the thought. Lieutenant Saberin had known Mrs. Bobaline when a Florida belle. Lieutenant Mera, and he, were ordered at the same time, to a post where her father, a surgeon in the army, was stationed. She was then engaged to the good practical man she afterward married, but, "the trail of the serpent," must glisten on the pansies, and heliotropes, and where the flower-of-love lies-bleeding, in that Eden too. The handsome Lieutenant Saberin arrived, and she fell in love, at first sight. He was equally smitten, and hunted, fished, rode, and walked with her, enjoying her wit and beauty greatly. She was in love with him *then*, and now that she showed such marked preference for his society, had he not a perfect right to be polite to her? He tore the bit of cigar in his fingers, to pieces, but Lieutenant Mera who stood looking at him, little dreamed what was passing in his mind. He frowned and curled his lips. He would have none of Lieutenant Mera's interference — and he would give him trouble the first lady he saw him take a fancy to. Such were his amiable thoughts. He turned suddenly on his heel, they left the room together, and walked in silence to the Colonel's door. He obtained a leave, and parting from

Mera, said gaily, as if in answer to the proposition he had
made before they came out, "I thank you, Mera, I'll
leave Madam Bobaline, and Miss what's her name — to
your tender mercies, — deal gently." Lieutenant Mera
looked as if he would like to demolish him — but he did
not. Lieutenant Saberin turned his sweetest smile on
him, as he said, good-night !

ARTICLE THIRD.

Posts of Field Officers.

LIEUTENANT Saberin, in order to keep away from Lieutenant Mera " cut tea," and going to his room, sat down to plan what he would do in the city. He drew his vade mecum, as he called his porte monnaie, from his pocket to make an entry, when out fell a lovely little note, he had received that morning. It was written in a lovely little hand. Lieutenant Saberin had been for years rather in the flowery toils of a very sweet village maiden — she had been a schoolmate of his, when he was a beautiful ingenuous boy. Now, he would consider such a man as he, too stupendous a sacrifice at such a shrine. He could not afford to marry so recklessly, though he loved her — heaven only knew how dearly! and regretted the necessity of such a course, but " was it not kinder to gradually drop the correspondence between them?" and she was too delicate, had too much pride to annoy him! He had gently checked her warmth by not writing to her, but within the past few months, some sweet little pieces of poetry had come to him through the mail, in which, though prettily disguised, he could trace the graceful Italian hand he had so often seen before. Yes, scores of pretty note-lets had he carried home in his book-satchel, when happiness put wing on his little heels.

Let us read over Lieutenant Saberin's shoulder. It has no signature — within lies the minnie ball! He glanced at the note and examined his pockets for one he had received a month ago — but as it was only poetry —

. he did not spend his time reading it — now, he wished to compare notes.

TO LIEUTENANT SABERIN OF WEST POINT.

*Na-gah-moo ! my lodge is lonely !
  The night wind's whisper in the pines
Sings to me only !
  No joy is mine,
  Dear, Na-gah-moo !

Na-gah moo ! my sweet voiced lover,
  Spring's soft wind,
And love-notes hover
  O'er †Me-Me's mind,
  For Na-gah-moo !

Na-gah-moo ! my lodge is lonely !
  No love-lit eye
Warms Me-Me ! only
  The watch-dog's cry,
Howls, Na-gah-moo.

Lieutenant Saberin paused, and the words of one **of** *her* songs, came to his mind.

" As he pauses awhile in the hush of some hour,
  Its tones will come o'er him, and prove
That the strife of the world cannot smother the power
  Of the song that breathes ever of love !
      Still love ! "

A great round tear lay like a diamond on the cheek of the calculating man of the world. He unfolded the last note, for there was something very delightful, and fascinating, in the new sensations he was experiencing — something akin to the pleasing pain the pilgrim feels, when doing penance for his sins, he opened the second note.

Suddenly, loud voices were heard on the stairs, giving sign that his sanctum was invaded. He deliberately folded the notes, put them into his pocket, and was sleeping in his chair.

* Na-gah-moo, the Indian for " sweet-voice."
† Indian name for " dove."

ARTICLE FOURTH.

Regimental staff.

FOUR or five officers, entered Lieutenant Saberin's room, all laughing and talking at once. He looked up pleasantly, and vowed he had pined for them, for the last three hours. Would they help themselves to seats, etc., or give him the extreme pleasure of helping them.

They would help themselves, to whatever his poor quarters afforded.

Lieutenant Alton, " a sweet young officer," as the ladies called him, walked to the cigar-case, took a cigar — lighted it, and sat down. Lieutenant Storme, set himself to do the honors of the toddy-glasses. Lieutenant Mera, leaned on the mantle-piece, and looked at the Florida scene.

Lieutenant Alton gave two or three whiffs, and addressed Lieutenant Saberin. " I can tell you we have had a stunning time this evening, at Tutes ! The young ladies *are charming*. That Miss Nora Kearney, Storme, that you stormed, is a perfect little beauty ; and *my* girl is tremen-dous ! Why, she started me on mathematics, and for a while I was ——— Alton, but she veered into the science of metempsychosis, which you are probably aware is not included in the branches taught at this life-taking institution, and when the accomplished scholar, and gentleman, Lieutenant Mera, came to my rescue, I was reduced to the uttermost farthing."

"What is her name ?" asked Lieutenant Saberin.

" Nora Kearney," shouted Lieutenant Storme.

" Look here, my dear fellow, your head is not quite straight, I fear you have tested the toddy too often ; we were speaking of t'other Tutes," laughed Lieutenant Mera.

"O, Miss *Bessy* Kearney, you mean, pardon me, I could not understand any one speaking of Miss Bessy, the same day they saw Miss Nora."

The toddy made, they all sat down around the table. Lieutenant Burlyton joined the party, and at three o'clock they still sat, smoking, drinking, and playing. Songs were sung, toasts drank, stories told — some that had better remained untold.

At four o'clock, good-night was said, by some, in a most pathetic manner, sung by others, very tragically; by all, in a way that would have astonished the performers the next morning. Dreams after such revels, are never rosy-hued, so you will please permit me to refer you to Robert Burns, Esquire, for a description of the flights those young men took on ebon mares, 'fu' fast that night, and the consequent fatigue, and disgust that half past seven o'clock, brought them. Ugh!

> "O, what noble minds were here o'erthrown !
> Like sweet bells jangled out of time and harsh ! ''

ARTICLE FIFTH.

Commands.

LIEUTENANT Saberin's sudden determination to get a
leave, was not simply an impulse without an object, as he
had wished Lieutenant Mera to understand, but was in
obedience to the following " commands."

NEW ORLEANS, May ——

Dear Old Saber——

I write on " the eve of my mar-
riage," as novelists and poets would say! yes, to-morrow
promotes me to the captaincy of one of the best drilled
little angels —

> • She is mine own ; And I as rich in having such a jewel,
> As twenty seas, if all their sands were pearl,
> The water nectar, and the rocks pure gold."

No small amount of charms, spiritual, and temporal, altogether " *very desirable.*" I assure you, old fellow, it is'nt
bad, to be made such a deuce of a fuss over! The day *is*
to be ——, and Lieutenant Charles Ambert and lady,
will be in New York on the 22d May, at the New York
hotel. Now you must — *must* is the word — get a leave
and come down. I have brought a wife up for you! she
is superb, she is! Talented, amiable, and by George! as
rich as an Indian princess; *very desirable*, like my wife,
in that respect. Get away, I say, and go to Washington
with us, for a few days — can get so much better acquainted
travelling, you know, and then you need not marry her unless you like! She is dying to see you, she says. The dick-
ins, I have not told you her name! Never mind! You'll

2

have the more to discover when you see her. What are you standing there *re*-reading, and dreaming over this letter for ? Why ain't you down on your bended knees, like Jacob, thanking heaven for sending a rich young woman into your very clutches, like the Patriarch Isaac ? Am not I a *true* friend ? Prove yourself as true by obeying these commands.

True as steel,

AMBERT.

Lieutenant Saberin's curiosity was keenly aroused for such a sovereign master of true melancholy. He would like to see the "Indian Princess" Lieutenant Ambert had so generously brought into his clutches! The fastidious Lieutenant curled his lips, and then his moustache. He must not fail ! conqueror-like, this must be a plumed victory. So we find him at Warnock's, before he goes to the hotel. Here he met Lieutenant Ambert, and after *chatting* awhile, they repaired thither.

When left by his friend, to bring down the ladies, Lieutenant Saberin paraded before the mirror, surveying his fine person with wondrous self-complacency. Will the " Indian princess " admire him as much as he admires himself? He thought she would. Not a doubt clouded the radiant face.

They came at last. Lieutenant Ambert, with the air of an Alexander, leading in two beautiful women.

" Kate, this is Lieutenant Saberin. Saberin — my lady wife."

Kate was majestic, dignified, and very beautiful. She met her husband's friend in quite a sisterly way.

" Miss Pauline De Saye, permit me to present Lieutenant Saberin — Miss De Saye."

She had been standing a little behind Mrs. Ambert, but an impatient glance was stolen past that lady, and the glow of admiration that mantled the loveliest gipsy face he had ever seen, was so visible that he was content to cast down his eyes in a very sentimental fashion, as he took the tiny hand so like a snow-flake, and thinking perhaps, of the right delegated to him, by his friend, retained it, till the cheek crimsoned like the setting sun — and the long, dark lashes fell, just in time to save the presumptuous warrior from a fate not unlike that of "certain" who cast the " three holy children," into the " burning fiery furnace," for the flame of those fervid orbs would have slain him, beyond a question.

Like a fine soldier, the gallant Lieutenant made a graceful retreat, and was immediately promoted to the post of monopolizer general, by his admiring friend Ambert, while, in her heart's judgment-hall the young girl pronounced him mighty nice !

On Monday morning, when Lieutenant Saberin was compelled to part with Gipsy, as he lovingly called her, he would have given his commission to linger at her side. He told her how happy he had been in her society — that he could never forget " that she looked happy by his side," and " woulded they had never met."

Gipsy told him she should cry when he was gone,— she was homesick at the very thought.

Homesick ! he was heart-sick, would go back only to live these precious moments over and over again, till he got his leave in June.

" And what will you do then ? Will I not see you again ? "

" I hope so ! many times it may be ; I shall call on *you* to decide that."

No reply.

Lieutenant Saberin went on.

" Where will you be on the 28th of August, Pauline ? "

" We return home about the first of September, and *may* be in New York about that time."

" May I compel Lieutenant Ambert to bring you to West Point for the 28th party ? Would you like to come ? "

" Like to come ? what questions you ask, Mr. Saberin. I would give all my visit north, for it ! "

" O, not so much as that, Miss De Saye, I assure you it

would not pay — it would not recompense you for all that! You could not get acquainted with *many* in one evening. Besides I should find an excuse for monopolizing you myself — you do not know how selfish I am !"

Miss De Saye simpered, " Have I not been happy for two days? I shall not care to know any one else !" (petulantly) " Why do you make me say these things ? "

He, (sorrowfully) " I was bold enough to hope, I might ask one more question, before we part — perhaps, forever; but after that, if it cost me the ' cherished hope of years,' I could not ask it." His tones were low, and sad.

Gipsy would have given all her worldly goods, to know what he was about to ask ! He adroitly turned the subject, not having any question to propound, he preferred giving scope to her imagination — well knowing the silly little head would balance the account in his favor. She followed him to the parlor door to say good night ; " Don't forget to make Lieutenant Ambert bring us to West Point ! "

ARTICLE SIXTH.

Principles of Wheeling.

He shook her little hand in a friendly indifferent way.

" I could not forget ! I may be back — but if I am not — I will find an excellent substitute, I will tell my friends that a bright southern bird, is to alight at West Point, before pluming her wings for her own sunny skies !"

" Is there a possibility that you *will not be back*, then ? I thought your leave expired on the 28th ; Lieutenant Ambert said so ! "

" It does. The ' powers that be,' *perhaps*, might grant an extension of my leave, but in case you came, I should not press an application for one since I hope to secure such a great inducement to return !"

O that deceit should dwell in such a gorgeous palace ! He seemed for dignity composed, and high exploit; but all was false and hollow! He held her hand, playing with a rich diamond ring, of great value. Pauline looked at his fine manly face, so full of thought and intellect, his Apollo-head, and locks! Her beau-ideal stood before her; she might never, *never* see him again! He raised his eyes to hers. Scarcely less bright than the radiant gem he was admiring so undisguisedly, and caressing so tenderly, were the flashing eyes she raised to his, saying, "Lieutenant Saberin, you *must* be at West Point, or I will not go," and taking the ring from her finger, she placed it on his — "and return this to me then!" she said with a pleading look.

"O, Miss De Saye, this is too valuable, it would be almost a fetter. I do not need such things to bring me back, I assure you," he exclaimed in genuine astonishment.

"You will enhance its value by retaining it, and render it valueless if you refuse it! Please wear it until we meet, it will serve to remind you of one you have — that can — of me!"

"That is all you need say!" replied the pitiless Cæsar; and he stole a very respectful look from the gem he was turning on his finger to catch the stars of fire in its depths, revealed by the light of the gas above his head, to the loving child-like face, and felt that he could lay him down and die for her. "May I not call you Pauline, to-night? Good night Miss Pauline, I will wear this until we meet!"

This time when he took her hand, she felt the metal of the ring — and he felt confident she appreciated the ring of the true metal. Poor Pauline ascended to Mrs. Ambert with the saddest "good-bye" on her lips, she had ever breathed. Lieutenant Saberin's visit had been "a success." He had said truly, he had enjoyed every moment, needing only the last few he had spent with Pauline, where he had "developed" her so *excellently* to add the "vici" to his "veni, vidi." He would make Lieutenant Ambert bring her to West Point for the 28th. That is the place to draw one's captives in triumph, at one's heels ! He would be *there !* Before then though, he would secure her for himself. She was too beautiful, too rich, to trust on West Point, unless well guarded, and he would be the protector. Lieutenants Mera, Burlyton, and Storme, all should know, *whose* the southern heiress was.

ARTICLE SEVENTH.

Principles of the Direct Step.

Upon this, Lieutenant Saberin acted on his return. He wrote a letter to Miss Pauline, a love letter of the most practical description, all that she could desire.

He spoke of army life — he would not expect her to brave any of its dangers or hardships. She should be the bright *particular* star, that through all should guide him on to immortality and fame ! He *had* had fancies, but beside the deep, enduring impression she had made upon his soul, they became aversions — here the ink paled to an unearthly hue, and " the lights in the chamber burnt blue ! " blue as the eyes of one of those fancies,— and strangely enough he thought of those blue eyes, and wondered if Pauline would love him as she had done. He did not doubt his predominating love for Pauline, but would she love. Yes, he thought she would; and he glanced at the glittering star on his little finger.

He sealed, and directed the letter carefully, and put it in his breast pocket, intending to mail it himself, and not entrust it to Weimer to post with the less important letters. He little dreamed of its fate.

TITLE SECOND.

SCHOOL OF THE SOLDIER.

General Rules and Division of the School of the Soldier.

Saturday on West Point! Who that has ever been there, will wonder at the note of exclamation? *Enchanting spot*, on that day! The hearts of three hundred cadets bounding at the thought of release from duty. Their joyful prospect of meeting loved friends from abroad! The calls to be made — all "*so* glad to see them." The strolls over the beautiful hill-sides; the paradisaical walk on the river banks. "*Flirtation!*" *— The putting into practice all they have learned during the week; "Modes of attack — means of defence — making slow and quick matches, and the "Manual of arms," in which all are versed. For example. 1st. "*Attention.*" 2. "SQUAD." At the second word the recruit will take a position in front of the eight-by-nine looking-glass, and arrange his hair. "*Shoulder*—ARMS!" he shall sew on his new chevrons. "LOAD!" He shall polish his forty-four buttons, put on his coat, button it tightly to the throat. "PRIME!" At this command, he shall adjust his cap *very far forward* on his head, a little to the left. "READY!" "*One time and three motions.*" The recruit advances to the front, and inspects the Plain, to ascertain if there is an enemy to be seen. He descends the stairs, grasps the tail of his coat, gives one energetic pull toward the heels. "1st *Forward!*" "2. MARCH!" "The recruit will retake a step of twenty-eight inches," until he reaches the hotel. On arriving, he will execute rapidly the several commands

* A name given by the Cadets to "Chain Battery Walk."

" *Present* — ARMS."
" *Secure* — ARMS."
" *Support* — ARMS."
" *Arms* — AT WILL.."
" *Eyes direct to the Front.*"

" Because this is the surest means of *maintaining a proper position,* an essential object, to be insisted on and attained."

Loading at Will, and the Firings."

In most cases, " *The direct fire,*" is all that is required; if this fails, " *Oblique Firing,*" is more surprising. Great *execution* attends " FIRE — KNEELING."

These may all fail — the recruit must not be daunted by the glittering ranks before him, though the foe, still " *Keep* — DRESSED," let him remember, *truth* is not all that is needed to secure the victory in war. He shall hoist foreign colors, till a proximity is secured, or more properly speaking, let him try —

" FIRE LYING."

Ellsworth's Zouaves are babes " in arms," compared with West Point cadets, in this exercise.

Who can bear testimony to this, better than the beautiful besieged, or in somebody's pretty, passionate language ; —

> " Oh ! only those
> Whose souls have felt this one idolatry,
> Can tell how precious is the slightest thing
> A ' Cadie ' gives and hallows ! chevrons and buttons
> Will long be kept, remembrancers of looks,
> That made each ' gift ' a treasure.''

Mrs. Bobaline was dressed to receive " cadet calls." Before she descended, she peeped into Isagone's room, and told her to dress herself charmingly and follow her down stairs, as it was very pleasant on the piazza. Desirous of pleasing her aunt, she bedecked herself quite bravely, a la San Francisco. Blue Canton crépe dress, rich lace on her neck and arms, a wreath of pearls and garnets, arranged in exquisite sprays, entwined in her light-brown curls, were gathered like a coronet on the top of her head. Quite abashed at the pretty face and figure she saw reflected in her aunt's cheval-glass, she trembled at the thought of venturing alone, to encounter the multitude of eyes, in every spot outside her chamber door. The house seemed to the terrified girl, one vast multiplying glass, eyes, eyes — everywhere. She ventured as far as the stair-case and peered over the balustrade, listening to the gay voices and then on tiptoe returned to her cell, as she called it. She wearied herself reading, and remembering her aunt's request, ventured boldly to the foot of the staircase. She could get no further, but stood leaning against the wall, till she had attracted every eye — from sheer want of nerve to move. Some giggled, and all scanned her curiously. She stood fire tolerably well for a time, but at length fled to her aunt's room again, and read an hour, when no longer hearing the hum of voices in the hall, "like the sound of many waters," she descended, and went to the door of the north piazza.

Color-Guard.

At the further end of the piazza, Isagone discovered Mrs. Bobaline enclosed in a "picket of Cadets," she termed her "color-guard." She had distributed to each of them a small bit of ribbon, of her favorite color, which fluttered from a button-hole of their flashy corselets, when they came to call on her. These were her especial favorites. One of them looked up and violating rule No. 38, "The color-guard will not fire but reserve itself for the defence of the color;"— and not observing rule No. 41* before firing, said, "Hallo, here is Madame Recamier reanimated, or Saint Agnes!"

---

* School of the Battalior, Part I. Vol. 2.

2*

They all looked, and Mrs. Bobaline recognised Isagone under the fanciful disguise, and laughed till her face was crimson. The thought of introducing such a figure, and such a name, was vastly more than Mrs. Bobaline's philosophy dreamed of, and she walked away around the piazza. Several of the young men followed her, while one or two, turned to reconnoitre the stranger.

They walked round and round her — but meeting her modest dignified blue eyes, they returned to Mrs. Bobaline, arm-in-arm, pretending to stagger, saying, "We be all dead men,— slain, énfiladé!"

"O, but isn't she pretty! I wonder who she is?" exclaimed Cadet Smith,

Mrs. Bobaline began to gather courage, and said, "She is a niece of my husband, she came last night." — The cadets looked at each other, and elevated their brows — "I will introduce you." And she gracefully led the way through the hall, to Isagone's side. "Is — I-one dear, allow me to present my friends. Mr. White, Mr. Brown, Mr. Grey, and Mr. Smith!" The fastidious lady could not draw the slow length of Isagone's quaint name out of her dainty mouth, and inwardly applauded her quickness of wit, in substituting the beautiful diminutive for it.

"Ione, my dear, I think Cadet Smith must be a relative of yours! Having the same name." This she added, to put the young girl a little at her ease, as she was truly appalled at finding herself surrounded by so many gentlemen in grey.

Cadet Smith said, nothing would give him more pleasure than to trace the relationship, and although her face became crimson at mention of her name, that had never been her admiration, Isagone was not sorry to find it belonged to the handsomest and most elegant of her aunt's admirers, and she thought they must be very smart, to be tolerated by her superb ladyship.

Mrs. Bobaline looked at "Ione," as she had named her so suddenly, (much to that young lady's surprise) and smiling said, "This is a young Californian," as if apologising for her peculiarity of dress. Cadet Smith liked this very peculiarity, and took possession of the stranger as no one but a West Point cadet *can.*

" Have you observed the view up the river, Miss Smith ? Was there ever so much beauty condensed into so small a space ? "

This remark drew Isa to the balustrade of the piazza. They did not join her aunt's circle again, but entered into the most animated conversation.

" Is this your first visit to the States, Miss Smith ? "

" O, no ! I was born in South Carolina, but my father removed to San Francisco, when I was a child. I am very proud of my native State, and claim to be a true South Carolinian."

Cadet Smith smiled quietly, " I think we must be nearly related, as I am from Ohio, no wonder I was attracted at once."

" Indeed ? antipodes in *that* sense ! "

He winced a little as he was as true an Ohian, but did not like the turn the conversation had taken. " This is just the place for antipodes to meet, and be attracted. " Let us drop our States, here, and take our Country."

Ione replied. " In honoring our state we honor our country, and I cannot see the propriety of dropping my state, even at West Point."

Mr. Smith would not reply, and flew to the " dernier resort" of West Point conversation. " Is this your first visit at West Point ? "

" Yes ; and every thing is beautiful, as it is new, to me ! "

" This is one of the most lovely spots in the world, and certainly one of the most interesting for strangers to visit."

" What a charmed life you must lead here." Said Ione,

" Yes ! its present attractions are very great, beyond a doubt."

" Its present attractions ? " questioned she, innocently.

"Yes, the visitors, to us — to you, the officers, and to some, our corps — but of course we do not see that."

Ione thought "if all ' our corps ' are as handsome and agreeable as Cadet Smith, that is an attraction indeed ! "

TO FIRE AND LOAD LYING.

"What is that marble pillar under the trees, near the flag-staff? "

"That ? — that, is — the famous ' Column of War.' It was brought from the ' Temple of Bellona,' at Rome. Whenever war was declared against an enemy, her priests threw a spear against it. There are many such marks of the spear. Some suppose them to be inscriptions."

"What a curiosity ! How came it here ? "

"O, it was sent a present to General Scott by — the Pope. When General Scott was up for President, the Roman Pontiff, wishing to flatter him, sent it to him — to hang on his watch-chain, — I suppose, but it proving a trifle too long, "our Chief presented it to the Academy."

This manual of "Fire Lying," was executed with such grace and skill, that Ione fell into the common error, of believing her senses. *It was her first visit to West Point.* All the "means of Attack," having been gone through, our hero should have been thinking of the "means of defense," against the bright revolvers directed at him — so dangerously near — when the drum beat for parade.

After his departure, Ione stood looking at ' column of war ', and determined to make a drawing of it, to send it to her mother — she would examine all the works she could find access to, and get its wonderful history. What a wonderful place West Point must be — for gaining information ! To see such curiosities, and meet people from all parts of the world, oh, she would enrich herself by the wealth of knowledge she would bear home on her wings, which she would hive like the toiling bee. Delightful thought!

Madam Bobaline stood gazing on vacancy, thinking of — Lieutenant Saberin. "Where is he ? Is he sick in New York ? "

Wheeling.

The reveries of both ladies were disturbed by Lieutenants Burlyton and Mera. They saluted Mrs. Bobaline, and were introduced to ' Ione ' (Mrs. Bobaline was enchanted with the nice name she had given poor Isa-gone!)

" Ho, for parade ! Are you not going out, ladies ? " said Lieutenant Burlyton.

" I do not care to go, unless Ione is anxious to see it."

" Well! young lady, have you tired yourself with the Cadies, too ? "

" Tired ? I don't know but one, are they all like Cadet Smith ? as clever as he ? " Ione replied, in a tone of surprise.

Lieutenant Burlyton shouted, " Ha ! ha ! ha ! O, mad-am, you *must* take her out to see what few more we have, of 'the same sort ; or permit me to play chaperone, I will bring her back safely."

Ione did not look very anxious to go, as the young gentleman's laugh made her shrink from encountering his wit again. She had nothing to say. Her ladyship thanked him, and told Ione to go by all means, she could not have a more delightful escort. He knew she spoke ironically, as the truth-telling Lieutenant was not a favorite of hers. He dropped his arms and made her a " first-class" school-boy bow. All laughed, as all always did, at every move-ment or speech of Lieutenant Burlyton. Ione walked off humming a tune.

" You have a Miss *Mimosa* there, madam."

" Yes, an original, decidedly," she said. Lieutenant Mera leaned on the balustrade — regarding madam, scarcely deigning to look at the new comer, whom he seemed to think was more like a Chinese than any one he had ever seen. The accomplished and lovely Mrs. Bobaline quite eclipsed all the young beauties of the petty court, and led captive the fastidious and reserved Mera. As soon as they were left alone, he asked Madam Bobaline if she would prefer to take a seat on the piazza, or go into the parlor. She would prefer the piazza, and he brought chairs and they sat down, near a group of ladies.

Lieutenant Burlyton sauntered to some ladies, friends of his, and told them to look out for the little Oriental he was going to drill — a new importation from the gold regions.

They did " look out " for her, as she came leisurely towards her aunt, her proud little head and neat shoulders enveloped in a rich lace shawl. Mrs. Bobaline looked, and was not ashamed of her. Lieutenant Mera glanced, and wished he had taken the wind out of Lieutenant Burlyton's sails, and asked her himself. He had brought his friend B. to do just what he *had* done, to take the young lady away from Mrs. Bobaline, as he imagined he had an ax to grind. " You are very quiet to-day, my lady; are you quite well ? "

" Yes, thank you ! " And she sat gazing on vacancy.

Inspection.

Lieutenant Mera's eyes wandered off, to a gentle girl in blue, who was looking wistfully after the Oriental, thinking to herself,— "|why do men always follow new faces, leaving those they pretend to love so much, for the first stranger \ O, man ! from your baby-hood you leave the dearest ones, from early morning, without a glance of regret, to linger all day, near those you hate, and fight, nor think of the loving and indulgent at home, till you have been whipped by some ' big boy,' or darkness, and your day's struggle after marbles, bring you home — to a supper, and good-night kiss from the neglected mother and sisters ! Later, the humble cottage, embowered in roses and jasmines — where you were petted, and waited for — where dwelt the fair face, and warm young heart, you

turned from so thoughtlessly, to play at a more momentous
game than marbles, in the great unloving world. At
parting, a warm embrace, and a few, very few words of
comfort and hope for the meek worshipper, who thought her
life too poor a sacrifice for so noble a divinity. Did you
ever return to the *sacred scenes?* Never, until a weary
man, you go back to sit on a little green mound, under
the very trees that waved softly over you, and a soft-
voiced loved one at your side, long years before, when you
promised so fervently to love and cherish that which is
now the wee handful of dust that rests beneath the grass
and violets. Why come back at all? To make happy
the heart that, weary with waiting, had broken? Have
you learned what it is to be alone? or has some perfume on the breath of June, transported you to the
year, the month, the day, the hour, you had that wealth
of love thrown away upon you? — such love as you
never since have known. Perhaps an irresistible impulse
has drawn you back, to permit the patient worshipper
once more to tell you how she loves to caress the weary
head; thinking perhaps, that you will condescend to tell
her that you love her; that she was not really forgotten
all these years! That you had seen her in dreams! —
yes! — in dreams the angels, in pity, brought to your
distracted brain. Your day-dreams were, position, wealth,
ambition! Love was for pastime — and must not inter-
fere with these! Too late! The knell is sounding
among the mournful trees — the peace you would have
brought, was all too late! Did God's peace come too
soon? These were the thoughts that sat in solemn con-
clave, in the upper room, just above those dove-like blue
eyes; some of them from observation, some from experience.

Lieutenant Mera nearly fell asleep, looking at the heavenly blue of those eyes, and forgot to grind his hatchet.
Madam felt neglected.

.

"INSTRUCTION FOR SKIRMISHERS."

" *To Deploy Forward.*"

'It is so very lonely to think of Lieutenant Bobaline being gone so long!—a lady cannot go anywhere on West Point without an escort; indeed, one might as well take the veil at once, as to be here, unattended."

Lieutenant Mera aroused, begged to be the humble servant of the ladies in such a deplorable situation, would she not call on him?

She bowed her beautiful head, and thanked him for his kindness: Yes, she would avail herself of his offer for Ione's sake, as she feared she should find it very stupid without her uncle; indeed, she dreaded the responsibility, as Ione had very much the air of a spoiled child.

Lieutenant Mera said " You should have introduced her to the officers first, as I fear the ' Cadies ' as Lieutenant Burlyton denominates them, will not give us a bird's eye view of her; but while they are making Miss Ione happy, you must make amends for the oversight, by not secluding yourself,— because the owner of the garden is absent, the fragrance of the rose must not be denied to the zephyrs.

. She raised her head in a haughty manner, and said, " I do not intend to seclude myself on account of my husband's absence, he would be displeased if I should; but I should not be missed where there are so many young girls."

" There is a mistake in your remark, my dear lady ! Your own observation should have taught you, that the unrestrained conversation of an accomplished and beautiful woman, can win a sensible man from the side of the most fascinating belle. I can bring witnesses!" and he looked out of the corner of his eye roguishly, at her."

" Of whom do you speak?" she replied, timidly.

Lieutenant Mera prided himself on his acumen in the

science of woman-reading; indeed, he was accustomed to say, that "he knew them by heart." He had not answered her, and she said, "You will not be anything but a witness against yourself, for you prefer the society of any one to mine!"

. "O, Mrs. Bobaline, how severe of you to say that to me! You must be perfectly aware that I prefer your society to that of any young lady. I left your side only when I felt that I was depriving others of a pleasure, whose claims were stronger than mine, or at least acknowledged."

"I acknowledge no one's claims, but Lieutenant Bobaline's."

She spoke resentfully, and Mera liked her none the less.

"SCHOOL OF THE COMPANY."

"*Countermarch.*"

Madame Bobaline and Lieutenant Mera sat for some time in silence, while their minds *countermarched*, musing over the field of the past. She knew he was a sincere admirer of hers, though, as he had never proposed, not a discarded lover. She however preferred the handsome, indifferent Saberin, and flattered him, and was delighted when they were stationed at West Point, together. Lieutenant Mera, while he had not quite recovered from the wound her bright eyes had given him, liked her frank, manly husband, and was very jealous for him; while, in point of fact there was little cause for it, as Lieutenant Saberin was too much absorbed in his own ambitious schemes, to pay much heed to her silly sighing for his society.

At length the lady yawned, and looking toward the long line of well-dressed ladies and their gaily caparisoned escorts as they returned from parade, exclaimed, "O, dear! what a tiresome. routine. I should think those people would weary to death of each other and of parades."

" Of parades, I suppose they do ; but of each other, a benignant Creator has kindly dispensed, that the more we see of our kind, the more indispensable we become to the complete happiness, each of the other. These are even Byron's sentiments, in the " Bride of Abydos."

> " To view alone
> The fairest scenes of land and deep,
> With none to listen and reply
> To thoughts with which my heart beats high,
> Were irksome ; for whate'er my mood,
> In sooth I love not solitude !"

When he turned to Mrs. Bobaline, she was just disappearing round the corner of the piazza. Lieutenant Burlyton and Ione came up.

" What have you done with Viola, Lieutenant Mera ? "

" Indeed, Miss Ione, I exerted myself to my hurt, to keep Madam here till you returned in safety, but was not sufficiently entertaining."

" Instruction of Officers."

Ione sat down to rest a moment. Lieutenant Mera said, " Did Lieutenant Burlyton do the honors of " Flirtation," for you this afternoon ? "

" The honors of what ? " she asked in astonishment.

" O, don't be putting those things into her head, she will learn them soon enough," Lieutenant Burlyton replied. Then turning to Ione, " *You* never flirted a mite, in all your pretty life, I'll bet my hat on that ! "

" No, indeed ! and I never intend to ! "

" Well, but every one has to, on West Point, do they not, Burlyton ? "

" There *is* a good deal of traffic in that line here, but as to the absolute necessity, why, that includes present company, and Miss Ione has found a paternal in me for the last hour, instead of a foolish flatterer as some of you young ones would have been. Miss Ione, you will find them out."

" Indeed, I should prefer finding people in," laughed she.

Lieutenant Merá rejoined, " *Colonel* Burlyton concedes great depth to us young men, which is quite flattering from such a veteran as he! I'll answer for it Miss Ione will find us out when she is out."

Ione smiled good-humoredly, and said she must seek Viola.

" Please say, I will wait for her, as the tables are full." cried Lieutenant Mera after her.

" Ha! ha! I'll squeeze you in beside me, Mera, rather than keep you waiting," laughed Lieutenant Burlyton. Mera hummed " Gentle Zitella," and threw himself on the sofa.

" DRESS."

Ione found Violetta reading. She laid her book down and arrayed herself for tea; asking, " How do you like Lieutenant Burlyton, Ione? Did he introduce you to any one? "

" No, he did not, the people stare so rudely, that one would hardly desire an introduction."

" O, don't be foolish! Yours happens to be a new face! every stranger has to pass through the same ordeal here."

" There are so few of them," said Ione, slyly.

" But now I recollect Lieutenant Mera said he would wait to take you in to tea. " I think Lieutenant Burlyton is too severe."

" Why, what did he say? Where did you see Lieutenant Mera ? "

Mrs. Bobaline had a habit of asking two or three questions at once, without waiting for a reply, looking the while at her hands, rings, bracelets, brooch, watch-chain and sleeves, arranging all these little affairs. I think all Mrs. Bobalines do this.

"In the hall,—he's so very elegant! don't you like him?" The last words were addressed to her own little face in the glass, as she was much amused to hear Viola's tiny feet, pattering away through the hall to tea, and the little face nodded a funny assent.

Mrs. Bobaline and Lieutenant Mera were standing in the hall. As she came down, she heard Viola say "after singing Tennyson's 'Miller's Daughter' to me, she first thought of you, sitting alone here."

Lieutenant Mera raised his killing eyes on Ione, till hers fell, before his look of scrutiny. "I will forgive Miss Ione, if it proves not the last thought she gives me," he said bowing apologetically.

Ione thought, I fear it will not, if I get glances like that, often.

When the trio entered the dining-hall, the attention they attracted, pronounced them a distinguished looking party. Mrs. Bobaline gave Ione a seat next to Lieutenant Mera. who proved that he could give pleasure to those with whom he conversed, if he chose. Ione was delighted with the grace and delicacy of his compliments. As they left the dining-room, he asked her if she would be disengaged after half past nine. She did not understand Rule 101 of West Point Tactics — That all ladies on "The Post" are engaged to Cadets till that hour, on Saturday afternoon, — and the officers seldom encroach upon their privileges, as they have very few, and said, —

"I have no engagement for this evening."

"Lieutenant Mera exchanged smiles with Mrs. B. at Ione's naïveté, and bowing said, "I'll see you then."

Cadet Smith came early, and promenaded on the piazza, with Ione, until ".Tattoo." He poured into her sympathizing ear the many privations and sorrows of the cadets, but she was perfectly *mystified*, with the militay terms and localisms. Lieutenant Mera waited to meet her, as Mr. Smith left her, and laughing, led her to a seat.

" REST."

" Now Miss Ione, rest thee awhile, you have travelled so far this evening."

" Travelled ? "

" I beg pardon, but how far do you think you and Mr. Smith could have walked, going at the rapid rate you have promenaded to-night ? "

She looked shyly at him, and he added, " Now rest thee well, and let us listen to the evening zephyrs, singing yon lovely river's lullaby."

" Sir Walter Scott ! " said Ione, laughing.

He sat in silence, or repeated gems from the poets in low rich tones, that bound the dreaming girl like a spell. He was a philosopher, and knew that after exercise, rest was welcome,— delightful, and after an animated conversation, silence, or loving words in low sweet tones, would be magical. The river was truly lovely. The quiet stars, those faithful watchers — reflected in the placid mirror, revealed the scenery, beautiful as a dream, portrayed in its perfectness, and the tiny ships and boats moving noiselessly on like a phantom fleet.

Ione enjoyed it with such intensity, that she " forgot all time," and it was eleven o'clock when Mrs. Bobaline came to say good-night, to them. She started to her feet, " You will not go without me, Viola ! "

" O, no, if you wish me to stay, but it is getting late, and as there is no one that cares for the smiles of a married lady, I conclude to retire."

The young gentleman winced, at having his own words turned against himself, but turning to Ione, he said, " Mrs. Bobaline expressed a kind fear that you would miss your uncle so much, that I offered to do all in my power, to fill his place. May I play uncle ? "

Ione looked mischievously at her aunt. " If Viola chooses."

" I fear Lieutenant Mera has not counted the cost. If we accepted, our very gratitude might become a burden."

" I see I am not to be uncle, may I try to persuade Mrs. Bobaline to take me for a nephew? I will be immensely dutiful."

It was Viola's turn to look mischievous. " If Ione chooses! " she repeated.

" 'So much to win, so much to lose, no marvel that I fear to choose,' " replied Ione in mock solemnity, and they said good-night.

Lieutenant Mera sat and smoked a cigar, in a trance of self love, till the stars waned. He had beguiled the pretty young girl into forgetfulness, he had wiled delicious flattery from his admired lady friend, and — and the field was all his own. No Lieutenant Saberin near to " spoil his heart-felt joy."

TITLE THIRD.

SCHOOL OF THE COMPANY.

Lesson First, Article First.

Mrs. Bobaline entered the dining room, on Monday, intending to sit at table an indefinite period of time, till her hero made his appearance; but was surprised to see him seated by Lieutenant Mera, in an earnest conversation. He arose, greeted her warmly, seated her at table, resumed his own seat, and said no more.

Lieutenant Mera called out, "Now our party is complete, can we not get up a sail to Cro'nest? it would be something new."

"Yes, as novel as a joke from Lieutenant Mera," shouted Lieutenant Burlyton.

Presently the door of the dining room opened, and some one took a seat at Mrs. Bobaline's side. Lieutenant Burlyton, who was seated opposite, looked up at Lieutenant Mera, and winked to him, saying,

"That Dora Bellamy will make some nice man a wife."

A low voice said, "Would I were Dora."

"No one spoke, and the tease bit his lip, and looked foiled. Lieutenant Saberin leaned forward, for a dish of asparagus, and glanced below him, but found his glance taken prisoner, by two sentinels in blue.

The room was very quiet till dinner was over. In the hall Lieutenant Burlyton whispered to Ione, laughed, and walked off tra-la-la-ing, to show himself "fancy-free." In the parlor the pretty rosy fingers of Mrs. Bobaline touched the keys of the piano, at first a little staccato, gradually growing tender, even mournful.

"Ione?"

Ione was gone.   Mrs. Bobaline arose and went to her
room.   Ione sat on the floor, reading a volume of illustrated Pickwick.   Viola silently arrayed herself in a
beautiful and becoming blue robe of foulard silk, and lay
down to take her siesta.   This was indispensable to her
existence, she affirmed.   She could not sleep.   She was
feverish and restless.

"Ione ; why did you answer that terrible Burlyton ? I
was quite angry ! "

" O, aunty, only to ' conciliate' him, as he calls it." And
she yawned, as if she would swallow Pickwick literally.

"Well please do not make yourself conspicuous, by
speaking to him again ; do not answer him ! "   She tossed
awhile, closed her soft eyes, but not to sleep — she peeped
through the long lashes at the bright face so wilfully happy, smiles, or a low musical laugh, broke like gleams of
sunshine from her heart, and lips.   At last looking up, she
saw her aunt was not asleep, and said,

" Who is Apollo, aunty ? "

" The man who owns the Apollo-rooms, I suppose, does
not Pickwick tell you ? "

" I was not reading — I was thinking."

" Pray don't call me aunty ! one would suppose I was
an old black.   I cannot divine how you ever came to woman's estate, so like a plant reared in a cellar, in body and
mind."

A merry laugh trembled out of Ione's throat, at the
queer image conjured up before her, and she sprang up to
look into the mirror, under the vague apprehension that
she should see a long, yellowish, white stalk !   She blushed
when she saw — no matter ! — yes, more mind than matter.

" Well, what vanity ! " said " aunty " who had near
wrung her neck, to see the cause of Ione's haste.

" Why au — I mean Mrs. — I mean, I was frightened,
lest I did look that funny way."

Mrs. Bobaline laughed in a very merry and natural
manner, for Ione's naïveté was irresistible.

" Why did you ask me who Apollo was ? "

" Because Lieutenant Burlyton asked me in the hall, if I saw Apollo looking at me, at dinner.

" Who did he mean ? "

" O, he was only laughing at that tall fellow below us, at dinner."

" What is his name, aunt — I mean — what *shall* I call you ? " and she sat down, like a penitent, on the floor beside the couch.

" Call me Viola ; his name is Lieutenant Saberin," and Mrs. Bobaline turned her face away, really hating herself for being so cross, but unable to control her unbridled temper. Ione murmured a sweet little home song, very low. Her aunt exclaimed pettishly,

" I beg you will not sing, when I lie down to take my siesta.

The head of Ione gradually drooped till it touched the couch, and she slept — instead of weeping as she feared she was about to do — the sleep of a heart at peace with all the world. Mrs. Bobaline heard her regular breathing, and turned to look at the gentle face at her side. The sweet repose that rested there recalled the time, not very far back, when she nestled her own warm young cheek on her mother's breast, and a tear stole from under her burning eye-lid. She gently stroked the silken head. " Indeed, I will be a mother to you, pretty one ! " she murmured.

Ione, aroused from her light sleep by the voice and touch of her hand, sat up. Mrs. Bobaline arose, and kissed her brow, and asked her to lie down. Ione thanked her, but she was quite refreshed, and she wondered what made her aunt so tender, all at once.

" I will be a mother to you ! " Ah, fair lady, you had not counted the cost of this beautiful impulse.

" Ione, would you like to go to parade ? "

" Of all things, dear Viola ! but I heard you say it wearied you to death."

8

" Well, it does sometimes, at other times I enjoy it very much, but everything must go just right."

" Dear me!" said the artless Ione.

They went to the hall, hats and parasols in hand. There, were no officers there; they walked into the parlor, and Ione touched the keys of the piano, and played the " Officers' call," which she had caught by ear. In a few moments Lieutenants Storme and Burlyton came, and looked into the windows.

" Here we are, lady fair! will you honor us with your commands?"

They came into the parlor, and Ione retreated to the window.

" Don't spring out, now! Permit me to present Lieutenant Storme; — Miss Smith. I believe you have the pleasure of knowing Madam Bobaline."

This lady looked daggers at him. She had not noticed what Ione was playing, and would rather have stopped in the house, than go out with the two gentlemen she was more indifferent to, than all the rest. " We are waiting for some friends," she observed in as quiet a manner as she could command.

" O, then you did not mean to call *us*, Miss Ione?"

" Call you?" echoed her aunt.

" Yes, she played the ' Officers' call.' "

Mrs. Bobaline's fair face darkened, and she sat down to play. While she was executing some of her finest airs, the gentlemen were enjoying a spirited conversation with Ione. Lieutenant Mera came in, and as he went directly to Mrs. Bobaline, the young men concluded the " friend " had arrived, and withdrew.

" DEPLOYMENTS."

" *Lesson Second.*"

As soon as they were gone, Viola turned, and looked at Ione; the girl became crimson as guilt.

"What did you do that foolish thing for? Now we shall be too late for parade."

Lieutenant Mera gave an inquiring glance at Ione. She smiled, and said, " I suppose it was foolish, but I caught the air, by hearing it, and scarcely knew I was playing it, and I assure you I knew nothing of their presence, or even what Lieutenant Burlyton meant till he explained."

Mrs. Bobaline still felt much annoyed, and left the room. Ione related to her companion, how she had offended. " I love that martial bugle, and have caught several of the little airs from it."

Lieutenant Mera bowed his head, and whispered " play it softly sometimes, and I will come, at least if you desire it."

" O, Lieutenant Mera, I could not do that!" and she blushed deeply, and followed her aunt, her companion joined her, and though they walked quickly, were unable to overtake the receding figure of Madam B., till she was lost among the crowd of ladies and gentlemen gathered about the iron seats on the parade ground. As they approached, they saw she had gained a seat, and that the Colonel was standing by her. He soon left her, and brought up one or two others, so that she was surrounded by officers till the parade was over. Ione went as near her aunt as she could get, but her ladyship took no notice of her, and though the Colonel turned to permit her to join the circle, Viola neither recognised nor introduced her, which greatly surprised and mortified her, and she stood in silence by Lieutenant Mera's side.

As soon as parade was over, Cadet Smith came and gave her a book to read, assuring her that it was a charming story. The Colonel and Lieutenant Mera walked with them to the hotel, the former gentleman bidding Mrs. Bobaline a very sentimental good-night, while the latter begged to accompany them to tea, and took a seat on the piazza after tea, with them.

Here Lieutenant Burlyton joined them, and having

saluted the ladies, said — "Miss Ione, what a fancy name you have, how came you by it?"

Viola glanced at her, and replied for her, "O, do not ask."

"Why?" he interrogated, curiously."

You are not sensitive about your name too, are you?" asked Lieutenant Mera.

"O, it is such a comical collection," laughed Madam.

"No, indeed, Lieutenant Mera, I am rather proud of it, amusing as Viola seems to think it."

Mrs. Bobaline could not suppress another musical laugh.

Lieutenant Burlyton said abruptly, "I don't know a more comical name than Bobaline!"

"But *her* name is Isagone Bobaline Smith — isn't that funny?"

They all laughed. Ione blushed and parried the joke by saying, her mother was French by descent, and that her grandmother's maiden name was Isagone Bayard, that her mother had given her the good lady's name in full.

"You never told me that. I thought the B. in your name stood for Bobaline," said her aunt, resentfully.

Lieutenant Mera rose in the awkward pause that ensued, and asked Madam to walk. As they proceeded, he very adroitly soothed her wounded vanity: "Any one can see at a glance that Bobaline is a change from Robert Alleine, the name no doubt of a brave French knight, of three or four centuries back; only that Lieutenant B. is such a noble, matter-of-fact fellow, that he never troubles himself about such trifles."

"Trifles!" cried the excited lady, "One's name is no trifle; and if it is so, why should not my husband attend to it? He ought, for — for *my* sake. I hate the name, and have never been addressed by it without feeling mortified."

"You must make him attend to it at once."

This delicate consideration made the humbled lady almost love the wily one, and he assumed at once the proportions of a man of taste and discernment in her eyes.

" Write your name B-e-a-u-b-a-l-l-e-i-n-e, — is not that pretty ? "

Mrs. Bobaline said she would ask permission of Lieutenant B., as she always called him ; she could not bring herself to speak the disagreeable cognomen, but to do her justice she had too much feeling to tell him so.   She was silent for some time and then said, " I don't see why his name was not Bayard, that is a sweet name."

" Lieutenant Mera bit his lip, and thought " how womanish ! "

" LESSON THIRD."

" Oblique Firings."

Lieutenants Mera and Saberin laughed merrily, as they emerged from the breakfast-room, the former had been amusing his friend by repeating the conversation of the evening before, on the subject of names.   They took their hats and walked to the north door of the hall.

Lieutenant Saberin asked, " What is the sum of Miss Smith ? "

" Not much, she is just so so," replied Lieutenant Mera shrugging his elegant shoulders.

" I perceive ; — one who plays round the head, but comes not near the heart."

" Precisely ! "

" Yet she seems rather brilliant in her tiltings with Burlyton."   Looking up, they saw Mrs. Bobaline on the piazza, and saluted her as Mrs. Beauballeine, with a very disagreeable look of mirth in their eyes.   But their own mortification would have been exquisite, had they known that Ione was seated in the private parlor, and had heard every word they had said.

The book Cadet Smith had given Ione the evening before, she had brought down in her hand when she came to breakfast, and had gone in the parlor to read it, while Mrs. Bobaline, supposing she had gone to her room, lingered on the piazza, to get a bow from her hero.

The gentlemen conversed a few moments with her when Lieutenant Saberin turned to go to the office, but stopped before entering the hall, and drawing a letter from his pocket, examined the address. Not a movement was lost on Mrs. Bobaline, who, in the pause of the conversation, heard him say, "She is mine, by Jupiter." She forgot to reply to some nice remark from Lieutenant Mera, quite piquing that young gentleman, who left her suddenly, just as Lieutenant Saberin turned from the telescope, at which he had stopped to take a peep at a yatch. He did not look at Mrs. Bobaline, but as he turned and entered the hall, a letter fell from his coat, and blew towards her. She snatched it up and throwing it into the parlor-window, retreated hastily around the piazza, in time to see Lieutenant Saberin going quickly towards the post-office.

The letter flew into Ione's face with such force, as to make her nearly cry out. Glancing out of the window and seeing no one, she concluded some cadet had thrown it, and flew to her room, without looking at it. When Mrs. Bobaline ran into the parlor to secure her treasure, she looked diligently for it, but no letter was there. She ran to the piazza ; had it flown out of the window ? No, there was no letter, she could scarcely credit her senses : but fearing Lieutenant Saberin's return to look for it, she fled to her room, and like a wretched culprit, locked her door, and wept violently, plead head-ache to Ione, and was invisible for the next twelve hours.

" LESSON FOURTH."

" *Fire and Load Lying.*"

"Ah, that falsehood should steal such gentle shapes,
And with a virtuous visor hide deep vice."

As Mrs. Bobaline and Ione sat on the piazza, Ione looked over the plain, and longed to become invisible, that she might have one grand romp over its beautiful expanse.

She felt like a poor prisoner, and heartily sympathized with the cadets. " Viola, let us go and take a walk."

" You are not used to the trammels of society, are you, Ione ? "

There was something terrible in her aunt's scornful little laugh, whenever the poor girl made a remark, and now she looked so disappointed, that her aunt condescended to say, " Why my dear, I could not walk across that plain for any consideration, without an escort. When I was a Florida belle, I knew Lieutenants Saberin and Mera, and I never went out without one or two officers in my train, and do you think I would let my old beaux see me walking like a servant, unescorted ? "

" Dear Viola, we need not care for any one. I am sure I don't, and you are married, aren't you ? " plead Ione.

" Hush ! do not let any one hear you express yourself so vulgarly."

" I've seen ladies walking alone, do, dear Viola ! It will be so charming."

" You see no person of distinction alone. I have never done it. I wonder the cadets do not come for *you !* " Mrs. Bobaline spoke severely and Ione felt it.

They sat a few moments and Mrs. B. arose and went to the parlor window ; there sat Lieutenant Mera, with a book before him, apparently fast asleep. She turned hastily and entering the hall door said, " Ione put on your things ; we will go out ! " Her voice and manner had changed magically. They were soon walking rapidly down the cavalry road, Ione lost in wondering what her aunt would do next. Near the chapel they met Cadet Smith. Madam gave him a sweet smile, and he turned and came to Ione's side.

" Where are your smiles to-day, Miss Ione ? you are walking so quickly and looking so demurely, I am afraid you are ' Wheaton-ing it,' or in other words, on your way to the hospital."

Ione smiled faintly, her aunt said tartly, " We are walking for our health ! "

" Indeed ? " he replied, then lowering his voice, asked

Ione, " how long since you have lost your health, and got that pretty consumption tinge on your cheek ? "

Ione laughed in a very natural way. Her aunt was shocked.

" Bless me ! Ione you certainly forget that you are in a civilized land, and think you are in San Francisco."

Cadet Smith bowed low to Ione, and said in his most impressive manner, " I will bless her forever, if she will always forget that she is here, if we are to be deprived of hearing that musical laugh by the remembrance that she is a prisoner too. Please laugh when you are with me, Miss Ione. Your laugh reminds me of my home, and my own sweet sisters."

The boy spoke with so much emotion, that it touched Ione deeply, and quite subdued Mrs. Bobaline.

Seeing the clouds returning to Ione's face, Cadet Smith began to draw upon his imagination to elicit another laugh.

" Did you ever hear the story of the poor ' Sep.' ? He had heard of the cadets foraging for apples and grapes, and not knowing about the fine fruit orchards of the Kinsley place below us, he supposed they were taken from the gardens of the professors, and seeing some tempting apples in one of them, crept in after dark, climbed the tree and was satisfying himself voraciously, when two young ladies came out to walk in the garden, and talk over their love affairs. They had walked and talked some time, when they cosily put their arms around each other, and in order to catch step, one of them said ' Hep !' The poor boy, losing all presence of mind at the dreadful word, started, let go his hold, and put his " little finger behind the seam of his pantaloons," and of course fell, in a very un- graceful manner, at the feet of the young ladies. They at first gave a little shriek, but after a moment's reflection, knew it could be nothing but a cadet, that would come tumbling, Ravel-like, from the clouds, and threw their shawls and rigolets over him. By the time the family came to their assistance, he was a prisoner between them. On

being asked the cause of the outcries, one of them said,
' We saw two stars fall from heaven.' The old professor
being a scientific man, took off his spectacles, glanced at
the clouds and said, ' he did not wonder at their fright, as
it was a very remarkable thing for to see falling stars when
the sky was not to be seen for the clouds. It was probably an ignis fatuus, rising from the low grounds.' ' No,
indeed!' she cried, ' it did not rise, it fell!' Here her
sister gave a scream of laughter, and the poor fellow,
alarmed lest they should betray him, broke from them,
throwing shawls and caps in every direction."

Ione shrieked with hysterical laughter, and Mrs. Bobaline could not control her own sweet voice from forming a
fine alto. Cadet Smith clapped his hands with glee at his
triumph ; when seeing Lieutenant Mera approaching them
from an opposite direction, he cried "Keep dressed ! "
here comes a blue-coat, and I must decamp! au revoir !"
and lifting his cap very gracefully walked away.

Ione really sorry to lose the gay youth, returned Lieutenant Mera's salute very gravely.

He had heard her musical laugh, and seeing her height-
ening color, and her beaming eye, it occurred to him, that
she was very lovely, and he said archly, " Ladies I have
fallen very deeply in love with a lady I just met ! "

The look of undisguised admiration he gave Ione, be-
trayed his meaning to Mrs. Bobaline, but the young lady
not feeling particularly interested in the announcement,
had turned a look of regret after the retreating cadet, the
wicked smile the elder lady gave, brought the gentleman
to her side. " Most beautiful and womanly of your sex,
how are you to-day ? "

" Lieutenant Mera, I always feel like calling for an explanation, when you address me ! " She said spirited-
ly."

" Ah, my lady ? that would be very cruel to your captive ! "

She stepped beyond Ione, leaving her next Lieutenant
Mera.

8*

" What are you thinking about, Miss Ione ? "

" I ? — I was just wishing I was over at yonder pretty cottage, feeding chickens."

" O, Ione! you are incorrigible !"

" And I wish I were with you ! which cottage will you have ? you can have any one you prefer." Said Lieutenant Mera rubbing his hands.

" I'll have the one near the wood, for I love the woods."

" Ione ! one might know that you were brought up in the wilderness, without trumpeting it forth on all occasions," sneered Mrs. Bobaline.

" I wish I had been. I have always longed· for the woods like a young squaw, but have dwelt in cities, as Miss Barrett says, " The blue sky covering me like God's great pity ! "

" And I," joined in Lieutenant Mera, " always think of Holmes' poor drudge of the city !

> How happy he feels,
> With burrs on his legs,
> And the grass at his heels ! "

" LESSON SIXTH."

" *Bayonet Exercises.*"

They reached a turn in the walk, and Mrs. Bobaline took a diverging path ; Ione did not see her and walked on. Lieutenant Mera stopped on the bank above the " Dade monument," and sighing heavily said, " How stern is the lot of man ; to plod the unbroken wilderness, bearing the heavy burden of life ; breasting its dark waves ; each for himself, alone ! "

" But the reward ! Glory, honor, undying fame ! —

> " I would spend my every breath,
> To live by fame forever, after death ! "

said Ione enthusiastically.

He curled his lip, saying bitterly, " Honor ! the huzzas of the stupid multitude whose voices when you are unfortunate, are a thousand times more clamorous to crucify, than they were when your sun shone in splendor, to deify you ! And devotion ! The simpering of some lovely belle before the cold slab, 'How beautiful that marble wreath is !' "

Mrs. Bobaline had joined them unperceived.

" Nonsense, Lieutenant Mera ! don't give us the blues, because you have them, it is unmanly."

His dark eyes glowed like coals of living fire ; she had snapped the last link that bound him to a vain, spiteful woman.

" Miss Ione, I beg you will pardon me, if I have given you pain, but 'tis true as gospel ! Content yourself to be a *belle*, and slay with the rest of the destroyers ! "

Madam walked away. Ione stood a little above him on the bank, subdued by the picture of the lot assigned to man by the stern soldier, her eyes filled with tears ; she laid her hand softly on his arm, " Caius Marius, take me down to see the monument if you please. Tuckerman says ' sepulchral monuments address the feelings both of love and pride, which bind generations of heroes together.' "

Lieutenant Mera took her hand, and helped her down the bank, and while she was reading the inscription, his eyes were fixed upon her with a cold scrutiny ; but when she finished, and turned away her head to hide the large tear that hung on her dark lashes, he took her hand, and drew it kindly in his arm. "By heaven, Miss Ione, I have given you pain ! and it is as Mrs. Bobaline says, *unmanly* of me ! What do you think of me ? "

" What do I think of you just now ? O — just now — you are a hero ! A ' stern heroic figure, self-sustained and calm, seated in meditation, amid prostrate columns which symbolize his fallen fortunes, and an outward solitude which reflects the desolation of his exile,' as Tuckerman so grandly says of Vanderlyn's Marius."

" Fallen fortunes, and exile ! " repeated he as if in a dream. " How truthful the picture."

They walked slowly, he stopped lest they should over take Mrs. Bobaline who was lingering for Ione. " And you, Miss Ione ! Permit me to quote your favorite Tuckerman also. His Ariadne, an ideal of female beauty, ' reposing upon the luxury of its own sensations, and yielding with childlike abandonment to dreams of love, how like a vision of pure love she seems.' "

" Lieutenant Mera, pray do not punish me so severely ! I quoted, because what you said, and your state of mind brought the picture, and the description, powerfully to mind."

" Indeed, indeed, Miss Ione, I was as powerfully struck with the resemblance to which I allude, the portrait is perfect."

Mrs. Bobaline beckoned to Ione, and Lieutenant Mera deliberately took her hand from his arm, held it a moment, raised his cap, and vanished down the bank toward the river.

Ione joined Mrs. Bobaline, whose burning cheek foretold a storm, " I am vexed beyond endurance that I came out to-day. When a man runs on as Lieutenant Mera did to-day, he must be intoxicated. I declare it is insufferable ! " She was ready to cry. Ione prudently forebore to reply.

PART THIRD. LESSON SECOND.

Marching Backward

A voice behind them, called, " Madam ! madam ! Please do not be my death, by making me run after you this way." A blush of pleasure suffused madam's face, while she waited for him, the gallant colonel being the pursuer.

Ione moved slowly forward, afraid to give her aunt an opportunity of taking vengeance on her by giving her " the cut direct," as she had done a few evenings before. Her silvery laugh evinced her returning self-control, and Ione was very grateful to the Colonel for his timely appearance, and powers of pleasing. A very polite little skirmish seemed to be progressing between them, but Ione did not turn her head, so did not see it was about a handkerchief *she* had dropped. She ascended the steps of the hotel, but not daring to enter lest she should offend the capricious lady, her aunt, she looked with the deepest interest toward the river, sweeping the plain with her eyes for Caius Marius, but he was nowhere to be seen.

The Colonel assisting Mrs. Bobaline, ran gaily up the steps like a boy of fifteen, left her, and approached Ione. With a bold stare of admiration, he presented her a handkerchief, saying, " I never in my life did hear of challenge urged more modestly !"

Ione's face became scarlet, she looked at the dainty article, held by the extreme corner, between his thumb and finger, — to her own hands and pocket, — then to her aunt, whose face was beaming with wickedness, she cast down her eyes, pained to a degree, took the handkerchief, courtesied very haughtily, entered the hotel, and her own room, and gave vent to her deep humiliation in a flood of tears.

After a " splendid time," with the gallant Colonel, Mrs. Bobaline went into the parlor, sat down to the piano, played and sang with her usual — not self-forgetfulness, but forgetfulness of everything but self. The Colonel said she must come out to parade. Well, where was Ione ?

" LESSON THIRD. '

" *The March by the Flank.*"

Mrs. Bobaline went to Ione's door. " Ione, I am going to parade, come ! " Ione did not answer. Madam opened the door. " Ione, you have spoiled your eyes, and are not fit to be seen ; and I want to go to parade. Never

mind, I'll disappoint you, when you are wishing for something." She turned to go away, but a new thought seemed to strike her. " I'll not be so annoyed ; just wash your
face and come along. If you do not, I'll never forgive
you ! "

" FACE. FORWARD. MARCH."

Ione rose, bathed her red eyes and nose, the nose had
the vote this time, and shewed its triumph, by looking like
an English ensign. To parade they went. A group of
officers hovered near, among whom she saw Lieutenants
Mera and Saberin. Her aunt's discomforture was complete, for after walking across the plain like a servant, *unescorted*, the Colonel had a party of ladies there, from
Cozzens, and did not even come to speak to her, and had not
the " odious " Lieutenant Burlyton joined them, she would
have had to leave the seats unattended. But she lisped
her sweetest phrases in gratitude for his attention. Ione
thought " sleek flattery and she, are twin-born sisters."
Her arts were lost on the sturdy soldier, who paid little
heed to them, but made the most of his time with " little
one," as he called Ione, and had, as he reported in barracks, " A perfect hocus-pocus time, with Mrs. Bobaline,"
spending the entire evening, much to that fine lady's chagrin. It never occurred to the matter-of-fact Lieutenant
that an officer of the U. S. A. could be anything else than
captivating to a woman. He told Ione what the color of
her eyes were, the quality of her hair, the imperfections
of her complexion, the shape of her head, etc., quite in a
friendly way. After he was gone, Mrs. Bobaline sat and
gave vent to her mortification by explaining to Ione, causes
and their effects. " The officers all court wealth, you see,
from the Colonel down to the cadet captain ; girls need not
come here, looking for attention, who have not splendid
homes to invite them to, or a grand party to accompany
them. That reminds me ; Lieutenant Mera asked how
you came from San Francisco. I did not know, and was

ashamed to say you travelled unattended, so I said you came on with a party. How did you get here?"

"As you say, with a party,— Senator Dasher's family — on their way to Washington. He put me on the cars at New York, under the care of Governor Morgan, to this station over the river."

"Is it possible?"

"Yes ma'am," replied Ione quietly.

"Well do bring it in, in some way, and tell Lieutenant Mera; I have been annoyed to death by questions about you."

"I cannot see why people should interest themselves about me, I never ask who they are, and shall certainly not take the pains to tell Lieutenant Mera anything about it; why should I? he is nothing to me."

"Yes, but we owe something to society; we must. all give a quid pro quo, for what we receive; if you pretend to be white, you must substantiate your claims to the considerations of society."

Ione's spirit was fast getting roused; hunted like a hare out of all her pretty resources, reading, walking, and music, which had always made her feel independent of the whims and caprices of those around her, she began to view life as a battle field, in which it was every one for himself. "I came to see you, and uncle, and have a pleasant little visit, and can be very happy seeing all these gay sights, hearing this delicious music, and walking through these enchanting scenes. I don't see why any one with the senses God has bestowed upon most of the human family, should not be happy, perfectly happy!"

"Don't talk like a fool, Ione! When you are with me, I do not care to fall into the shade, or be dragged into invisibility, by having those around me of such poor aims, and no ambition!"

"I view life in a different light: I cannot see the necessity of making myself wretched, because Lieutenant Mera minds his own affairs, at least a part of his time. I suppose they are *not* gentlemen at their leisure; each one seems to have his imperative duties to attend to, and when at liberty, why should they be obliged to rush for me, or I be blue, and feel slighted, because they walk with, or talk to another lady ? "

" Ione, you are too much ! You view life ! When your mother sent you here, away from home, I warrant you she had an object, and a very important one, that is, to get you settled in life. It is natural to suppose so. A poor widow's daughter should try to do what she can for herself." She looked at Ione out of the corner of her eye, and saw a very perceptible curl on her lip. " To be sure, you might do better in San Francisco than here, and — "

" And, as you say, the officers are like sleep —

> ' And ready visits pay, where fortune smiles ' —

" — Let me, a poor widow's daughter, be grateful for the crumbs of flattery, and smiles, that fall from these fortunate belles' table."

Mrs. Bobaline out of temper and patience, could give no more advice to one on whom the valuable commodity was only thrown away. She retired to her room without deigning to say good-night.

Ione went to her prayers, and was very penitent that she had vexed her aunt, and promised to be more dutiful in the future.

" LESSON FOURTH."

" *Wheeling and Turning in Double Quick Time.*"

(Lieutenants Saberin and Mera conversing on the piazza of the hotel.)

Lieutenant Saberin. " You call that Miss Smith so artless ! She was going to walk with her Cadet Smith, the other evening, they went off the piazza, when she looked back and saw me, and immediately returned, and went up to the parlor-window and called to Miss Dora Bellamy, ' I hope you are not to stay here alone, come with us? ' but kept glancing at me, while she was talking, and her eye was more eloquent than her tongue, but I stood fire like a statue, and did not take the hint. I thought, my little lady, I'll foil you for once. Dora went with her, who by the way, I consider much the prettiest of the two, — Miss Smith turned her head twice, as much as to say, Can you resist?

Lieutenant Mera asked slily, why he did not go with her, as he did not doubt she had a message from Madam, for him, adding, " you conceited fop, she is as far from being a flirt as a fool, which you are trying to make her out; besides, she does not admire you at all, she told me, you always reminded her of a bachelor friend, who, reveled the majority of his time in the sulks, and in those moods flew into a vehicle, which he called in an eminently proper manner a ' sulky,' which he nearly lived in."

Lieutenant Saberin was not flattered, and said he did not see the application.

" Never mind the application ; " said Lieutenant Mera, delighted to have vexed him, for his conceit. They arose and walked. Presently they met Miss Smith and Lieutenant Burlyton ; truly enough, Ione looked wistfully at Lieutenant Saberin. Lieutenant Mera was profoundly puzzled. He had thought her too modest and sensible to show such public admiration for any man ; could she have taken it into her head to try to attract that unsocial and aristocratic fellow by this folly? This was simply absurd, no, there was something going on under this pretty pantomime. He tried in vain to convince Lieutenant Saberin of this, who thought Lieutenant Mera jealous, told him he need have no fears, he could not condescend to rival him. Lieutenant Mera was offended, they parted, Lieutenant Saberin taking refuge in the impregnable sulks.

PART SECOND.

" *Ready.   Aim.   Fire.*"

Lieutenant Mera entered the parlor, one day after dinner, and found Mrs. Bobaline and Ione seated with Lieutenant Burlyton, and a lady—a new arrival—a Mrs. Mor-
dant Maryglot.   English by birth, and a great traveller,
she was a George Sands in propriâ personâ.   " Bless you!
had seen all the world!"   A lover of the fine arts
a great worshipper of glorious queen Bess!   They all
seemed insane with mirth.   He drew a paper from his
pocket, and sat down to listen, and for a time, thought the
two ladies destitute of soul and sentiment, and was rapidly
losing faith in their truth and humanity, so much did
they appear to enjoy the quizzing Mrs. Maryglot was un-
dergoing from Lieutenant Burlyton.

Mrs. Bobaline laughing gaily at some lively sally from
the witty stranger, called to Lieutenant Mera to sit up
and join the party ; but he, rather offended than flattered,
politely declined.

Mrs. Maryglot looked slighted, and remarked in a low
voice to Ione, " Pœnus est," " he is a Carthagenian !"

Lieutenant Burlyton glanced at Mrs. Bobaline, and replied " Oh, you must speak in his own tongue to him !
You recollect Charles V. used to say, ' you must speak
Spanish to the gods, Italian to the ladies, French to gentlemen, German to soldiers, English to geese, Hungarian to heroes, and Bohemian to the devil !' "

"Dear me!" said the learned lady, "and which am I to speak to your friend, Bohemian?"

Lieutenant Mera rose and walked away in high dudgeon, followed by peals of laughter, just catching Mrs. Maryglot's pleasant remark, that she should have taken him for a Bœotian. She then fell upon Charles V. with true English vigor, "confounding him for his impudence, — an illustrious Bob Acres, milksop, whiteliver, nidget &c." revenging the insult to her chérissable mother-tongue.

Lieutenant Mera avoided the terrible party of humorists for some time, and returned to his strolls with Lieutenant Saberin. They often saw Ione with cadets, her aunt or Lieutenant Burlyton, she always looked at Lieutenant Saberin till Lieutenant Mera was forced to yield that she was making a fool of herself about his friend. A fine development of such a character as he had conceived Miss Ione Smith to be! So beautifully consistent as she had been in nearly all the phases of her nature. "She is a woman, and that is enough to account for her imperfections, how could she be faultless?"

"Charge — Sabre — Bayonet."

Four o'clock had already passed, and Cadet White had not come. Lieutenant Burlyton passed and repassed Ione on the piazza, as she sat waiting for him; at length stopping and bowing before her with his coat-skirts spread out repeated like a school-boy, "'Oft expectation fails, and most oft there when most it promises; and oft it hits where hope is coldest, and despair most sits!' why comes not your tardy cavalier, fair lady?"

Taking refuge in one of Viola's pretty caprices, she did not answer him, but rose, went directly through the hall, and ran down the path to the river-side. Loitering along dreamily, she entered a tempting spot, shaded so lovingly, that the sun's rays were completely excluded. She stepped from rock to rock, and seated herself quite among the tops

of the evergreens growing on the crags beneath her.
Here she sat perfectly enchanted by the delicious, quiet
beauty of the scene, and purity and balminess of the air!
So rapt was she, that she forgot her own existence for a
long time, but the fact that there was a Miss Ione Smith,
was forced upon her when, " with wild surprise she stood "
and listened, most unwillingly, to the conversation of two
gentlemen on a path below her. She could not see them,
but as they addressed each other by name, she discovered
that they were Lieutenants Mera and Saberin.

" O Saberin, I succumb, the old witch certainly was
right! I am a Bœotian! I never was so deceived in a girl!"

" Ha! ha! Love is a celestial humbug!" laughed
Lieutenant Saberin. "Faith, I am sorry for the little
thing, but I am to be gone so soon, and then she'll fall
back on her cadets! She's ambitious, Mera! she's ambitious!"

" Bah!" was Lieutenant Mera's reply. Ione wished
for wings, but had not got hers yet, poor girl!

Lieutenant Saberin sang

> " Cupid is a knavish lad,
> Thus to make poor females mad!"

Lieutenant Mera said " bah!"

Lieutenant Saberin laughed. "O, gentle Protheus,
Love's a mighty lord!"

Lieutenant Mera turned fiercely, " What do you mean;
that I am in love with Miss Smith?" His *friend* did not
answer, and when Lieutenant Mera spoke again, his voice
was husky with rage. " Saberin, you are a puppy!"

" Go wretch! and give a life like thine to other wretches
— live!" shouted Lieutenant Saberin in mock tragedy, —
their voices mingled in a boisterous, heartless laugh, and
they moved on. Ione was petrified. She had not the power to move. She gradually recovered from the shock, but
had undergone a metempsychosis; she found herself seated
on her bedside in her own room, marvelling at the extraor-

dinary chance that should have led her to that spot, the first time she had ventured forth alone.

She sat still till her aunt came, having searched the house for her. " Why Ione, you look as if you had seen a vision ! where have you been child ? " Mrs. Bobaline exclaimed in unfeigned anxiety.

" Only a stroll down the bank ; and have tired myself out ! " she replied petulantly.

" Well, arrange your hair for tea, as I am going down ! " She found her aunt talking with Lieutenants Mera and Saberin in the hall, and sweeping past them with the erect head of one who was perfectly aware that she was misunderstood, and maltreated generally, she entered the tea-room alone.

After she passed, Lieutenant Mera said, " what's up ? "

Mrs. Bobaline smiled, and replied " she did not know unless Ione was in love ! She had been wandering away down ' flirtation walk,' alone for hours, that afternoon."

The friends glanced at each other. They went in with Madam and sat by her. Ione however never raised her eyes, and answered a question Lieutenant Mera put to her, in such a way that they saw she meant to be uncivil, and they became in consequence very polite to Mrs. Bobaline. Ione left them at the table, and went into the parlor, where a lady was singing, and as the sweet notes stole through the house, the two young men heard it, and both being fond of music entered the parlor together, the first time since Ione came. The sweet singer left the piano, and Lieutenant Saberin to amuse himself with the " love-sick damsel," advanced to her with his most fascinating bow, and asked her to favor him with a song.

Ione simple and natural as a child, said she knew only one or two old songs, and that she feared to sing after the lady who had just sung.

Lieutenant Saberin loved old songs and home-singing best, and led her to the piano. She was frightened, but this only lent a tender tremulousness to her naturally fine voice. She sang the old song :

" Oh, no, it never crossed my heart,
        To think of thee with love,
    For we are severed far apart,
        As earth, and arch above !
    And though in many a midnight dream,
        You've prompted fancy's brightest theme ;
    I never thought that thou could'st be,
        More than a midnight dream to me ! "

" A something bright and beautiful,
        Which I must teach me to forget
    E'er I can turn to meet the dull
        Realities that linger yet !
    A something girt with summer flowers,
        And sunny smiles, and laughing hours ;
    While I, too well I know would be
        Not e'en a midnight dream to thee ! "

As she rose from the piano, Lieutenant Saberin, really penetrated, offered her his arm, and led her to the piazza.

She had longed for this opportunity, and abruptly began, " Lieutenant Saberin, you lost a letter, some time ago ! "

Startled out of his sentimentality, he replied, " Yes ! "

" I found it, and have been very impatient to return it," Ione went on rapidly, lest he should interrupt her.

" Impatient ! could you not have given it me at first ? " It is sometime since I lost it." And genuine surprise made the tones of his voice imperious, and harsh, and Ione quaked like a culprit before her judge, when she supposed she had acted a Solon's part and would be completely at her ease.

" Yes," She faltered, " but now — now that you have it in safety — and I have tried to act for the best, is not that enough ? "

" This is very strange ! " replied Lieutenant Saberin. " Where did you find it ? When did you find it ? "

Ione evaded the first question, but replied to the second, " Perhaps not ten minutes after you lost it ! "

" Where ? " demanded Lieutenant Saberin.

" Near where you lost it, I suppose ! " she said timidly.

"Miss Smith, you are evading my question! I don't know where I lost it!"

"Did you not drop it on the piazza?"

"Did I?." said he impatiently.

"I suppose so; but now that you have it, is not that enough?"

"Did you know that it was mine?"

"No indeed, Lieutenant Saberin!"

"Your aunt knew it!"

"Yes, but she did not speak to me of it."

"This is very unaccountable! Strange that your aunt did not find it, I left her there!"

"I told you I found it," she replied really distressed. "I don't know that my aunt even saw it. I will leave you a moment and bring it you." And she vanished into the hall.

Lieutenant Saberin was confounded, and quite incapacitated for his adroit plan of cross-examination, which poor Ione would certainly have undergone under other circumstances. She came out in a few moments, and handed him the letter and was retreating precipitately, when Lieutenant Saberin caught her sleeve. "Stay!" She involuntarily stopped. He offered her his arm, saying, "I must know more about this!" Ione tried to draw her hand from his arm, he would not let her go, but said slowly and deliberately, "Is there any mystery about the finding and detaining of my letter from me, all this time?"

Ione felt that she had fallen into the hands of an inquisitor-general, but her pride came to her aid, and she told him that on the morning he lost it, she had a pleasant book to read, that she went from the table before Viola, to enjoy it awhile, in the parlor, alone. She did not know her aunt was on the piazza, till she heard the gentlemen address her, she felt no necessity for retiring, but sat absorbed in her book, till she was startled by a smart blow in her face, and a letter fell on the floor. She sprang up and looked out of the window, saw no one and supposed at

once, some person had passed and thrown her a letter.
She thought of her cadet friends, up at the hotel without a
" permit ;" she ran up stairs without looking at the address,
when about to open it she turned it, and saw it was not
for her.   She was just going to tell Viola about the sin-
gular circumstances, when her aunt rushed past her and
shut her door violently.   " I thought she was ill," she continued, " and as she likes to be alone when she does not
feel well, I went to my room, and concluded to keep my
own counsel till I heard something more about it, and if
possible restore it to the loser.   A good while after, Violetta said to me, ' I would give anything to know what
became of that letter.'   I replied, what letter?   She
looked surprised, and said ' Lieutenant Saberin has lost
a letter and every one in the house has been looking for
it, have you heard nothing of it ? "   I said I had not
heard a word about it.   And ever since I have been trying to give it to you unseen."

" But why unseen ? " he demanded.

" Lieutenant Saberin, please do not ask me any more
questions," she plead, in a piteous voice.   " Only don't
mention it to any one, now that you have the letter — is
not that enough ? "

" Not at all ! the letter should have reached its destina-
tion long ago, and now it cannot go at all ! " he grumbled
in a petulant tone.   " I don't see why you should be so
very careful of anything belonging to me, unless you
wished to place me under obligations to you ! "

" O, no ! " was all the poor girl could say, and tried
again to disengage her hand.

He dared not let her go offended, it was no part of the
young gentleman's policy to offend any one, and certainly
not a lady, as he desired to be a general favorite.   He
changed the subject.   " Now, my little friend, tell me
where you have been this afternoon ? "   Ione shuddered
perceptibly, which determined Lieutenant Saberin to
satisfy his misgivings on this subject.   " You are very in-
trepid to venture forth alone to the river-side ! " he said
in his sweetest tones.

" Who told you I was alone ? "

" You will not tell me anything ! and you want me to tell you everything," said he playfully. She did not speak, he added, " I will be more frank than you ; your aunt told me."

Ione concluded that her aunt had raised the house about her, and said, " I was weary of waiting for a friend, who promised to take me down to the river-side, and ran down by myself — and — "

"And, what ? " said he eagerly.

" O, I profited marvellously by my adventurousness — saw the world in quite a new phase ! and came home a wiser, but I fear a less charitable person than I could wish myself."

" Should such an ardent young lover of nature be uncharitable ? " he asked.

" It was with regard to human nature, that the bandage was so rudely torn from my eyes. Inanimate nature *commands* our love and admiration, for that is as it came from the hand of Divine wisdom ! "

" You say the bandage was torn from your eyes, yet you were alone," exclaimed he.

" Yes, but I was made the unwilling listener to a conversation, painful in the extreme, between two gentlemen, respecting myself."

She ceased speaking, and Lieutenant Saberin was for once in his life humbled in his own eyes ! What must this young girl think of his vanity and presumption ? She had heard him say that *she* was *ambitious*, in falling in love with him ! and Heaven only knows what else, for his ideas were not nearly as collected as they generally were, when conversing with young ladies, neither could he gather his scattered wits, to attempt the slightest vindication of himself. He led her to some chairs at the dark end of the north piazza, and said quietly, " Sit down, Miss Smith ? "

Ione declined very haughtily, and turned to go back to the parlor, Lieutenant Saberin walked at her side to the door. A fine looking young man sitting near the door,

4

remarked " That has been a tip top flirtation ! " He had
been watching them closely. Lieutenant Saberin bowed
low at the parlor door, and said, " Permit me to see you
for a few moments to-morrow at any hour ! "

She left him without appointing the hour, and entered
the parlor. The flashing eyes of her aunt terrified her,
and she went to her own room. It was late when Viola
came up. She heard with great surprise, the most hysterical sobs and sighs escaping from her aunt's room.

" Remarks."

Ione sprang from her couch, with a vague apprehension
of something still to do or bear. Ah! how she sighed
for her sacred quiet home. How she dreaded to meet her
aunt! Why, she could not have told. Violetta was
very beautiful, exquisitely so, to Ione's mind, and certainly
she was so to others. The elegant Colonel always gave
her one of his grandest bows, and often called on her,
though Ione had never been introduced to him. Why
should her gay, witty, lovely aunt, weep? Ione thought
if any one in the world had cause to weep, *she* had. Had
she not tried to please every one? Her mother told her to
be perfectly unselfish, and then she would forget to be
homesick. Had she pleased anybody? no, she had succeeded in a matchless degree in arraying every one, like
so many antagonists, against her diminutive self! What
could it mean? There was Lieutenant Mera, a superb
man, that God had made " on purpose," to protect little
defenceless maidens; he met her with a grand dignity of
manner, that would have frozen the blood in the cheeks of
fifty sachems. What had she done to him? Then there
was Lieutenant Saberin, to whom she was an " entire
stranger," accusing her of compassing heaven and earth,
to make him fall in love with her ! *Horrors !*

Cadet Smith too, what had she done to him? Had he
not made " ever so many," engagements with her, and
kept none of them? Yet she had seen him lingering beside

a lovely girl, carrying her shawl and parasol — all devotion to her. Here she nearly screamed aloud, in deep sorrow for herself, and imagined she was broken-hearted! She shook her head, to get these disagreeable thoughts out of her little brair, as if they had been so many wasps, and sat down to write to her mother. "Dear mother!" But she had taken more time to dress and dream, than she thought.

"To Mark Time. March."

A smart rap on the door informed Ione that her aunt was in the flesh, and going down to breakfast. She made haste, and joined her in the hall. She was surrounded by a group of officers, chatting in the liveliest mood with them, and Mrs. Maryglot. They all turned so suddenly upon her, that she blushed deeply.

"Charming!" murmured Lieutenant Mera.

"The blushing beauties of a modest maiden!" brayed Lieutenant Burlyton, "nay, will you not deign me one smile?" and he intercepted her way to the dining room.

Ione laughed, and said "'Think not thou, no smile I can bestow upon thee, there is a smile, a smile of nature too, which I can spare, and yet perhaps, thou wilt not thank me for't.'"

Lieutenant Burlyton assumed an attitude of mock humility, and responded, "'Heaven help me! to beg of thee dear Violet! some of thy modesty!'" All laughed, and he pointing in fine tragic style to the dining-room door, quoted Miss Barrett. "'On the door you will not enter; I have gazed too long — adieu!'" and left them.

Madam Maryglot followed him saying, "Partons! Je ne vous retiendrai pas plus longtemps!"

This was the most delightful morning Ione had had since her arrival; everybody seemed in their best humor, and the hour was one of unalloyed pleasure. The officers left them, and the ladies were all talking and laughing at once, when the colonel entered.

" 1st. Forward. 2d. March."

The colonel took a seat beside Mrs. Bobaline, called for a cup of coffee, and whispered to her to introduce him to her cousin. Mrs. Bobaline spoke to Ione, and introduced them.

The colonel rose with his cup in his hand, went to the other side of the table where Ione had seated herself, and sat down beside her. She looked painfully conscious of having robbed her aunt of her finest feather, which highly incensed the penetrating lady, for she read quite plainly, " Dear Viola, I — I don't want the Colonel ! " Madam concealed her chagrin behind a sprightly mischievousness, completely disconcerting the poor girl, so that she scarcely knew what she was saying.

" Fair lady," began the colonel, " may I presume on a few moments of your precious time, since all the fascinating younger men are gone."

Ione looked at Viola, a blush and a spasmodic working of the mouth, were her only reply.

" Will you take a turn in the carriage with me this bright morning ? "

Ione dared not raise her eyes, but answered, " I'll ask Viola."

Mrs. Bobaline laughed loudly. " Do as you please, Ione, one would suppose I was an old beldame, keeping watch and ward over you ! "

The colonel turned his eyes from Ione's burning face, in pity, — bowed in the most courtly manner to Mrs. Bobaline, and replied for Ione, " Ah, Madam ! do not such injustice to yourself ; who will bear the bell when you think it not worth your while to wear it ? "

" We'll have it put on the cat, to frighten the old rats away ! " sneered Mrs. Maryglot. Mrs. Bobaline laughed rudely. The colonel was not easily foiled ; he begged to change the selfish drive into an excursion across the river, to visit the home of the sweetest of our poets, ' The Homer of America ! ' nestled so lovingly in the bosom of the grand old mountains."

" O, yes! let us make up a party," cried Mrs. Bobaline eagerly, "and permit me, colonel, to make out a list
of those to be invited?"

" Certainly!" said the colonel, "if you will include
sweet Ione and I," and he folded his napkin very carefully. Mrs. Bobaline curled her pretty lip. They adjourned to the piazza. The Colonel lingered beside Ione
for an hour, saying many flattering things, till Mrs. Bobaline descended from her room, with the list, on which she
had written Lieutenant Saberin's name twice. "The
party," she said, "should be a rechercher affair!"

" Indeed it will be, if you have two Lieutenant Saberins,'" laughed the Colonel.

Mrs. Bobaline blushed deeply, and drew her pencil
across the name. "Now, Mrs. Maryglot, *you* must leave
your quiver at home, and be your own charming self!"
she said.

" Diana without her quiver?" asked Ione. The colonel
declared that Ione was Diana's self, and she needed no
other arrows than her eyes, "and I shall be your beau."

Mrs. Viola bade him not spoil Ione by saying those silly
things to her.

" My dear lady!" said the colonel demurely, "pray do
not call one of my most poetical efforts silly!"

" Poetical? ah, yes, they are what they call blank-
verse," laughed Mrs. Bobaline.

Mrs. Maryglot came on the field armed and equipped for
the excursion, and immediately began to warn Ione against
her new admirer, telling her she would find the officers
and military men, "an unco squad, an muckle they will
grieve ye."

Poor Ione looked really alarmed, as her own experience
corroborated the good lady's words. Her shrinking ti-
midity interested the colonel very much ; he drew her hand
in his arm saying, "There's ae wee faut, they whiles lay to
me, I like the lassies, Gude forgie me!"

Mrs. Bobaline had made out her list, but it was quite
another affair to muster her forces. The ladies were mostly

pre-engaged, or disinclined to take such a tiresome trip,
and the officers were still more unattainable, each one
positively engaged, except Lieutenant Saberin.

" It will give Lieutenant Saberin great pleasure to accompany Mrs. Beauballeine's party." The lady read and
re-read the " charming note." She would not let Ione see
it, and secure to herself this coveted escort. But what
shall she do with Mrs. Maryglot? She saw Lieutenant
Burlyton just descending the steps. She flew to him, told
him Ione was crazy to visit the home of the " Horace of
the age ; " that they were making up an excursion party ;
that he was indispensable to her happiness, with much
more to that effect, all of which Lieutenant Burlyton, the
generous, as he should have been styled, believed, and fell
into the snare at once, saying " All right, I'm ready."
Eleven was the hour named, and all were to meet on the
piazza. The colonel took his leave of the ladies. Ione
and her aunt, arrayed themselves very tastefully, for reasons
best known to themselves. Ione did not know that Lieutenant Saberin was going, but was greatly flattered by the
devotion of the colonel. They were soon reminded by the
untiring Mrs. Maryglot, that the hour had arrived but not
the beaux! The ladies descended, and were not a little
annoyed to find only Lieutenant Burlyton, with whom
none of them happened to be in love. Presently, Lieutenant Saberin came, and took his station by Ione. Mrs.
Bobaline could not have this ; she beckoned her into the
hall, and gave her a little *motherly* advice. " The colonel
had invited her to go, and she must show a little character,
and not bring superior officers into juxta-position with sub-
ordinates, that they might fight and kill each other!"
Ione was ready to cry, and begged to stay at home. Madam laughed in her bracelet, and said, " O, by no means,
only be a little discreet, I'll give you hints occasionally !"
She promised to obey, and they set out.

The tardy Colonel came directly to Ione, and apologized
for his want of punctuality in not meeting her precisely at
the hour.

Lieutenant Saberin looked sulky and greatly inclined to " back out," but Mrs. Bobaline came to his rescue, like a skillful general. " Colonel, I would like to consult you for a moment," she cried after him. The Colonel turned to her, and Lieutenant Saberin took the post he wanted, while Lieutenant Burlyton shouted behind her, " How can the queen of love and beauty bear the fatigue!" Lieutenant Saberin put his hand in Ione's arm, and walked faster to get away from them, and when far before them, was silent and gloomy. Ione at first felt resentful, but glancing at his proud, dark face, the thought entered her innocent heart, " Perhaps he has some deep sorrow, that lies buried in his own breast." And forgetting her pride, and that he was a reserved young officer, expecting to be amused, she warbled lowly and sweetly,

> " Ne'er tell me of glories serenely advancing ;
>   The close of our day, the calm eve of our night ;
> Give me back, give me back, the wild freshness of morning,
>   Her clouds and her tears, are worth evening's best light."

Lieutenant Saberin started from his reverie, and begged her to sing the whole song for him. She did so ; he was delighted with it, and the rest of the party joined them. Mrs. Bobaline looked eloquently at Ione, and she gravely took her seat in the boat beside the Colonel. Lieutenant Saberin looked questioningly at her, and at every one else, but saw no solution of the enigma. There lurked a very bewitching smile about the mouth and downcast eyes of Mrs. Bobaline. Lieutenant Saberin thought, " The little one is stupid, Madame sees it, and Madame is very appreciative, and by George! very pretty," — and he seated himself by Madame. In a few moments they were exchanging those nameless little courtesies, which seem to constitute such a spell of enchantment over the minds of the members of the " Mutual Admiration Society," and by the time the boat reached the shore, they set off together, apparently perfectly satisfied with the arrangement. Lieutenant Saberin had a method in his madness, however,

for the idea had entered his brain, to sound Mrs. Bobaline
about Ione. "She is rather interesting, and amusingly do-
cile — *but is she rich?* How came she to West Point?"

Violetta evidently did not care to show her off, she had
avoided introducing him to her. Was she ashamed of her
family? She had waylaid him to introduce him to Miss
Arnold." All these things passed in review before him,
and made him curious to fathom her ladyship's designs.
He said to himself, "I will begin sarcastically; that will
either please, or pique her, and draw her out.

"Ha! ha! Miss Ione reminds one of Cunningham's
"'Nannin O,'" sae saintly and sae bonny O."

"Yes, she *is* very demure; unaccustomed to society, I
imagine," answered Mrs. Bobaline.

"You imagine? do you not know? Is she some princess in disguise, 'some fay from fairy-land?'"

"She certainly is no princess, though the Colonel ap-
pears to think her a fairy or something of the sort, he
talks such nonsense to her!"

"Who is she? What is she?"

"Well, she is the child of Lieutenant Bobaline's only
sister; her mother is a poor widow — and — and I sur-
mise, sent her here to get a settlement."

"Ha! ha! a poor place to get a settlement!"

A long silence followed "the short and simple annals"
of poor Ione, and Lieutenant Saberin set his sails to in-
vestigate for himself this terre incognita, and falling into a
ruminating state of mind, he walked on without speaking,
chagrining Madame extremely, for she saw that she had
overstepped the bounds of policy. She certainly had
shown no kindly feeling for her young ward, and that to a
man to whom, above all others, she would fain appear an-
gelic; she was far too selfish and "beautifully impulsive,"
to be mistaken for an angel by any one who had seen her
often; and she had shown such undisguised admiration for
Lieutenant Saberin, that a secret contempt had crept into
that gentleman's mind for the poor infatuated lady; still,
his human nature could scarcely resist the worship of such
a pretty woman.

"*Change Step.*"

Mrs Bobaline showed signs of fatigue, supposing Lieutenant Saberin would offer her his arm; but she was disappointed; for he begged her pardon, and arranged a seat for her, to await the coming up of the company. They sat quietly enjoying the scene, apparently, but each was busy with the darling scheme, — Lieutenant Saberin plotting to get possession of Ione; and poor, imprudent Mrs. Bobaline smothering the sighs, and crushing back the tears, that nearly found their way to the hot cheeks several times, was building a Jacob's ladder to regain her lost elevation in his eyes.

"Ho! Saberin," shouted Lieutenant Burlyton. "Given out?"

"Yes," he answered gruffly.

Mrs. Maryglot had performed the walk in true English style, and pranced up, glowing like a rose, to the panting Mrs. Bobaline, "Up, up!" cried she "labor vincet omnia."

"Miserere mei!" affectedly murmured the exhausted lady.

"Ipse frueris otio," continued Mrs. Maryglot.

"Pray, Mrs. Maryglot, speak German, we don't understand you!" said Lieutenant Burlyton, looking very drolly at the learned lady.

"Very well;" she replied "after this, you shall converse in your native tongue, 'German to soldiers!' I think you said."

"*My* native tongue? I hope you don't take me for a Dutchman! Ha! ha!" and Lieutenant Burlyton lay down on the grass, and rolled.

"Mrs. Maryglot has just told Mrs. Bobaline, that she beats an omnibus; Colonel, what do you think of that?" Seeing Mrs. Maryglot taking aim at him, he went on, "not in so many words to be sure, but as near as he could understand her," and he laughed immoderately.

"Speaking of omnibuses," said Mrs. Maryglot, "re-

minds me of those that run between Berlin and Charlotten
burg, a delightful little drive of an hour or less; ah, 'tis
charming! the perfume of orange groves, and such associa-
tions gilding every spot your eye rests on. What a tame,
humdrum country is this!"

" Humdrum, madam!" screamed the Colonel, turning
scarlet, " is it possible that your mind is in such a *benight-
ed* state?"

Lieutenant Burlyton had arisen and drawn near the
belligerents, enjoying the prospect of fun. " When Greek
meets Greek," he shouted.

Mrs. Maryglot fell into a tragical attitude, grasping the
shawl that was falling from her shoulders, so that almost
unconsciously she assumed the grand grace and dignity of
a Roman senator. Waving her uncovered and finely
moulded arm to and fro, her voice rang out, " What, what
are your barren hills, and chaotic scenery, compared to
classic, storied Europe, where we breathe the air of Eden
and behold the foot-prints of an Alexander, a Julius Cesar,
a Frederick William? What are your savage haunts compared to such scenes?" Her nostrils dilated like those of
a war-horse. Ione drew near the place of conflict, and
laid her hand softly on the Colonel's arm.

" Madam! madam!" cried the infuriated man, " was
Washington a savage? Are not his foot-steps more — more
— yes, more?"

" Yes, yes," echoed Lieutenant Burlyton.

Just at that instant they were shocked by peals of laughter from Mrs. Maryglot. She pointed beyond them, they
turned, and saw Lieutenant Saberin with his cap nicely
adjusted on a crotched stick, preparing to photograph the
group. Squinting over it, he cried in the most business-
like tone, " Eyes a little oblique, · Colonel." They all
laughed, and good humor was restored. Lieutenant Saberin
put on his cap, and advancing to Ione, took the wild flowers from her hand, in a quiet brotherly way, and offered her
his arm. " Poor little girl! those furious people have terrified you to a degree, I'll be sworn you are glad to get
under my wing."

She could think of nothing just then, but the gravity with which he had enacted the daguerreotypist; and her laugh rang through the air, awakening the echoes among the hills, and rather throwing Lieutenant Saberin on his dignity. She explained that it was his cleverness that amused her, and he rewarded her, by throwing off the magnificent officer, and donning the fascinating young gentleman, and succeeded beautifully. Their walk was at an end, much too soon for either party. Mrs. Maryglot was with the warlike Colonel, who was anxious to retrieve his character in her eyes, by enlightening her dark mind, as it regarded the hallowed ground she was treading. As they approached the home of the poet, she asked "If the village was built on the General's domains; — were they his tenantry?" Mrs. Bobaline and Lieutenant Burlyton were directly behind them, and enjoying their conversation very much, but this was too much for the fun-loving Lieutenant, he gave forth one of his sonorous neighs, making both ladies shrink with affright The Colonel, unwilling to lower this grand idea to the democratic fact, darted a savage look at Lieutenant Burlyton, and said gravely, "There are several estates joined here, I believe."

"What great man owns and cultivates these enormous hills, or do they cultivate them?"

"O, yes; there are many cottages built at intervals, and there are fine graperies, and orchards of rare fruit, and — such things."

She thought this very fine; saying it was quite a respectable country. She was indignant that the General did not preserve acres and acres of park and green-sward around his mansion, and have herds of deer, and ponds for fish, and swans, etc. she could not forgive him for it! Lieutenant Burlyton ground his heel in the earth, and leaning over it examined it closely. Mrs. Bobaline bit her lip politely, the Colonel led the way into "Undercliff."

"Undercliff!" murmured Mrs. M. "the home of an American poet."

"Yes," responded Lieutenant Burlyton, "'Woodman spare that tree.'"

The lady looked in every direction, and turning to him said sharply, " What tree ? "

" O, I was quoting." Making a grimace at his companion, for her stupidity, as he said in an " aside." They walked in, and around, rather lawlessly, as the family were absent. Mrs. Maryglot pronounced it quite " homelike," but was disappointed that she could not see the poet. They strolled far above the place on the hill, and were now weary enough to return. Ione and Lieutenant Saberin had reached the boat.

" Have you taken the tenderest care of Mrs. Bobaline, Colonel ? " asked Lieutenant Saberin, which consideration, flattered the lady into sprightliness, and she said quickly, " Indeed, he has ! " and pointing to Ione she quoted, " ' To this great fairy, I'll commend ’thy acts, make *her* thanks bless thee, — O, thou day o’the world.' "

Lieutenant Burlyton, who had to drag the weary lady every step, as he afterward said, dropped his head, rushed from her side, stepped into the boat, and giving Ione his hand, seated her cosily by his side, leaving the rest to take care of themselves. Mrs. Bobaline stood back and let the Colonel help Mrs. Maryglot in, and seat her, he turned to Mrs. B. " O, never mind me ! " she said ; but he still stood up in the boat.

Lieutenant Saberin regarded Mrs. Bobaline curiously. " You are going, are you not ? " he said, but made no effort to assist her. She blushed, did not answer, but sprang forward to get into the boat unassisted, stepped on the edge, as it was swaying about from the restlessness of the tall Colonel, it upset at once. The whole party were in the water in an instant. Lieutenant Saberin had leaned forward to catch Mrs. Bobaline, lost his balance and fell after her head-foremost into the water also ; he righted himself quickly and caught her up, as being the object of his pursuit, but was unconscious that any one else was in the water till he had landed Mrs. Bobaline ; what was his dismay to see the half-drowned Colonel clinging to the boat, and the Lieutenant and Mrs. Maryglot rolling over and over each other like playful porpoises, while Ione was drifting away, with a piteous look on her death-like face. He could not reason, he rushed into the water, and after a sharp struggle secured her with one arm, while he attempted to reach the shore with the other. Many persons had gathered to their aid, and but a few moments elapsed till all were safely on terra firma again. Ione was nearly exhausted, but Mrs. Maryglot shouted so lustily that "she was drowned," and Mrs. Bobaline was really so nearly dead with fright and the chill, that she received but little attention, till she saw Lieutenant Saberin advancing to her with two men, and a large chair between them, to carry her to a house for dry clothes, and to get warm. She begged he would take Mrs. Bobaline, but he resolutely refused, and taking her up, seated her in the chair, ordered the men to take her to the hotel. Her aunt was at once endowed with new energies, she rose, put her arm in that of Lieutenant Burlyton, gathered her wet dress about her, and said "Take me after Ione." He led her to the hotel, and Madam Maryglot coming up with the Colonel, they were confided to the care of some women, and were presently arrayed after a very droll fashion, in garments " a world too wide," too long or too short, too large or too small. Their own wet habiliments parcelled together, and they parcelled into the boat, to the amusement of the spectators.

"1 Squad Backward. 2 March."

" They spake not a word, but like dumb statues or breathless stones, stared on each other, and looked deadly pale." The accident occurred so suddenly, that no one appeared to know how the boat was upset. The by-standers had told a variety of stories, some that it was the Colonel helping a lady in ; " other some " that it was Lieutenant Saberin, losing his balance and falling forward when helping a lady, but Lieutenant Saberin saw and understood the whole affair, that Mrs. Bobaline would permit

no one to help her, but him, while his vanity allowed him
to mortify her, and thus it happened that the boat was upset. Every one was sullen or thankful, and even poor
Madam Maryglot had not a word to say for herself, except
that, "It was a wonder of mercies that they were not going home dead corpses!" in a very quiet, christian way.
Lieutenant Burlyton's chin was buried in his wet bosom,
which heaved and shook at this sally, like a disturbed jelly,
but his mouth was serene as usual. He however had fun
enough, marshalling and marching them up to the hotel,
which they reached unseen, but there, ye gods!

> "The handsome bar-maids stare, as mute as fishes ;
> And sallow waiters, frightened, drop their dishes!"

The servants ran out to see them, but the ingenious
Lieutenant B. asked them if they had never heard of people going in swimming, or bathing, before, attitudinizing
before them he repeated,

> "The torrent roar'd ; and we did buffet it
> With lusty sinews ; throwing it aside,
> And stemming it with hearts of controversy."

They retired abashed.

The Colonel complimenting him in prose, "Well Burlyton you *are* a great fool!" bowed to the ladies, who were
disguised like washer-women, and each took himself to
his retreat as quickly as possible. Mrs. Bobaline kept her
room and her bed for some days, really sick from the effects of her impromptu bath.

"LESSON THIRD."

"Two."

Lieutenant Saberin felt a languor and depression unknown to him, for some days, and avoided every one. In one of these new phases of his character, he seated himself in the loneliest spot he could find. Here Love, the mischievous boy, brought to his side a pretty blue-eyed girl, just as he had adjusted his lorgrette to peep at a black-eyed one, from New Orleans. Of course he could not expose his infidelity to the intruder, so he politely offered her a seat at his side to admire, as he knew she would, the lovely scene around him. The little lass was "fond and fair to see."

She asked him if he had a little notelet in his "vade mecum," he had never read. With a rueful tinge on his ingenuous face, he drew out the little book, and among the leaves discovered,

"The Lost Bird."

"My bird has flown away,
 Far out of sight has flown, I know not where;
Look in your lawn, I pray,
Ye maidens kind and fair,
And see if my beloved bird be there !
His eyes are full of light,—
The eagle of the rock has such an eye,—
And plumes, exceeding bright,
On his smooth temples lie ;
And sweet his voice, and tender as a sigh !
Look where the grass is gay
With summer blossoms — haply there he cowers —
And search, from spray to spray,
The leafy, laurel bowers ;
For well he loves the laurels and the flowers !
Find him, but do not dwell,
With eyes too fond, on the fair form you see,
Nor love his songs too well :

Send him at once to me,
Or leave him to the air, and liberty !
For, only from my hand
He takes the seed into his golden beak.
And all unwiped, shall stand
The tears that wet my cheek,
Till I have found the wanderer I seek !
My sight is darkened o'er,
Whene'er I miss his eyes that are my day.
And when I hear no more,
The music of his lay,
My soul, in utter sorrow, faints away !''

When he looked up, the blue-eyed one had vanished, or
he saw her not for the tears that, "stealing from his eyes
in large, silent drops, without his leave," "dropped on his
doublet as Nature had intended them for ornament!"
Long he sat, in contrite sadness. "If she would only
hate me! I hate myself! The pure and lovely angel!
She would be as happy as a bird in Paradise with me
here! — but that can never be! No, no! I am commit-
ted to Pauline. Heavens! I could drown myself." His
monologue was interrupted by the voice of Lieutenant
Mera, behind him.

"That little piece of poetry, if you please, Mr. Saberin."

Lieutenant Saberin turned upon him like a "tiger chafed
by the hunter's spear."

"Mera ! "

Mera's frank, manly face saved him. Ne'er had Al-
pine son such need," for Lieutenant Saberin was ready to
dash him down the rocks, had he not been arrested by the
majesty of Lieutenant Mera's mien, and the lion-like, de-
fiant look of his large, dark eye.

Lieutenant Mera divined at once, that his friend supposed he had heard his soliloquy, when he had that moment dropped upon the grass at his side, the damp green-
sward muffling his tread, so that Lieutenant Saberin, buried in such an intense depth of thought, had neither seen
nor heard him. He supposed the last exclamation addressed
to himself, as a prefatory remark to some confidence about

to be placed in his keeping; and seeing the poetry lying on the ground, asked familiarly, and as he thought, facetiously, for it.

Lieutenant Saberin covered his flashing eyes with his hand, snatching the paper from the ground, turned and walked away. Lieutenant Mera, generous as brave, arose, followed him, and laying his hand in his arm gently as a girl, began in low, loving tones, to tell him some of his own plans.

They walked on till, coming in sight of the hotel, he said, " Hallo! Ladies? Who are they?" They could not see, till near the hedge, when they discovered they were Mrs. Bobaline and Ione; the former looking lovelier than ever, in a white robe. Lieutenant Saberin, really pitying her, had looked for her reappearance, to pay his most deferential respects to her. He now ran lightly up the steps, and without noticing Ione, greeted her warmly. His tactics said that he could not pay one lady a proper compliment, without sacrificing another lady to her. He expressed his delight that her bright presence would make the house inhabitable again, he had scarcely been in the house since that unfortunate affair. A pearly tinge overspread her pale face, showing that his barbarity to her had not drowned the love of flattery, or dethroned the idol in her weak heart.

" *Four.*"

" Ione, here are invitations to a party given by the Coldes, Wednesday evening," said Mrs. Bobaline, entering Ione's room, " and, darling, if you have no pretty evening dress, we must get one up, as you must look nice on your first appearance at a party, here."

" Thank you, Viola, I have some evening dresses in one of my trunks, I believe; but what sort of an affair is it to be? Who will I see? I mean, will the cadets be there, or, poor fellows! are they denied the pleasures of attending a stupid party?"

" Why no, Ione, of course cadets cannot go. It is strange you prefer the cadets to the offcers ; yet I don't know that it is, as they prefer the society of married ladies to that of girls, they are so stupid and silly ! But for your own sake I beg you will not insist on identifying yourself entirely with the cadets ; they are nice enough, but for a poor young girl, who should think of establishing herself, or of something beside flirting, the young officers are much more available. There's Lieutenant Mera ; be more polite and attentive to him ; he has spoken to me of you several times. You are altogether too independent with the officers, to be fascinating ; the cadets like it because they are not independent, but the officers hate an independent woman."

" Why, Viola, there is nothing an officer so much seeks as an heiress, I have heard you say so yourself ; and surely she is independent of them."

" No, Ione, she may show her dependence on them for their assistance, in a thousand ways, their opinion, or their affection, to enhance her own happiness ; if she does not do this, she is not loved."

" Then," said Ione laughing, and seating herself cosily on the carpet, " I will insist upon Lieutenant Mera giving me his arm, or I shall not be able to walk across the room ; do you think that will be taking ? "

" Yes, such airs would come very well from an heiress, but a poor girl must be very sweet, and kind — not to make a fool of herself though, and show one particular officer that she wishes his attentions alone."

" O, don't I wish the bonny boys in grey were to be there, and not a shade of blue should tinge my sky ! "

Mrs. Bobaline arose looking offended, and said as she reached the door, " I suppose Miss Ione will not object to a few invitations to dance, from the shades of blue."

" No — but what are they to me or I to them, sweet Viola ? all you married ladies are constantly ding-donging it in our ears, that the officers avoid a poor girl as they would the — the — small pox. Pray permit us to enjoy what we can have; the cadets *are* generous, and come away from the barracks to see us '*poor girls*,' while the calculating officers, would not walk across the hall to see one, unless you go and carry them in your arms, as it were!" and Ione laughed merrily.

"Innocent!" exclaimed Mrs. Bobaline, shutting the door with a click.

When Ione was alone, she ruminated. "Lieutenant Mera has spoken to me of you several times," yes, and he spoke of me to Lieutenant Saberin, "so so," with a shrug of his manly, elegant shoulders. Did that mean love, or any desperate degree of admiration? Not in her poor estimation. So she chose not to think about the disagreeable creatures any more, but took out one of her dresses. She would dress herself prettily this afternoon, as she was to go to walk at four o'clock with a "bonny boy in grey." Her toilet completed, she did not stop to speak to Viola, fearing to displease her by her elaborate attire; she ran hastily down the stairs, hoping she might not encounter any one to detain her, as she must meet her cavalier more than half way, just outside the north door, which she had chosen, to avoid being seen.

"INSTRUCTION."

"ARTICLE FIRST.   FOR SKIRMISHERS."

"*Relieve Skirmishers.*"

She met Lieutenant Storme.

"Oh, Miss Ione! how glad I am to see you. I was just going to send up for you, (a white lie) there is to be riding in the hall this afternoon, I thought you might like to go, and now you are all ready and looking as lovely as Wenus. Let us start down here, and take "Flirtation" in our way."

"Thank you Lieutenant Storme, but I have an engagement to walk, at this hour."

"With whom, may I ask?"

"Cadet —" began Ione.

"O, never mind. Where were you to meet, outside the hedge?"

Ione bowed.

"Well, we can go on, and if he is there, we shall meet him. Will that do, Miss Ione?" It would be a pity to lose the riding and walk too, as those young men are not the most reliable persons in the world.

Lieutenant Storme knew that Ione's cadet was in the south parlor; and if he could get Ione outside the hedge, they could not meet, and he would take the little beauty where she would be seen, and he envied, by officers and cadets.

Ione was positive that she should meet Cadet Smith at the hedge, and accepted Lieutenant Storme to that spot; but was astonished at not finding him there. He glanced in every direction.

" You see the young man is not as good as his word."

Ione looked annoyed, and replied, " I fear your remark is too true, they are unreliable."

Ah, well, Miss Ione! I will do my poor endeavors to atone for the young man's delinquency, and do " Flirtation " in good cadet style, and then *I* can take you to see the riding, which Cadet Smith could not do ; so please be consoled, and don't look so doleful."

" How can you, Mr. Storme, make fun of me so cruelly! I am sure he has not neglected to come, and I feel there has been some mistake; and I would not appear to disregard our engagement, for the world."

" O, Miss Ione, do not you know that young ladies should not make engagements with cadets ? Their great subordination renders them liable to receive orders from their superiors, at any moment."

" Their superior officer, if you please, Lieutenant Storme," said Ione, vexed.

" *That is* better ; I would not have you suppose that Cadet Smith has his superior on the Post, except in rank ; and I dare affirm has not willingly neglected his engagement," he said cunningly; " and I will give you his excuse very soon."

" You will be saved the trouble, for I think we shall meet him."

" He is very unlike me, if he gives up the chase, with such a prize at the end."

" Which way are you going ? this is not the way to ' Flirtation.' "

" No, but I did not wish to leave the hedge too soon, so I thought we would take a look at Fort Clinton, and then return to the hotel, and so around ; have I your approval ? " He said this very earnestly.

" O, yes, Lieutenant Storme, you are very kind ; and if we do not find him on his knees, at the entrance of the hedge, ' let me see his eyes, that when I see another man like him, I may avoid him ! ' "

All this time Cadet Smith was in no amiable mood :

thinking he would be a little *civilized,* or do as civilians
would think it only civilized to do, — go to the hotel for
her, he entered just as Lieutenant Storme stepped out
of the north door; so he went into the parlor, to
await Ione, thinking he would see her passing the door,
and not run the risk of being reported, he waited some
time, walked to the window, and could scarcely credit his
senses when he saw Lieutenant Storme and Ione walking
deliberately past the very spot he had appointed to meet
her. Burning with indignation, he went out on the piazza, repeating " When was woman true ? " He saw them
go to Fort Clinton. Had he felt indifferent, he would
have given chase and claimed her from the superior officer, but he was not ; and turned on his heel, more wounded
than angry — very sentimentally indignant. In the door
stood a young lady, an old friend of his, her jaunty little
hat hung over her shoulder by the strings. Cadet Smith
asked her whither she was bound. She replied,

" O, anywhere for a walk ; I thought it a pity to stay
in this pleasant afternoon, — where are you going ? "

He would invite her, take her to meet Ione, and give
her the cut direct.— " Nowhere ; I came to see a friend,
and *found her out !* Permit me to accompany *you ?* "

" O, no indeed. I will not take you away, perhaps your
friend may come in, and be disappointed."

" Why, what in the world could a fellow have to do
that would be pleasanter than to take a walk on such a
delicious day with an old friend, Miss Lizzie."

" Thank you for the *old* part of the compliment, just
wait till I ask mamma, and tell her who I am going with.
She ran through the hall to the parlor.

Cadet Smith thought her pretty and graceful, and chided
himself for having shown her so little attention since Ione
came : she would not have behaved as his new fancy had
done — he would treat Miss Ione as if he had never known
her, so he would.

Lizzie Arnold was a formidable rival for any young
lady. An officer's daughter, with a brother in the corps,

she was at home on West Point. Her mamma, a very lovely woman and very wealthy, won a large circle of friends among the best people, for her beautiful and natu ral Lizzie.

She soon returned to Mr. Smith. He proposed Fort Clinton first, but they were too late for Ione and her beau, for while Lizzie was gone to her mother, the Lieutenant had returned with Ione, and gone down the steps to the far-famed " Flirtation." Ione thought Lieutenant Storme handsome, but could not judge of his brilliancy, as she had only been introduced a short time before, since which time he had only bowed to her in the most formal manner, manifesting the greatest indifference about becoming " better acquainted " with her. What power had placed him in her path this afternoon, good or ill? His familiarity frightened and piqued her. If she was astonished at his invitation and evident wish to atone for Cadet Smith's non-appearance, she was still more so at his conversation. He flattered her in the most delicate manner,— told her amusing stories, and commented most freely upon all the residents of the post,— mentioned who were his favorites among the young officers, in short, was confidential to a most complimentary degree.

Ione, between perplexity as it regarded the conduct of Cadet Smith, and not knowing what to make of Lieutenant Storme, was in a perfect maze of emotions. Cadet Smith had been very polite to her, she had found him unvarying in his attentions, manly and straight-forward — their little interviews on the piazza, and one or two strolls, she had enjoyed very much ; and now, to her amazement, she found herself entertained in an equally agreeable manner by one of " the shades of blue " that only the day before she should have protested she was not acquainted with ; and her friend had broken an engagement that he seemed to think his existence hung on arranging! O, West Point ! would it not take a longer head than unsophisticated Ione's, to understand your tactics ? and how much more your accomplished tacticians !

Lieutenant Storme had succeeded in making himself so entertaining, that Ione had almost forgotten her disappointment, in her mirth at his ludicrous stories, when at the turn in the path, near " Gee's Point," they met Cadet Smith and the young girl she had noticed with him at the hotel. All parties look surprised. " O, conscience, conscience, man's most faithful friend ! " Cadet Smith saluted Lieutenant Storme, but did not look at Ione. Miss Arnold gave Lieutenant Storme a pleasant bow, and poor Ione looked petrified.

" Is not that the young man you were to walk with ? "

" Yes, Lieutenant Storme," trembled on Ione's lip. " What have I done to offend him ? "

" Please don't mind the freaks of a boy in this way, he has given his conscience a vacation. Really, if you insist on looking so miserable, I shall be tempted to turn, and in the face of the pretty girl, give him a sound thrashing ! "

" O, Lieutenant Storme, you would frighten me to death. Indeed, I don't mind, only I fear he has something to blame me for, or he would never treat me so."

Lieutenant Storme's heart melted at the sight of her pretty distress and trembling lip. " It may be he has been a little late, and some one has told him of our going out together, and the young scamp has seen fit to vent his vexation in this ungentlemanly manner; and in such a case the best way is to take no notice of him ; he will come to his reason if he is worth the interest you take in him."

Poor Ione heard, but refused to be comforted. When they reached the riding hall, the ladies and officers concluded that was a case past help, a clear case of a proposition accepted, they both looked so demure.

" Load at Will."

When they were seated, Lieutenant **Mera** joined them. — " Miss Ione, your aunt is half crazy about you, she has had criers out, all over the plain ! "

" Weeping cadets ! " interrupted Lieutenant Storme.

—And has had a detachment detailed to fire a ten-inch columbiad, to bring you to the surface, if you had gone desperate and leaped into the river."

" It would take more than a columbiad to bring Miss Ione up, this afternoon," said Lieutenant Storme.

" But really, is Viola coming to see the riding ? " she asked.

" Yes. Fearing her last remark had offended you, she thought you might have gone off on a high horse; she will soon inspect the riding-hall, assisted by Lieutenant Saberin."

Ione looked troubled. " She could not think that I would be offended at that; she meant it for my good, no doubt."

" But, Miss Ione, all do not attribute such disinterested motives to the interference of others, particularly if — shall we let Lieutenant Storme into our family secrets ? "

" It is no secret, what were you going to say ? "

" Particularly if — " said he, nonplused because Ione had not fallen into the snare he had laid for her, and fearing to betray his utter ignorance of what she meant, and only intending to be witty, stammered again,—" Particularly if it calls in question our — our — What word shall I use, Miss Ione ; can't you help a fellow ? "

" Get Lieutenant Storme to help you, *he* is in the ethical department. I never was felicitous in expressing my own thoughts.

Lieutenant Storme laughed, pleased to see Lieutenant Mera fairly matched. Ione, never doubting that her aunt had told him *something*, and fearing that something was as wide of the mark as usual, dared not commit herself.

" Help me, Storme."

" Certainly, certainly, — deliquescence — calls in question our deliquescence ; that will do."

They laughed, and at that juncture the gallant boys in grey came into the hall.

" LESSON FOURTH."

" *Firings.*"

Lieutenant Smith whispered to Ione, " The fourth cadet is Smith, Miss Ione."

She looked at him just in time to catch one glimpse of recognition, but no bow. Not a moment did she lose sight of him, even the entrance of her aunt, who touched her shoulder as she seated herself behind her, did not attract her notice. Cadet Smith's horse was very vicious — one he had chosen — as their standing entitled the young men to a choice — among the high-bred animals this important Post always commands. He rode well, took the ring every time, cut the heads with a will, and his " firings " were terrible to the unstrung nerves of the uninitiated Ione. Two cadets were thrown, but she did not show much alarm until his horse, on starting out, reared, plunged, reared again, and fell, falling on Mr. Smith. The dragoons soon brought the horse to his feet, but poor Cadet Smith lay senseless. The cavalry officer ordered a litter brought, and he was lifted like a dead man, and taken from the hall,

Ione had risen at first, and now stood holding by the iron railing, as white as marble. Not one sound escaped her lips until most of the people were gone, she then asked in a suffocated tone, " Do you think he is killed ? "

" No, Miss Ione; pretty seriously injured though, I imagine; shall we go ? "

" Where is Viola ? I have not seen her."

" She has just left your side, with Lieutenants Saberin and Mera."

They left the hall, but her aunt and her escort were far up the hill, so they did not overtake them before they were at the hotel. At the door, Lieutenant Storme left Ione, saying he was sorry their afternoon should have commenced and ended under such unpleasant circumstances."

" LESSON FOURTH."

" Cease Firing."

Ione went to her room, the little sanctum, to think over with astonishment, the unaccountable changes she saw in people, each day ; and wept over those changes, and offered fervent petition to Heaven, that she might be a steadfast friend and discreet woman. She found Cadet Smith a dead weight on her heart. She was anxious to know how severely he was injured. She took off the brilliant dress she had put on with such pleasure, folded it, and put it in her trunk, wishing never to see it again, she put on a black one, which Viola had begged her not to wear again, as it made her look like a sister of charity or a widow. She looked like both, as with her hair drawn back in bands, her plain collar and sable robe, she descended to the piazza, where she found Viola, talking with a lady friend about the party. " What should they wear, who should they see ? " Mrs. Bobaline said,

" Well, Ione, have you gone into mourning because Cadet Smith was thrown from his horse ? "

" Yes, Viola, have you heard if he is alive ? "

" Why did you take off that lovely dress ? you always choose such unbecoming dresses to wear to parade."

" Please don't chide me, did I not dress within an inch of my life, to go out with Colonel Storme ? "

" I think you are looking very saintly," said Miss Priest. " What will you wear to Mrs. Colde's party ? "

I don't know what ; I have some dresses mamma packed for me."

Miss Priest looked as if she did not believe her. " When she decides, you must make her show it to me, Mrs. Bobaline ; her dresses are so unlike ours, they have quite an oriental air about them." With this elegant compliment, Miss Priest said good morning to them.

Alone ; Mrs. Bobaline looked Ione full in the face.

" Ione, what made you tell Lieutenant Mera what I said
to you this morning about cadets and officers ? "

" What you said ? I never told him one word. He
came to me and said you were afraid I was offended at
your last remark, and was in search of me. I only said
you could not think I was angry, as you meant it all for
my good. The conversation then turned into a joke, and
nothing more was said.

Mrs. Bobaline seemed annoyed. Mera had shown himself very acute, for from her, instead of Ione, he had
elicited the entire conversation. Ione laughed, and begged
her not to mind, but come out to parade.

> " O'er the battalion like a tent,
> Cloudy-ribbed the sunset bent,
> Purple-curtained, fringed with gold,
> Looped in many a wind-swung fold.
> While for music, came the play "
> Of West Point's glorious orchestra."

Ione felt that she *must* learn how her injured friend
was, and hoped to hear, from some of the cadets, before
parade was over.

" *Position of the two Ranks in the Oblique Fire to the Right.*"

Mrs. Bobaline went to speak to some friends, and left
Ione, in West Point parlance, " supporting a tree." A
party took their station in front of her ; they were talking
of the terrible accident which happened in the riding-hall.
One very pretty girl said, " Yes, he was my favorite cadet. Last year he was very polite to me, escorted me
everywhere, and to think of just getting here in time to
see him killed, is too aggravating. He saw me, and bowed *so* sweetly." Her party seemed quite interested, until she came to the sweet smile, when they all laughed.
She blushed, and asked if her father had heard how much
he was injured. He said he had not, but would ask the
surgeon when he saw him. " Do, papa, there he comes,
now."

On being questioned, the surgeon said he could not give a definite decision; he was badly hurt, but reckoned he would not die, and glancing at the young lady's interested face said, " He seems to have some one to live for."

The ladies begged to know what he said; but he replied very pompously. O, but doctor, did he mention any names ? just tell me the name ! " persisted the girl.

"No, no, Miss, I cannot tell the name ! It might be yours, and it might not; and I fear he would not thank me in either case, if he got well."

That "*if*" sank deep into Ione's heart. The consolation of knowing that she had not offended him, was denied her. " Too late ! " she murmured. " He, poor fellow, lies raving of some one he loves, and they are far away; no one but strange men to take care of him ! " She shivered at the thought. She sought her aunt, and saw her walking toward barracks with her friends. Ione strolled toward the hotel, round the little path that winds on the brow of the hill; she left the direct one to avoid the file of ladies and gentlemen slowly wending their way up to tea. She lingered to look at the lovely sunset clouds, the dark mountains, the pretty little village buried in the bosom of the hills — the island home of the gifted ones — which brought visions of another little struggling heroine, in the " Wide, Wide World," to Ione's mind. As she stood, all became quiet. The cadets had gone to their noisy " mess," the band, with their glittering instruments, the drum-major's nodding plume and measured tread had descended below the hill, the officers' quarters opened to admit the groups of chatting friends; and the hotel had received into its brilliantly lighted hall, and its dimly lighted, but dangerous piazza, the many; and Ione stood alone, wondering that she was not happier, or rather why she was so miserable, where there was so much that was beautiful, to admire. She turned, surveyed the plain, and saw the twinkling lights that sparkled beneath the trees, in front of the fine quarters, and wondered if it were joyful and happy within those walls, as they appeared a few

moments before, at that beautiful spectacle,— the evening
parade.   Should she like to dwell there ?   Who with?
She did not " hand in " the answer to the superintendent.

" *Position of the two Ranks, in the Oblique Fire to the
Left.*"

As Ione approached the hotel, the sound of cheerful
voices on the piazza, the light streaming from windows and
doors, and music and laughter, greeted her, and she sighed,

> " Leave, if thou would'st be lonely,
> Leave Nature for the crowd ;
> Seek there for one, one only,
> With kindred mind endowed."

Some one at her side continued :

> " Heart-wearied thou wilt own,
> Vainly that phantom woo'd,
> That thou at least hast known,
> What is true solitude ! "

She recognized Lieutenant Saberin's voice and fine
form, in the deepening twilight.   She smiled, and asked,
" Did your lady love teach you that, Lieutenant Saberin ?"

" *My* lady love !   'From early youth War has my
mistress been, and though a rugged one, I'll constant
prove, and not forsake, e'en now !' "

" Surely you love some one better than War, do you
not ? "

" O, no !   Minerva will not have a rival.   When you
swear allegiance to her, all other idols must be dethroned."

" And where comes in a mother's love ? "

> " My mother ?
> Already for her son her tears of bitterness
> Are shed.   When first I had put on the livery
> Of blood, she wept me dead to her ! "

" How heartless ! "

" Southey *said* it, Miss Ione ; I only echo it ! "

Well, I shall echo Proctor:

> 'I hate the camp,
> 'I hate its noise, its stiff parades, its blank
> And empty forms, and stately courtesy,
> Where between bows and blows, and smile, and stab,
> There's scarce a moment. Soldiers always live
> In idleness or peril. Both are bad.' ''

And I expect that Miss Ione's ' I hate the camp,' will end as Theodora's ' I hate the soldiers ' did ; and I shall see you encamped around by stiff parades and empty forms, and loving them as much as I."

She laughed : " Do you know that I am dreadfully hungry ? "

" Poor Miss Ione ! May I not take you in to tea ? "

She declined, but he insisted, and they entered the glaring hall together. The picture was scarcely inferior to the one just left. The beautiful young girls, the elaborately attired matrons, the gay uniforms and fine figures of the officers intermingled, formed a most charming tableau vivant ! The supper table was almost deserted, and they seated themselves at the north end of the table, so that they could look up the river and see the beautiful moonlit clouds. Ione was too intent on her supper, and content with her fascinating companion, to see the envious glances of mammas and daughters, as their promenades caused them to pass and repass the doors and windows ; but Lieutenant Saberin saw it, and felt that if he was not making a very deep impression on Ione, he was on the spectators.

After she had satisfied her West Point appetite, Lieutenant Saberin proposed a promenade on the piazza. As they arose she percieved, for the first time, that they were not unobserved, and laughingly said " others have enjoyed our tete-a-tete as much as we ; why did you not close the door ? "

" I was very unselfish, I opened the window, that you might enjoy the divine, and left the door open that others might have the same privilege."

She walked in silence at his side for a few moments, he

asked if she was going to Lieutenant Colde's party. She
said yes, she thought she would. He asked if he might escort her thither, as Lieutenant Mera intended proffering
his services to Viola. She hesitated, then accepted, but
thought how will Viola like this? What can have made
him ask me, and Lieutenant Mera to ask her? I know she
does not want him, and am still surer this fine gentleman
cares nothing for me. If I only had the power to divine
their motives!

While she was occupied with these thoughts, Lieutenant Saberin was equally busy. What a queer little character this is; she must be perfectly indifferent to me, she
accepts my invitation as a matter of course, and will not
take the trouble to converse. " I wonder if she is rich ? "
He glanced down at the slight figure at his side, the glossy
hair, the rich bands, the high white brow, the exquisite
mouth and chin, the round white throat encircled by the
spotless linen collar, caught by a cross of diamonds.
"Strange ! " murmured he, caught by the same thing,
" that I should not have noticed, that she can be no plebeian."

Sure enough. The beautiful ornament glowed like a
lunary rainbow in the moonlight, while the sweeping folds
of her black dress, gave her the high-born air he had but
that moment detected. " There is none of the plebeian
about the graceful bend of that intellectual head, and dignified carriage of those pretty shoulders ; and if not rich,
she is certainly high-born."

Piqued by her silence, he went on, " What the deuce
do I care ; she can't compare with *regal* Pauline ! " But,
Lieutenant Saberin ! is not this little black-robed image
the first woman that ever treated such advances as you
have made, with such indifference ? " Yes, but she shall,
she must be conquered, she must recognize my claims to
every woman's devotion."

" *Commence Firing.*"

Lieutenant Saberin was not accustomed to Ione's man-

ner in a woman, and could not resist the temptation to
turn her perfect ease and self-possession into bashful timid-
ity, at a look of admiration from him.   Ione spoke first.

"A penny for your thoughts, Lieutenant Saberin."

"What was Miss Ione thinking of?   Her thoughts will
be worth repeating; while my gloomy cogitations could
give little pleasure; please, Miss Ione!"

She paid little heed to the killing manner this was said
in, but answered without reserve, "I was thinking whether we would be the happier if we knew the motives that
pompt every act; and if our esteem for each other's characters would be raised thereby, if we knew the *why* of
all their acts?"

"You would be infinitely happy in such a case; *you* do
not doubt motives surely!" drawled he affectedly, as one
would with a forward child.   She did not notice it.

"Well, please tell me why you invited me to go with
you to Mrs. Colde's party, and not Viola?"

"Simply, because I wish the pleasure of your society!
motive — *Selfishness* underscored!"

"I think that is nearly always the ruling motive, with
gentlemen?   Is it not? yet Wordsworth says, 'It is a joy,
to think the best we can of human kind.'"

He looked down tenderly at her, and said with mock
humility, "Will not Miss Ione begin by thinking the best
she can of me?"

She felt the glance, but ere its influence had formed the
tender reply, she thought of "she's ambitious, Mera! she's
ambitious!" and turned away her head.

"The best I can?   O yes, that is not asking much!"

He stopped, and leading her to the edge of the piazza
where the moonlight shone on her face, he leaned his
elbow on the railing, his head on his hand, and looked into her face with his peculiar smile, while he scrutinized
her closely.   She bore it bravely, looking off on the river,
as if she was unconscious that his eyes rested on her.   He
said:

"So, I am not asking much!   It may be more than

5*

you think, Miss Ione, it might be more than even I could wish ! "

The color went and came in her cheek during these remarks, her eyes flashed, then fell beneath his bold look, she dared not trust herself to reply, she felt paralyzed, had not the power to raise her eyes, but stood a marble impersonation of helpless indignation.

Perhaps it was well she did not look at him, for he never looked better, his black eyes blazed like two small torches, his high white brow, partly shaded by his cap, beneath which lay the dark clustering curls, dashes of silver light on them, where they were touched by the moon-light, his graceful attitudes — all would have captivated the imagination of the young girl. She did not see, she only felt this and trembling for her own weak heart, she almost flew from his side along the piazza, through the hall, up to her room ; he slowly followed, and as she vanished, he said in his sweetest tones, " Good-night, Miss Ione."

In his retreat, he met the Colonel, " O, Saberin ; you are just the one I want ; Storme, and Burlyton, and I, are going round to Dumpain's, and we want you to go with us."

" Thank you, Colonel, I have letters to write, and my lessons this evening, and I must be excused."

" Never mind the letters and the lessons, come along, Saberin ? "

" Indeed Colonel, it is simply impossible, this evening," in such a tone that the Colonel left him, and he set off for barracks, thinking, " I have found a hard case to subdue, and I fear she will be still harder to dispose of after she is won, but entirely too fascinating to be let alone. I'll play off against Mera, and be magnanimous, and sacrifice my happiness to his ! That will be all right — afford me a little pastime, and get Mera a nice little wife, and Ione a fine husband."

"FIRE BY RANK."

MRS. COLDE'S PARTY.

Ione had not heard from Cadet Smith since the conversation at parade, and was every day and hour more anxious to know his true condition. Wednesday morning she concluded she would take a walk down to the hospital, to get something for a headache, from the steward, and casually inquire after the young gentleman that was hurt ir the riding hall.

After giving her something for her own affliction, the polite steward informed her that the young man was a little better, but still very bad. Her aching head was about in the same condition, — it certainly felt less tight about the temples, when she knew that he was neither dead or dying! She would send to New York and get him some flowers, they would cheer his solitude. The question now was, how and when could she get them? She had heard her aunt speak of Mrs. Simpson as a " good angel " in all cases of tribulation, and she did not stop till an arrangement was made with the good lady, to send for them that very afternoon; they should come as if for Ione to take to the party. Ione knew that Viola would be asleep at that hour, and she should have a grand opportunity to send them.

At half-past three Viola sent Ione to her room to arrange her dress for the evening, but she sat waiting for her flowers till four o'clock, without giving her dress one thought. They came, — the beautiful, bright messengers

of love and good wishes — thanks to the indefatigable Mrs.
Simpson! She sat and worshipped them, and blessed
Mrs. S. Such rosebuds, heliotropes, lilies of the valley,
geraniums, calycanthus! Were there ever such clusters
of sweetness mingled before? No, clearly no! Her
trembling hands arranged them in a box, directed them to
" Cadet Smith, Hospital," the air was intoxicating with
their fragrance. The boy was dispatched with them and
she found it parade time. She hastily snatched one dress
after another from the trunk, and chose a rich cherry
silk, trimmed with golden flowers. She thought, it is very
bright, but Viola says this is my first appearance, and she
did not wish to be ashamed of me. Lieutenant Saberin
is so very grand, he will subdue it. She ran down to tea,
and found Viola already there, talking to Lieutenant Mera,
who drew a chair near him for Ione.

" So you are one of the sensible young ladies, who can
eat if they are going to a party."

She replied, " It takes more than a party to spoil my appetite."

" Yet you seem greatly elated."

" Yes, but it is not the party."

" The escort! " said Mrs. Violetta.

" It requires a woman to penetrate her sex," said Lieutenant Mera.

Ione blushed deeply, and said, " At fault for once, Viola. Judge not."

The eyes of Lieutenant Mera rested on her, as if they
would fain have penetrated the secret joy so apparent on
her face. Tea over, they went to walk on the piazza, and
met Cadet Allen. " O, Mr. Allen! how is poor Cadet
Smith ? "

" *Poor* Cadet Smith! why, Miss Ione, he is the richest
fellow in the corps to-night, any of us would change places
gladly, with him,— a wealth of flowers! Such a friend as
he must have! "

" Who may his kind friend be? " she asked, assuming
great indifference.

" Of course there was no name to it, but I think he suspects Miss Arnold ; he murmured something like ' dear kind Lizzie ! ' "

" Miss Arnold ! " exclaimed Ione, and her voice trembled a little in spite of her disguised tone.

" Perhaps he thought of her because he wished it to come from her, there was not a clue to them, no name," said he.

Mrs. Bobaline laughed.

" The more fool she ! "

" I wish I knew the sender, any way, I would cultivate her acquaintance," cried he, and bowed himself away.

Ione was mechanically saying, " Yes, it may be so," when Mrs. Maryglot, who seemed to be omnipresent, certainly always near enough to join in any conversation going forward, whether on the north or south piazza, either parlor or hall, now smirked up to Ione, and whispered loud enough for every one to hear, " Never purchase love or friendship by gifts ; when thus attained, they are lost as you stop payment."

Ione started. Mrs. Bobaline said, " What do you mean, Mrs. Maryglot ? certainly not that Ione sent the flowers ? "

That lady saw she had gone too far, and replied, " O, only a little good advice."

Ione saw she knew more than she chose to tell, and resolved to question her little flower-porter, Mike. She ascended to dress, but was not long making her toilet, and looked very lovely. A golden butterfly with ruby wings caught back her glossy hair on one side, to all appearances ready to take flight, and leave the rich waves to veil her completely.

Viola sent to Ione's room to say Lieutenant Mera was waiting, and it was quite late ; Lieutenant Saberin had not come, would she go with them ?

She would go with them, and soon appeared, hooded and cloaked. She thought it very strange that he was late, but never imagined that he would not come at all.

Mrs. Lieutenant Colde's quarters looked very brilliant

that night.   Her own good taste and discrimination in her invitations, gave *her* parties an eclat that rivalled all competition. She only invited those she wanted,— the lions, the
brilliant, the witty, the rich, the showy, and those she dare
not leave out.   Ione was delighted with the glitter.   Mrs.
Bobaline was proud to say, "She's my husband's niece,
from South Carolina," — she had heard Ione say she was
born in Charleston.   She was secretly pleased with Ione
for not caring that Lieutenant Saberin had not come for
her, remembered the happy face at tea, and the flowers ;
and putting that and this together, was confident she was
not at fault now, and — "Ione liked Cadet Smith ! "

Lieutenant Mera thought Ione a vision of loveliness, and
so thought another tall individual rather elegantly leaning,
half concealed by the sweeping folds of the long lace curtains, that draped the window.   He was talking to a lady
who seemed rapt, but not too much so, to lose sight of the
handsome Lieutenant Mera and the exquisite Mrs. Bobaline, and draw the attention of his lordship to them.   He
looked and wondered at the superb dress of the "ambitious," young lady.   He was surprised to see her fairly
eclipse the "regal Pauline," her joyous face told the vain
man that her heart was in the right place, and not out skirmishing for him.   His eyes followed the party to Mrs. Colde,
he saw a yellow light gleam from the hazel orbs of the
fashionable Miss Vera Colde, a sister of the Lieutenant,
who kept a strict account of every woman entering the
lines of the forces stationed at that post.   She was staring
at Ione, as an old lady would at a comet, seen for the first
time, just over her head, "as if her soul had suffered an
eclipse ! "

Ione released Lieutenant Mera, who danced with Mrs.
Bobaline, and she was left to the tender mercies of Miss
Vera Colde.

"Have you been long on West Point, Miss Smith,
have you ever visited it before, etc ? "

Ione replied in the most innocent and courteous manner ;
and when Lieutenant Mera claimed her for the dance, the

interesting Miss Vera knew where she came from, who she knew here, where she had been, and nearly everything she knew herself. Each question was followed by such an eliciting smile, and such a winning "yes?" like a "patient fisher, his angle trembling in his hand," it would have wiled Jonah out of the whale's maw.

" Miss Ione, you dance ' The Lancers,' of course?" said Lieutenant Mera offering her his arm. She took it, and as they moved off asked,

" Please tell me, Lieutenant Mera, who that young lady with the *Vera* peculiar name is; I verily believe she knows this blessed minute more about me than I know about myself."

" O, Miss Ione, how *Vera* severe! that is one of our belles; she excels in the dance, but I ought to have warned or saved you from that catechising; we all succumb to her and yield up all our hoarded secrets, as tamely as the prey of the famous Miss Ann O. Conder, yields their breath!"

" You call me severe, and say such things!"

" There are clouds of witnesses to corroborate what I say; beware!"

The music began, and Ione saw Lieutenant Storme and Miss Nora Kearney were their vis-a-vis. Lieutenant Mera bowed to Ione, and then to Miss Nora, in a very finished manner; and Ione quite delighted him with her grace and knowledge of the dance. Lieutenant Saberin, still unseen by her, watched with great pleasure the glidings of the little figure. Could she possibly forget that he was in existence? Very likely; carried away by the novelty of her situation, it might be the perfection of her cunning to pretend not to see him, — she knew he was there, or she would be looking toward the door, for him. She would do that from mere curiosity — to know why he had not come for her.

The laughing nod that Lieutenant Mera was just then giving, was in answer to Ione's question, " Has Lieutenant Saberin come yet?"

"Lieutenant Saberin is here, and standing at the extreme end of the parlor, conversing with Miss Kate Kearney, or Miss Tute, or some one — but, by George! it is not you. Shall I call him?" and he bowed low before her.

She was amazed at the dark, flashing eyes he raised to her face. "Certainly not!"

He offered her his arm for a promenade in the hall. As they left the parlor he said, "Are you quite content here, so far from your home?"

She sighed a very little sigh: "My home, my home, my happy home!" she warbled under her breath.

"Tell me about your home."

"There is very little to tell, Lieutenant Mera. My home is beautiful, and my mamma is in it to-night without her Ione, and I am a little homesick."

"Shall I take you to Madame Bobaline?" asked he, in his measured tones.

"Why, no! You are very funny, Lieutenant Mera!" laughed she.

"Thank you, Miss Ione! are funny people apt to make their friends home-sick?"

"Queer, I mean; you have not made me home-sick."

He led her to the sofa and asked her to excuse him a moment. She replied, "certainly," very much perplexed by his manner. The gay Lieutenant Storme rushed up, "O, Miss Ione, make me the happiest of mortals, by permitting me to dance with the loveliest of women!" She rose and made a very low courtesy with the gravity of a dowager-queen, and laid her hand on his arm. She felt very grateful to him for taking her just then, as she thought Lieutenant Mera had to resort to a ruse to get rid of her; and while watching the whirling figures in the redowa, was feeling that she was a stranger, in a strange land.

"*1st. Front rank. 2d. Aim. 3d. Fire. 4th. Load.*"

Lieutenant Mera made directly for Lieutenant Alton. " I would like to have your assistance in relieving Saberin ; I would like to introduce him to a friend, and he has been stuck with Miss Bessie Kearney ever since he came."

" Stuck ! I am not sure he won't knock me once for my officiousness. How do you know he would like to be relieved ? " with the blandest smile in his light blue eyes.

" That's not the subject under consideration just at present, Lieutenant Alton ; we will leave that for a collateral investigation," drawled he in the most measured tones, as they confronted the object of their observation. Miss Bessie bowed a lovely salute to the young gentlemen, and thought herself a belle. Lieutenant Alton *generously* undertook the relief, while Lieutenant Mera stood, and did execution with his eyes. Lieutenant Saberin not understanding anything but an intrusion, was vexed to notice the pleasure Miss Bessie evinced, at the addition to their party ; but unwilling, at any cost to his feelings, to be the " mournful third " in any place, said with a subdued voice, " I have been very selfish, Miss Bessie ! " and left her. Lieutenant Mera allowed him to get away a few steps, then followed, " *O, Saberin !* I would like to introduce you to a friend of mine, if you have no objections."

" Certainly not, my dear fellow, where is she ? "

He led him into the hall, and round into the door of the front parlor, to the sofa. They confronted my lady Maryglot seated just where he had left Ione. A broad smile played over Lieutenant Saberin's face, — Lieutenant Mera muttered " Le Diable ! "

" Thank you," said Madam, " I have the pleasure of his acquaintance ! " Lieutenant Saberin threw back his head and gave a very undignified " Ha ! ha ! " Lieutenant Mera echoed it on a very high key.

" You seem amused ! Think'st thou, I could live

> ' So long in this bright Eden,
> And not know its master-spirit ? ' '

" Oh, madam ! " said Saberin, " How would'st thou be,

> ' If he who is at the top of judgment, should
> Judge as you do ? Think on that : and
> Let mercy reason justice ! ' "

Lieutenant Mera bowed maliciously. " I leave you in
good hands, Lieutenant Saberin, I'll bring the gentleman
to you."　 Lieutenant Saberin did not know that he intended to bring him to Ione, but saw he evidently did not expect to see Madam Maryglot, and enjoyed his discomfiture
very much.　 Mrs. Maryglot pulled his sleeve as he seated
himself by her, " Look ! look ! at Ione Smith dancing
with Lieutenant Storme, she looks like an houri ; why are
you not dancing with her, instead of getting into the
clutches of Apollyon ? "

" Madam, I dare not trust myself near the blaze, lest I
get my wings singed ! " said he solemnly.

" Don't like that red dress ? "　 She exclaimed indignantly, " I think it beautiful ! if your wings get no worse
singing than that little angel would give them, you will
have to be shy of such introductions as your friend gave
you a few moments ago."

" I could face the cannon's mouth, with my friend's
friend as the artillery-officer, easier than trust my untried
soul amid such dangers ! " cried he heroically.

" Where were the glory of an even combat? The splendor of a victory is where the odds are fearfully against
one."

" But, Madam, there are cases where a victory would
be a vexation of soul, and it would be more manly to suffer defeat, than to conquer !　 What could I do with such
a prisoner ? "

" Imprison her in your heart's core ; and if she is not happy, hang her round your neck ! "

" Mrs. Maryglot, _I_ am not a killing man ! Tell all this
to Lieutenant Mera ; one of his subduing glances would en-
slave her for life ! "　 His eyes followed her as she left the
parlor with Lieutenant Storme.　 " You know where the

citadel is ably garrisoned, the beauty of an assailant cannot effect a great deal!"

Mrs. Maryglot's curiosity was aroused. "Now tell me Lieutenant Saberin, have you a sweet-heart? and is this bona fide constancy in you?"

He laughed at her eagerness; "Now Mrs. Maryglot, is this bona fide interest, or — or — "

"Interest, indeed! anything, only tell me! Where does she live? Who is she? *Rich*, I'll wager."

"Yes, Madam! rich in charms; dark and royal as the queen of night! A Southern bird in gold and purple plumage," said he, really warmed at thought of Pauline.

"By George!" exclaimed she indignantly, "Not a killing man! Gone down South and manacled some beautiful young creole, and come back here with your eyes full of ink, and your heart full of ebon tresses! Now I give you fair notice, if I see you pointing the smallest of your arrows at our bird of paradise, I'll tell her about your black bird bird down South."

Lieutenant Saberin was very much amused with Mrs. Maryglot, and would have lingered by her side a good part of the evening, had not the Colonel come and beseiged him, to dance with a stranger, his vis-a-vis. He found that the Colonel was dancing with Ione. The young lady to whom he was introduced was very pretty; he bowed in the most formal manner to Ione, never addressing one word to her, but executed the " manual of arms " in splendid style, with his partner.

"Ione did not show that she felt this treatment, but there was a little rebellion in her heart. She had not studied West Point Tactics, and the damper thus thrown on her, made her spiritless, while Lieutenant Saberin's partner, kept both gentlemen alive with her sallies. Ione wished herself at home many times; and when the march announced supper, the Colonel was gone, and she had no escort, and was nearly alone in the parlor, when Miss Vera Coldë came like an icicle, to her side, with a glare of surprise, offered her arm, to take her to supper. "You alone!" conveyed as much as Ione could well bear. They entered the room, she found a seat beside Mrs. Brown, and Lieutenant Burlyton came and brought them cream. All the young ladies were chatting so gaily with agreeable officers, or in cheerful groups, but Ione felt alone. She left the refreshment room with Mrs. Brown, and listened to a sad amount of gossip.

At length Mrs. Brown, feeling fatigued, grasped Lieutenant Brown by the coat-tail as he was passing her, with one of the professors, to the supper room again; and insisted upon being taken home immediately. They went with Ione to Mrs. Violetta; Lieutenant Mera came to them, and they were soon on their way home.

Mrs. Bobaline was very quiet. She had seen nothing of the "star of the evening." If she was in one room, he was unavoidably in another,—he had not once sought her. Ione was silent too—fatigued, and angry at Lieutenant Saberin's treatment of *her*. Lieutenant Mera was enough for all. He had evidently fortified his spirits with "seven others, more wicked than himself." His tongue was loosed, and his usually measured tones were made to skip like lambs. He made love to Ione, and fun of Mrs. Bobaline, in a most reckless style. Madam did not deign a reply, and attributed his behavior to the right cause. Ione paid little heed to his flattery, but could not but be amused at his wit and brilliancy. As he said good night he took a rose-bud from his coat and gave it to Ione, saying very gravely, "Well, Miss Ione, keep this in remembrance of all I have said to night. I have meant it all." She took the bud, and turned to follow Violetta, who had gone instantly to her apartment, when he whispered "Stay, Miss Ione! here are a pair of lovers, sure enough!" She looked and saw Lieutenant Saberin and Madam Maryglot coming up the steps. Madam cried out, "Contez-nous je vous prie, ce qui s'est fait?" "Ce n'est pas la question à faire!" retorted Lieutenant Mera. "Je n'aime pas, cet homme-là," whispered she, aloud, to Ione. Ione replied, "C'est mon meilleur ami!" Lieutenant Mera bowed to the floor, " Vous êtes bien bon ! " " Quel dommage," sneered the old lady. " Adieu, jusqu 'au revoir," said Lieutenant Saberin, in a very melancholy tone, and gave his hand to Ione. She courtesied low without taking it, and went up stairs. Mrs. Maryglot clung to her dress, vituperating the whole affair, in every known tongue.

" Cease Firing."

As Ione's door closed that night, it shut in as sad a heart as could be imagined. She sat down on the side of her bed, and inquired what Lieutenant Saberin could mean. How could he behave in such an unmanly manner? In San Francisco, her most casual acquaintance would call him to an account for it. Indeed, in any *civilized* society he would be held responsible. She would treat every man on West Point with the indifference they deserved, and henceforth she would look to something else than these " braves " for her happiness; and she threw the bud Lieutenant Mira had given her in such a spiteful way, that when she saw it disappear in the toe of her little slipper at the side of the bureau, she laughed outright, and took it out tenderly, and told the pretty thing, that it was only its misfortune to have fallen into the hands of a naughty man, she would put it in water for its own sweet sake, making a cologne-bottle serve as a vase. Although Ione's fit of vexation ended in a laugh, she was none the less resolved to wage war with the *braves* as she had named the officers, and the very determined little face she confronted in the toilet-glass certainly did not look like forgetting those vows, ' ere the dawn of the morning ! '

" TO FIRE BY RANK. READY."

Ione appeared at the breakfast table in her most becoming morning-dress. She did not wish to attract anybody's
attention, no indeed ! It was self respect ! There was
not a smile nor even a look of recognition for those she
knew at table, except Mrs. Maryglot. This was very
sweet, to shew those braves what they had forever lost !
She was learning life's lesson of masking her best features,
as a miser hides his gold. The bright smile drew a chair
out at madame's side, and in a very motherly tone, " How
did you sleep, my dear ? "

" She slept well enough, but dreamed of icebergs, all
night ! "

The good lady replied at the top of her lungs, " I fear
my dear, you are finding the *knight airs* cold here ! "

Ione's lips curled a little, and she said, " You see I intend to defy them ; I have donned my " ægis," and she drew
a superb camel's-hair victorine closely around her shoulders, the long white waves sweeping over her white arms
and blue robe, made her remind you of — of — well — of
an angel with her wings folded on her breast, but I most
solemnly aver she was not conscious of all this. She only
knew that she felt like a second Minerva, having left the
" hermit pity with her mother; had her armor buckled
on ! "

Surprised that Viola was nowhere to be seen, she hastened to her room, and found her still in bed. As she approached, Mrs. Bobaline cried out in a very-well tone of
voice,

" Whose is that superb cape ? let me see it, Ione ! "

She threw it to her aunt. " It is mine ; are you sick
Viola ? "

" Yes, I have an awful headache, and have sent for my
breakfast. But do tell me where you got this from, it is
the most elegant thing I ever saw."

Ione had gone to the window to see the braves go out from breakfast. She did not turn, but laughing, said, " O it fell to me from — the clouds; don't you see how fleecy it is ? " then coming up lovingly, " but dear Viola, you are not going to remain in bed all day ? "

" No, I shall get up by and by. Who did you see at the table ? "

" No one to speak to, but Madam Maryglot — all were there."

Violetta thought, " she is such a belle, I supposed they would have besieged her, when she was alone," and the thought that no one came to speak to her, nearly drove away madame's vapors.

" O, it is a glorious morning ! I wish you were well and could take a walk with me."

" Indeed, I cannot to-day, but you can go without me. Change the book from the library and get another," said Mrs. Bobaline in her sickest accents.

" That will be pleasant; what shall I get for you ? "

I do not care for any, you may get one for yourself."

" She could add nothing to Viola's comfort, so left her enjoying a cup of tea, a pyramid of toast, and three boiled eggs. As she went out Viola said " that cape, I fear, is too dressy for the morning, have you no plain mantle to wear ? "

" None that just suits me, for this morning, it is so soft and warm. Good morning, Viola ! "

The hall she found full of ladies and gentlemen, a number of her cadet friends were there, they were going to dance in the parlor, all rushed at her to join in the dance, Ione could not resist, and was soon mingling with all her heart in the merry whirl.

" Rear Rank."

Where, but at West Point, could you find the gay belles the morning after a party, in their muslins and slippers, at this early hour, whirling through the redowa, and bowing through the " Lancers," with all the airs and graces and a wealth of bright smiles thrown in, usually attendant on gas-light alone. What wonder the cadet returns to the tent sighing " ever of thee," after such a romp with lassies in white and blue muslin wrappers, lovely in real roses, with musical, heartfelt laughs, and the acme of zests given to all, that they could not stay half so long as they wished. Cadet Allen escorted Ione to the library, and made her promise to walk with him at four o'clock. She remembered Lieutenant Storme's advice, " These young gentlemen are not reliable ! " and replied, " I'll ask Viola, and if you come, perhaps ! " she said laughing.

" If I come ? that's odd." She made no explanation, he gave her a book he was reading, with a charming story in it — " Lady Lee's Widowhood." Lieutenant Alton was in the library, and followed her out, and walked to the hotel with her.

"1 *Front Rank*. 2 *Aim*. 3 *Fire*. 4 *Load*."

And at five P. M., Viola was herself again, and Cadet Allen came. Ione went to do " Flirtation," with him. Returned — he gave her an introduction to Quartermaster Corridor, his particular friend, telling her he must leave her, but he would consign her to his friend, to whose kind keeping everything precious was entrusted. As they approached the seats, she saw Viola sitting there, and Lieutenant Saberin at the back of her seat, talking to her; she did not venture near the two people she wished of all others to avoid, but walked on down the front, and back to " Barracks." Here she met Madam Maryglot.

" My dear, I have just invited Lieutenant Mera to take us down to the famous little Church of the Holy Innocents, I knew you had never been there, so used your name, without your leave."

" I am very glad you did, I should so like to go. But

why ask Lieutenant Mera, will it not annoy him to walk so far ? "

" I have not invited him to walk, but to ride, my dear, in the most splendid turn-out West Point can afford. I think his highness may condescend to accompany us under those circumstances."

" O, how kind of you to think of me."

" Not at all, child ! ' They that do an act that does *déserve* requital, pay — first themselves, the stock of such content.' "

Ione was fast becoming sincerely attached to Mrs Maryglot, malgre her peculiarities. If she felt sad, she found herself at Madam M.'s side. On their return to the hotel Lieutenant Burlyton met them and said, " There is to be a " shin-dig" down at Cozzens' to-night, and I will do you the honor of taking you, in an omnibus, Miss Ione, if you know no good reason why I should not."

She thanked him — would go if Viola went.

" Of course Viola is going. Did I not hear her say, " Thank you, Lieutenant Saberin, I shall be delighted !" He squealed this out, pretending to mimic Viola. " Come, Madam Maryglot, you must go too ; we'll show you how it's done at a *fashionable* watering place, so go and put on your best bib and tucker ; may be you'll catch a whale ! "

" O, do, Madam Maryglot ! " cried Ione.

" Ah, non sum qualis eram," said she mournfully.

" What's that, now ? " said Ione.

" ' I am not now what I once was,' child ! Why do you forget your Latin ? "

" Judicium Dei," replied Burlyton, and that means it is God's judgments on her."

Here she flagellated Lieutenant Burlyton in Italian, German, and French, selecting the choicest phrases she could think of ; to all of which he bowed and smiled as if she were complimenting him, in the most polite language.

Ione rushed off to dress, delighted that she was to go with the amusing Lieutenant ; she had come to like him far better than any of the officers. The beautiful road that wound through the trees down to the home of the *princely Cozzens*, seemed like Chestnut street, it was so full of promenaders.

They all gave a good-humored smile to the joyous load in the omnibus. The hills echoed with " Benny Havens O," " Dixie's Land," and the classic strain " Pop goes the weasel!" The gay party made an entrance among the fashionables decorating the sofas and chairs surrounding the magnificent saloon, quite surprising to behold. Lieutenant Burlyton skipped up the steps, as if he were assaulting a garrison. " Entre deux vins; E pluribus unum!" exclaimed he, hoisting Mrs. Maryglot up by both elbows, running down again for Ione, he introduced himself and her, as les enfans perdus! Mrs. Maryglot fell into a fit of laughter, holding her sides, while a continuous fire of oblique glances from one distinguished group to the other, queried, "Are these an importation from the lunatic asylum?" Mr. Cozzens however modified their terror by giving each of the gentlemen one of his glorious welcomes.

The Colonel had in his care a superb white embroidered crape dress, tied on with Solferino sashes, one of the F. F. D. C's. Lieutenant Storme consoled himself in Nora Kearney's absence by promenading assiduously with a terrible beauty in a cloud of blue lace. Lieutenant Burlyton danced with every mother's daughter that smiled at his lively sallies, which kept him busy, as he told Ione going home. Lieutenant Saberin promenaded most of the evening on the piazza with Mrs. Bobaline, inviting Ione to dance but once, quite as if it were a civility he owed her on her aunt's account. Madam Maryglot did catch a whale, a real spermaceti — one that had engulphed half a dozen ships, and swallowed all their treasures! The ride home was quite as musical as their coming, and a trifle more boisterous.

"Church Call."

Ione was awakened by the band playing for "Inspection." She stood at her window listening to the sweet notes of "Stabat Mater;" it was a lovely Sabbath morning, and the revel of last night seemed like an unholy dream. She made many good resolutions, and among others that another Sabbath should not pass disregarded by her, she would go to church. She descended to breakfast, and found Viola sitting talking to Mrs. Maryglot, who had just invited her to ride down to the Church of the Holy Innocents, with them in the afternoon. Mrs. Bobaline excused herself, as she should lose her "nap."

Ione asked if she would not go with her in the morning.

"No, I think not, I was up so late last night; if you wish to go, the soldier will show you a seat."

"I will go," said Ione. As she descended to the piazza she thought " oh, if my mamma were only here, how much we would enjoy this delightful Sabbath-day together. What would I not give for her counsel and guiding hand, in this maze of — I know-not-what-to-do! Alone, where I most need a friend. Saddened by these thoughts she stood looking off toward the plain, slowly pulling on her gloves. She heard the "church call," its sweet notes echoed among the Academic Halls, and adjacent hills, calling many weary home-sick ones, and many a reluctant truant, to hear the words of consolation, of counsel and warning. Bentz, the bugler, vied with the birds, and Ione thought it was a pity that the bugle should not be sounded as a church call in all churches. She saw a lady on the path before her, as she descended the hotel steps, and at once recognized Mrs. Maryglot. She hastened, and joining her, they entered the chapel before the battalion. The old lady stared around her as if she was in a museum, quite mortifying Ione, by her perfect indifference to the attention she was attracting.

" Where is the soldier to show us a seat ? I don't see him," said she aloud. " There's the Colonel," she continued marching up the centre aisle, " He'll give us a seat." Hearing his name mentioned he turned and saw the ladies, rose and motioned them round to his seat. Ione's face was scarlet before they reached the polite Colonel. Madam stood some time surveying the church, then seating herself, she leaned over Ione, saying to the Colonel, " I see you ape the English. Who is that man and woman, over the chancel ? " meaning the painting by Weir. Here the cadets came in, and she sat up and stared in dismay, at the shout of command within the walls, the clang of sword and bayonet, the tread of three hundred men, as they marched to their seats. She asked the Colonel as the chaplain came in, " Is it customary to reserve the best seats for those boys ? I supposed they were for the superintendent's family and other distinguished people." The cadets that heard her, laughed, and the Colonel elevated his shoulders, and looked like a saint. Her investigations did not cease till the fine voice of the chaplain resounded in her ears. " The Lord is in His Holy Temple."

She was greatly impressed with his fine reading, and whispered to the Colonel to present her after service. They lingered long examining the painting. She wondered if a mortal could be admitted to his studio. The flags — they had their right place — were they arranged by the excellent taste of the Colonel ?

He regretted he must give the honor where it was due, " To an artist upholsterer from New York."

" I was in hopes I could compliment your taste in something about the post, Colonel; what have *you* done? "

" Here? " said he in a discomfited tone.

" Anywhere, anywhere! " He stroked his moustache and beard. " Tell me of some of your feats in arms, were you never in a battle? "

" No very renowned field," said he deprecatingly.

" Yet you conqured Mexico? "

" Yes," said he, drawling a little, as if ashamed of the unequal contest. " But you know Mexico is not formidable like England or France."

" Oh, I know, but tell me about some of those battles, they were hugely trumpeted at the time. Were'nt you there? "

" Yes, Madam, but a — but suppose you tell me some of the feats your ladyship has performed," said the gallant Colonel.

" It reminds me, ' merit was ever modest known! ' " she replied drily.

" Really now Madam, it would be delightful to hear some of — "

" Arnold was one of your heroes, where is his tablet? " she asked maliciously, displeased at the Colonel pointing out the Yorktown flags. He showed her the blank tablet. She seemed struck with the idea, and repeated from her idol poet, " Thou art a traitor, and a miscreant, too good to be so, and too bad to live! "

" Me, Madam?

> ' Lies it within the bounds of possible things,
> That I should lend my name to that word — " Traitor? ' "

" No, no! I was speaking of that other hero," said Madam, and left the chapel repeating

> " Is there not some chosen curse,
> Some hidden thunder in the stores of heaven,
> Red with uncommon wrath, to blast the man
> Who owes his greatness to his country's ruin? "

Ione was conciliating the Colonel, who had lost his bland elegance of manner. Madam always ruffled his plumes, as Lieutenant Burlyton cleverly observed.

Dear reader were you ever becalmed? Mrs. Maryglot had been on the coast of Spain; and she likened the hotel on a Sabbath after dinner to one in such a case! she could not endure it, and ordered the carriage early, and the garçon tapped at Ione's door, " Madam was in a hurry." She found Lieutenant Mera looking as bright as if he had been just bought at a hair dresser's, and in a delightful mood. They drove out of the Black-gate and up the Fort-Putnam road, while Lieutenant Mera entertained them with many stories about the points of interest; and Madam Maryglot was an inquisitor general at getting information from all sources, and she found a pleasant and intelligent companion in the man she had pronounced a Bœòtian. As they drove up under the trees in front of the church, Madam exclaimed, " Ah how lovely and home-like! A wee handful of old England set down in your untamed country." She was wild over it. After prayers she lingered reading every inscription, and left the " delicious pet of a church " with a sigh.

As they returned home, Lieutenant Mera asked Ione if she had ever visited the cemetery at West Point. She had not, and they drove to it. Mrs Maryglot said as she had been there, she would leave them to walk home.

Ione admired the monuments, and wandered among them, reading the inscriptions with a subdued enjoyment that greatly interested her companion. He led her to the graves of the " Innocents " to whose memory the church they had just left, had been raised as a monument. They sat down to rest, and Liuetenant Mera took from his pocket Butler's poem on this grave-yard, and read in his low musical tones, one of the sweetest things ever written.

" And here at last who oould not rest contented;
    Beneath — the River, with its tranquil flood,
    Around — the breezes of the morning scented
    With odors from the wood.

Above — the eternal hills, their shadows blending
With morn and noon and twilight's deepening pall,
And over head — the infinite heavens, attending
Until the end of all."

As he finished, the holy hush of the place was entrancing; the soft low tones, and sweetly solemn words, harmonized with the day, the hour, the scene; and now the distant notes of the band, at evening parade, stole over them with a dreamy blessedness, that Ione recalled years after as an oasis in her West Point experience. They slowly wended their way back to the hotel.

"LESSON FIFTH."

"Fire and Load Kneeling."

Ione's evident depression of spirits gave Mrs. Maryglot as much uneasiness as she was capable of feeling; accordingly, after she was arrayed for the evening, she tapped at Ione's door saying, "Come pet."

Her heart nearly rushed out at her eyes, at those "sounds of home," but she gave a little swallow, and squeaked out "Yes," and joined her queer, but sincere friend. Madam leaned affectionately on Ione's arm, as they rapidly "reconnoitered" as she said, to see, "Who were where." They walked twice around the piazza, and through the crowded hall. Every eye followed Ione, whose heightened color became crimson, as they walked on, by hearing one *lady* remark to another, "*She* engaged to Lieutenant Saberin? I don't believe it! He would'nt have her."

Madam put her arm softly around Ione's waist, and darting a look at the lady that reminded her of an old superstition about the evil eye, she fairly growled, "O, yes, that's devilish woman! She must give her *slap* if it breaks the hearts of half her sex."

"O, how I have coveted that lady's friendship!" said Ione plaintively.

" Who is she ? " asked Madam.

" Colonel Tee's lady." And the great drops forced themselves down her burning cheeks.

Mrs. Maryglot drew her to the steps leading to the glen behind the hotel. " Now what a little einfaltig liebling," she said in a choked voice.

Ione laughed through her tears. " What is that? do talk English to me, Mrs. Maryglot ! "

" O, that's nothing bad ; its a sweet word. Liebling ; darling, favorite, etc. Now why do you cry ? "

" Oh ! Mrs. Maryglot, I want somebody to tell something to," and she sobbed outright.

" Then tell me ! I'm just the one to keep it, and counsel you. Well ? "

Ione remembered that her mother had often said to her, " Aye, keep something to yoursel' ye ne'er will tell to ony," and trembled at the thought of confiding in a stranger ; but still more so, at going on unguided by a wiser brain than her own. She fairly threw herself into Mrs. Maryglot's arms. Oh ! Mrs. Maryglot, I am — I am engaged to Lieutenant Saberin."

Mrs. Maryglot really rejoiced at this splendid announcement, as she thought ; looked at her with a quizzical face, " Well, and what is there so horrible about that? he is a magnum bonum thrown down to you; and — and you're another ; " and she hugged her very much as a bear would have done.

" Oh ! — Mrs. Maryglot — O, — But then you know, — I don't love him ! — I'm afraid of him ! I know he's not good ! "

" Oh ! — ah ! that's another thing ! Sie solten sich vor ihm scämen, liebling," and she held her at arms length and looked at her.

" Why will you persist in talking Greek to me ? you know I don't know what you say," cried Ione, pushing forward, and hiding her burning face in Mrs. Maryglot's neck.

" It's not Greek, child ; but most excellent German. Why don't you understand German ? "

"Because I never took a dozen lessons in the horrid language."

"Well, well, you must begin at once to study it, it is the finest language in the world." (After a moment.) "Well, and you don't love him? what next? Girl-like you love somebody else — eh?"

Ione looked up very wildly. "Who told you so?"

"'O, there's nothing lost to him that sees, with an eye that feeling gave,'" madam replied adroitly, for she knew nothing about it.

"Well, does everybody know it?" said the einfaltig liebling.

"No, no! no one but me! But how in the name of the 'fiery Alps, rocks, caves, lakes, fens, bogs, dens, and shades of death' did you get engaged to him, without loving him? I did not think you such a milk-sop, such a — a —" rattled on she, in a merciless way.

"O! Mrs. — dear madam, pity me!"

Madam looked like a stone jug, and the confession began.

"You see, Mrs. Maryglot, I thought like Mrs. Tee, that he was very high-minded, and — that I was doing something grand, till I found I did not love him — that I was afraid of him, and then I knew I had sinned!" and the sobs broke forth anew.

Her friend took her hand, and caressed it.

Ione leaned her hot cheek on madam's shoulder. "What can be done, my dear friend? I'll write to mamma, to send right off for me!" Still no reply from her *dear friend.* Ione moaned piteously.

At length Mrs. Maryglot said, "And who is the other?"

"Oh, do not ask me that! Perhaps I only think he is good, perhaps it's only because I am not afraid of him, and he don't care a pin for me." She sat down on the grass, dropped her hands in her lap in a very hopeless way, and began in a low voice; "For some reason I shrank from him from the first; there was a curious impertinence in his eyes from the first time I ever met them. Then all

6*

at once he became very polite, and was sure to seek me
when I was away from Viola. I was flattered, and thought
I had formed groundless prejudices against him, but I
fought my heart every step. One evening I ran down
from my room to look for Viola or you, and saw no one in
the hall, but advancing hastily to the north door, I turned
my head thinking I heard some one coming out of the parlor, while hastening on, I ran right into some one's face ;
I gave a little cry, and Lieutenant Saberin caught me in
his arms ; he saw me coming, and stood at the side of the
door, to frighten me. He said he had been waiting an hour
for me. There was no one out there, and I was very indignant that he should behave in that way, but he fell on
his knees and called me — oh, a great many — everything
— said I was his life — oh — you know ! I was so surprised and trembled so that he thought it was all — love, I
suppose. He held my hand and would not release it till I
would become engaged to him. I said no, no — he plead
for three weeks, and then if I did not like him — or, at
last, would I be engaged for fifteen minutes. I laughed,
and then he said we were engaged."

" Well ! " said Mrs. Maryglot.

" O, well, I said nothing, and he said that meant, *yes*."

" That, was when ? " asked madam.

" A week ago, but I have not walked with him, or
scarcely seen him since, for I fear him. When he finds me
alone, he calls me his petite jolie fiancée, and says he likes
me all the better for my shyness ; but before others he
throws me kisses slily off his finger-tips." Here she
curled her pretty lips. " He says, now we are cheating
Lieutenant Mera, beautifully ; and that is just what I
don't want ! O, I'm not engaged to him one bit ; that is,
my heart's not." Here she buried her face in her hands
and wept bitterly. " I wish I was with mamma. I wish
he was hung ! "

Mrs. Maryglot looked to her like an old toad, sitting
on the rocks, with a brown and steel color shot-silk, her
fat face, and great double chin, she appeared as uncon-

cerned as if she were listening to the cry of the whippor-
wil, she now turned her eyes on the tear-stained face of
Ione, and broke into a laugh, that made the young girl
almost spring from her seat. She laughed on, till Ione
was offended. Seeing this, she very quietly said, " You
have never before had a *beau*, as these girls call a lover,
and I can assure you, Lieutenant Saberin was only playing with you."

Ione looked like an enraged lioness, at this flattering
insinuation. " I am excessively angry at you, Mrs. Maryglot ! '' and she turned her crimson face away from her
searching gaze.

Madam pitied her " liebling " too much to prolong her
misery, so applied the knife at once, like a skillful surgeon.
She saw that Ione was in his toils, though *she* was not
aware of it, and determined to dethrone the fop at once
from the heart of this sincere child of nature. " You see
Ione, if you were the daughter of a general, he would
proclaim the engagement on the hotel-top, and lead you
about like a captive queen ; as it is, he is playing with
your most sacred feelings."

" But why should he disrespect me ? I have always tried
to deserve the respect of every one," whimpered she, with
a look of despair.

Madam laid the fingers of her fat hand tenderly on her
cheek, " Be very thankful things are no worse, liebling ;
now if you really loved him and he were going to be *hung*,
you can see, things would be much worse — '' but seeing
the tears stealing silently over the rosy face, she added,
" What do you care for the gavache ! un âme de boue ;
you know what that is, ' a soul of mind,' — wait till I get
at him."

" O, dear Mrs. Maryglot, pray do not let him know that
I have told you a word, for worlds. Indeed, I shall fly
away home ! ''

" A la bête à bon Dieu, as the French call the lady-
bug. No indeed, but a beau jeu beau retour ; that is, one
good turn deserves another. Now for some plan ! If you

were only an heiress, I should delight to punish the dis-
honorable — the unmanly fellow!" She mused long,
thinking, "What better could I do with my money than
to give it to Ione, and make these prigs all scramble for
her, for they all admire her, as who can help it!" At last
she said " I have a plan ; you keep near me, all the time,
and we will attach the prettiest girl we can find, to our
party : and if he comes we will introduce him, and seize
every opportunity to leave them alone."

"Ah, Mrs. Maryglot, could I be so cruel ; to get another into the same trouble I am in ? "

" Never you mind, little innocent, I'll get some one that
has seen the world ' à bon chat bon rat.' "

" Ah, Madam ! ' Aquila non capit muscas.' "

" Bon ! bon ! brava ! ' when did you learn latin ? "

" You see I am learned, too. I wrote off a whole gram-
mar when I was ten years old. But you wont do anything about this affair of mine, will you ? "

" O, I see. The idol holds his seat ; but ' Bonis nocet,
quisquis pepercerit malis,' and that means, ' He hurts the
good, who spareth the bad,' leave him to me, for ' cæca
regens vestigia filo,' or ' leading his blind steps with a
thread,' O, wont that be b-l-i-s-s, now that I know my gentleman ! "

" Mrs. Maryglot, you frighten me to death ! Would to
heaven I had suffered in silence ! "

" No harm done, pet, I'll handle him gingerly ; trust
me ! " She drew her to herself affectionately, then leaning
on her arm, they walked to the river bank. The moon had
risen, fairly eclipsing the twilight ; and now Ione's spirits
rose to the highest pitch, since she had once cast off the
burden of her young heart on such able shoulders, and
she sang in a low voice, from Moore.

> " Hark, 'tis the breeze of twilight calling
>   Earth's wearied children to repose ;
> While round the couch of Nature falling,
>   Gently the night's soft curtains close !
> Soon o'er a world, in sleep reclining,
>   Numberless stars, through yonder dark,

Shall look like eyes of cherubs shining
  From out the veil that hides the ark !
Guard us, Oh ! Thou, who never sleepest,
  Thou, who in silence throned above,
Throughout all time, unwearied keepest
  Thy watch of Glory, Power, and Love.
Grant that beneath thine eye securely
  Our souls awhile from life withdrawn.
May in their darkness, stilly, purely,
  Like ' sealed fountains,' rest till dawn ! ''

As they stood at the close of the song, Ione's hand clasped in Mrs. Maryglot's, madam compared the Hudson to the river of Damascus, named by the Greeks Chrysorrhoas, or ' the golden stream,' flowing through the beautiful valley called the ' Orchard of Damascus,' told her of that famous city, which the Arabs consider the first of the four terrestrial paradises, believed by the Bedouins to be the most ancient city in being. " Now we are abroad, shall we, as Dr. Thompson says, quoting from the Arabs, ramble on ' ala bab Allah, toward God's gate.' This they say when they neither know nor care where they are going. " Ah, my love, we think we are mere automatons here, but alas ! in Arabia they are daily, hourly insulted by those who love them best ; even little boys treat their mothers and sisters like slaves, and are esteemed the cleverer for it. The women wear such a profusion of ornaments, it would sicken you of them — thousands of piastres strung around their foreheads, in various coins ; their shoes too, you would break your precious neck with them, wooden sandals, raised on bits of ornamented boards a foot high, they go clattering along."

Ione forgot her griefs, in those of her Arab sisters, and wished she were the Great Mogul, to punish the men for their cruelty.

Mrs. Maryglot affirmed there was no necessity of such a state of things if the women would only stand up for themselves, but it made her so mad to see her sex " show the white feather " at the very time they should exhibit proper spirit — the men would respect them more. " Now

just hold your head up with the gallant Lieutenant, and
your heart up too — don't throw it at his feet because he
deigns to smile slily on you, or he'll trample on it and turn
again and rend you."

"Indeed, indeed madam, my heart is snug enough
in the right place; I assure you the Lieutenant has not
possession of it as he supposes."

"There now, that is what they call caprice and cruelty ;
becoming engaged, and hating and fearing them, all in the
same breath!" madam replied with some severity.

"But you can see my dear madam, that I am not engaged to him — that I did not say yes, as he said I did,
silence was not consent, was it ? "

"Of course not, but why had you not spirit enough to
say ' you are *very* greatly mistaken, sir ! '" If I am not
mistaken in the man,

> "He is strangely bewitched by that sort of renown
> Which consists in becoming "the talk of the town,"
> And to hear from the gazing, and mouth-open throng,
> The dear words "that is he " as he trudges along,
> While beauty all anxious, stands on her tip-toes,
> Leans on her beau's shoulder, and lisps ' there he goes ! ' "

Ione laughed merrily, and the welcome sound of the
gong reaching their ears, Madam Maryglot, in a comical manner arranged Ione's head erect on her shoulders,
" as like the lid of a coffee pot as life," drew down her
upper lip, etc. throwing her into spasms of mirth, with the
benevolent purpose of setting her at her ease in a rencoun-
ter with those " prigs of officers."   They climbed the hill-
side.

"Now dear Mrs. Maryglot, I have forgotten all you
have told me, and shall just go on and make a fool of myself as I did before."

Madam stopped to laugh. "Why don't you tell me as
the king of Sparta told the ambassadors, ' the former part
of your address was too long, that I have forgotten — the
latter part, being unconnected in my mind with what

you said before, I do not see the propriety of that, and shall not feel bound to act upon it.' "

Ione said Madam was a great deal too wise for her comprehension, she could not see the wit of the half she said.

" Vi capisco perfettaménte," replied the old lady.

" Well," said Ione " Well, — what? The English, if you please ; you forget that you must enlighten me when you speak in your foreign tongues." ·

" O, it seems so foolish that you cannot understand such a simple sentence ! I said I understood you perfectly."

" Madam Maryglot, you are mighty provoking ! How should I know what you are saying, when you are talking in every lingo that was spoken at the tower of Babel, in the same sentence."

" Grazie !." replied the imperturbable lady.

As they ascended the steps of the hotel they saw a group of strangers. A very pretty girl formed one of the party.

Madam stoped the waiter-boy Mike, who was darting past. " Chi sopo quelle signore ? "

Mr. Mike was a great character, a great reader, a subscriber to the New York Ledger, and read that *invaluable* sheet, to waiter-dom assembled, every night. He was also what has been greatly eulogized, a·good listener, and had often heard the learned lady discussed by the gentlemen in the office, and felt more elevated by the implied compliment he conceived she was paying him, than he had ever been by the generosity of his superior officers. He bowed as nearly like those nonchalant young gentlemen, as his age and the surprise which he must have felt, would warrant one in expecting — and said, " Oui, Madam ! "

" Oui, — what ? — dunce ! " she said, and glared on him. Poor Mike ! He seized his nose with his doubled dexter hand and rushed past her, for the kitchen.

Lieutenant Burlyton who was reclining on the balustrade near, conversing with some ladies, stood up to look at the farce that was enacting, and when Mike disappeared, fell into a spasm of laughter.

Ione caught a glimpse of Lieutenant Saberin ascending the front steps, and escaped to her room. She sought Viola in vain ; and now she must retrace her steps alone. " Why did I not stay by my old general, Mrs. Maryglot ! Dear me, I will nestle under her wing all the time, yet I don't know what moment she will expose me, as she did about Cadet Smith's flowers : dear me ! " and she leaned over the railing to see if Lieutenant Saberin had gone in to tea. He had not seen her in her flight, and went directly into the dining-room.

Madam Maryglot losing sight of Ione, bounced into tea, quite in a fury at being made " the laughing stock of fools," as she informed the party on the piazza when she flourished away from them into the hall. Her indignation blinded her to the absence of her liebling till she saw Lieutenant Saberin enter alone, she then arose, went into the hall, and looked up at Ione, who stood leaning with her elbow on the railing, her hand covering her eyes. Madam Maryglot's great heart ached for her. " Ione," she whispered, " come, come ! "

Ione started, and the brightest of smiles made her face radiant. She skipped down to her friend, and kissing her wrinkled cheek, followed her into the room, a blush mantling face and neck, for she was sure every one at the table knew just as much as she knew herself. She felt the burning glance of Lieutenant Saberin's dark eyes on her face.

Mrs. Maryglot rehearsed her grievances to her in an undertone. She glanced at Lieutenant Burlyton, and his droll face quite upset her gravity, and she fell to devouring her crusts in a very unlady-like fashion, that the irate lady, might not detect the " aid and comfort for the enemy," lurking in the dimples of the corners of her mouth. Lieutenant Burlyton joined them as they left the table, and promenaded the piazza, by the side of Viola, to whom he portrayed in living, glowing colors, " the best thing of the season,"—Madam Maryglot addressing Mike in Italian. That earnest old lady, however, had her plans laid, and was busily carrying them out. She sailed round and round the party she intended to attack nearer and nearer each time, till she cast anchor within grappling distance. Ione saw the manœuver, and fell behind just in time to meet her terror, Lieutenant Saberin.

" Well, Miss Ione, I heard your warblings at the riverside, and we wished you were in the boat with us."

" You, where were you ? "

" Not far below, and lingered till the song was finished, it was ravishingly sweet ; we were afraid of startling you, or we should have entreated for more."

" Who was with you ? "

" My better half, Lieutenant Mera ; he was melted like gold in the crucible ! "

Madam Maryglot had by this time cried, " Ship ahoy," and " Whither bound ? " etc., and as the rest of the ingredients were brought near, hastened to stir them together. " Ione, my dear, this is Miss Randolph ; Miss Randolph, Miss Smith. I thought Southern girls ought to know each other here ! Lieutenant Saberin, don't run away, we want you." The haughty cynic curled his eyes and lips, and knit his forehead ; and had she been a man, would have curled his fingers too, at this great liberty, but came forward, and gave a lordly recognition of the introduction. " A Randolph of Virginia ! " cried she, smirking in his face with the air of a very enthusiastic antiquarian, bringing to the day the crown-jewels of Semiramis, from the viscera of Ninevah.

Ione and Miss Randolph, cooed like young turtle-doves over each other, and amused Lieutenant Saberin so much as to restore his self-complacency, and he volunteered to take them to the Observatory. This was a treat indeed. Lieutenant Saberin left them to bring his friend, an officer who had promised that Ione should visit the Observatory the first cloudless night after the new moon. They spent a delightful evening, thanks to the unwearied exertions of good Mrs. Maryglot, and at the hour appointed they took their flight to the moon. They descended as far as advisable into the volcanic crater Tycho; they saw none of the inhabitants, and returned without attempting to visit the reverse side, or even to gather specimens of lava from the crater.

" Fifty miles in diameter!" shouted Mrs. Maryglot, " I'll not believe my own eyes!" She tucked Ione under her arm, as if she had been an old eagle, and could carry her eaglet to terra firma in sublime style. "Lieutenant Saberin, you take care of Miss Filista," meaning Celeste, Miss Randolph's christian name. Lieutenant Head stepped forward, and led the ladies down. The laughing echoes scintillated around their heads from those left behind, and Ione heard Lieutenant Saberin say, "Madam has let me fall into the hands of the Philistines truly; and you are laughing at me Delilah-like!"

Celeste said he ought to be able to carry her down on his shoulders, such a Samson as he supposed himself to be.

"PART THIRD.'

"LESSON FIRST."

"*Alignments.*"

The prospect of witnessing the Grand Review for the first time, drove all else from Ione's mind. She was invited with her aunt to the collation at the house of the Superintendent, given for the "Board of Visitors." Cadet Corridor had asked Ione to await his coming after review, and he would accompany her in to the Superintendent's. Mrs. Bobaline was seldom seen without two or three of the young officers, but he whose presence gave most pleasure, was rarely with her. This morning Lieutenant Saberin met her at breakfast, and said he hoped to meet her at the Colonel's. This brightened the day for the poor lady, and she was radiant; that meant that he would pay his respects to her there, and no pains were too great to adorn herself for such a triumph. Her chief charm was not her unexceptionable toilet, or perfect features, but an indescribable air of elegance, and a charmingly gracious attention to the person with whom she happened to be conversing. She was surrounded by so many distinguished gentlemen, that Ione enjoyed the crumbs that fell from her "feast of reason," not a little. The review was very grand. The throng of spectators, lining the side-walk in front of the "quarters," and on the path under the trees, from the academic building, to the flagstaff, formed an exquisite embroidery around the finely cut green-sward of the parade ground. The "Board of Visitors," black-coated, and profoundly dignified; the

"academic Board," in all the grandeur feathers, sashes, swords, epaulettes, and white cotton gloves can im-
part, were there. Then the cadets, — mammas' charming
boys ; daughter Carrie's devoted admirers ; the young
officers' formidable rivals ; terror of professors ; the amusing, abused, heart-breaking cadets ; the fine looking engineer corps ; the artillery, the dragoons : a most formidable
array ! And now the miniature army scours the plain to
the most inspiriting music ; once, twice, three times.

Ione's eyes danced with delight. In vain she tried to
recognize Cadet Corridor, but when the "double-quick,"
brought them before her the last time, she was startled by
a look of recognition she received from him, in an oblique
glance.

The review over, Lieutenant Mera joined Ione, and
asked if she was going in to the collation.

"Yes, I am waiting for Cadet Corridor."

"Really, that's a novel idea — for a cadet to engage a
lady to go to a collation." Does that signify that he is to
monopolize every word and smile, this afternoon ? "

"O no ! " she replied, "I suppose he thought it would
be pleasant for me to be sure of some one to bring me
cream."

"Anxious you should not lose your cream ? I reckon he
was only anxious not to lose the cream of the guests himself ! " laughed he. "But I must go and get a drink ;
good-bye, Miss Ione," and he dashed across the road. He
raised his hat as he entered the gate, looking as if it was
no paradise, when leaving her outside.

She started as she turned and found Cadet Corridor at
her side, "Oh, Miss Ione ! 'present or accounted for ' in
the body, but heart and eyes 'running it,' I will beat the
long roll, and ' hive and court-martial, the truants ! ' "

"What *are* you talking about ? I don't understand one
word ! " said Ione, as bewildered as possible.

"Never mind, come, they will eat up all the goodies,
before we get there."

On entering the hall Ione noticed a crowd of officers,

around a table apparently examining with great interest something on it. She asked what it was.

" That? that's a great curiosity ! It is an ancient bowl, used at the "fountain of youth," and is still supposed to retain its magical properties, that is to say, it changes any liquid poured into it, into a rejuvenating beverage. You would be surprised to see the change its icy contents will effect on the *staid*, — those that linger after the rest, I mean, — professors and officers. They lose the wrinkled brow of wisdom, and martial tread, and frolic and dance as if the prayer had been answered in their case.

> " Oh, for one hour of youthful joy !
>   Give me back my twentieth spring !
> I'd rather laugh a bright-haired boy
>   *Than reign a gray-beard king !*
> Off with the wrinkled spoils of age !
>   Away with learning's crown !
> Tear out life's wisdom-written page
>   And dash its trophies down.
> One moment let my life-blood stream
>   From boyhood's fount of flame !
> Give me one giddy, reeling dream
>   Of life, all love and fame ! "

While the youthful sage had been raising the curtain for Ione to peep behind the scenes, they had become wedged in, near the door. As he finished his quotation, she glanced over her shoulder to watch the devotees around the Helicon fount ; and saw a slender white hand raise a glass above the heads. A laugh followed the toast, and she knew the hand by a signet-ring she had seen Lieutenant Mera wear. " I wonder what the sentiment was," said she mechanically.

Cadet Corridor had heard it, and replied, " It was a mathematical joke, ' Here's to the mixed Professor — ! ' " Ione did'nt see it, but soon found herself a link in a chain of bowers and scrapers around my lord and lady Superintendent.

The lady said, " Mr. Corridor take your friend into the next room, you will find it full of young people."

Mr. Corridor thanked her, but had no intention of losing his friend in a crowd ; and said, " Here is just the cosiest spot in the world, in this south window, hung with roses and honeysuckles, and the band will play just near us — could this be improved ? "

" No indeed, we are very fortunate," she replied. She felt at ease, and the wit and easy flow of words on simple subjects, gave a charm to her intercourse with cadets, she never knew when, in momentary fear of saying something stupid, or not fearfully interesting, she weighed each word before she spoke it to the officers. Cadet Corridor went to get Ione some cream, when Lieutenant Saberin immediately took his seat.

" Where is Viola ? " said Ione.

" Surrounded, like Saturn, by worlds of admirers, till I, like an eighth moon, was compelled to move into space, as I could not get near enough to catch a gleam of her flowing robes."

" But really, have you not seen her ? "

" Why, Miss Ione, has she anything to tell me ? "

" O no, but she expected to meet you, and I fear she will be disappointed. How strange, that those we most wish to see, are the ones we never can see ! "

" In that case, Miss Ione is as disappointed as her aunt ! "

" Please, please, Lieutenant Saberin, I did not mean any thing of that kind ; but really, I would rather, if you could only see one of us, that she should not be disappointed."

" I understand, but cannot consent to be driven away, even by so lovely a compliment."

Cadet Corridor returned, looking very wistfully at his seat, so dangerously filled. Lieutenant Saberin showed no signs of vacating it, and he took his position at the back of her chair. She conversed about the strangers, addressing most of her remarks to Cadet Corridor.

At length Lieutenant Saberin arose saying, " Miss Smith, shall I have the pleasure of listening to the music with you this evening ? " in the most nonchalant way.

She bowed her head in very much the same style, and drew a long breath, as Cadet Corridor resumed his seat. At parade Ione watched for the newly recognized position of her cadet friend, and found it by the most comical little signal that could be imagined, the slight movement of the white glove on the left hand. Ione's eyes must have borne testimony to the recognition as plainly to Cadet Corridor, as if she had waved hers in return. At supper Ione saw plainly by Viola's manner, that she had not been entirely forgotten by Lieutenant Saberin. She liked him all the better for not having failed Viola, and when he came to her in the hall and said, "Miss Ione, music has commenced," and offered her his arm, she vouchsafed a very sweet smile, which he did not attribute to the right cause. They did not speak, till they reached the iron seats.

Lieutenant Saberin broke the silence. "Did you ever see such a night? this is happiness! Just look at the shadow of the trees on the grass! and the moonlight on the hills across the river. One ought to be very happy in this beautiful world."

"One is, is not one?" she answered.

"No; I am a great way from it. I do not know what the sensation is, it is so long since I have experienced it."

"Lieutenant Saberin blue?" she exclaimed in a tone so like the one he remembered in Lieutenant Mera, the night before he got his leave to go to New York, that he started. "I did not know that you were ever unhappy, if I were a man, I would throw sorrow to the winds!"

"If you were a man; Miss Ione, you would have no sorrow. The good are always happy!"

"Then you cannot be very unhappy, you are not very bad are you?" said she anxiously.

"Yes, my profession is a killing one, you know! And then I must always be wishing some one out of my way as I would like to be promoted; so I don't see how I can be good like such as you!"

"You are just talking nonsense, there is nothing wicked in being a soldier, *you know;* and in deserving promotion!"

"Deserving? the deserving are not the ones that get it. Those that fawn on the men in power; that go to Washington and distinguish themselves in the redowa and lancers, that ride and flirt with the honorable Brown, Smith, and Jones's daughters and nieces, are the ones that add the bars to their rectangles."

"Then it seems Lieutenant Saberin is too good to gain promotion in that way."

"Which is worst, to break hearts among the ladies, or to wish the men out of our way ?"

"Lieutenant Saberin, you are too metaphysical for me ; I am afraid you are taking cold under the trees."

"If that solicitude were really felt how happy I should be. But in what am I metaphysical ?_what does meta-physics mean, Miss Ione ?"

She fairly grew out of patience and said quickly, "See metaphysics call for aid on sense."

"Then I shall not call in vain to-night," said he.

"I wonder why they do not leave the flag up, on moon-light nights," said Ione, determined to change the subject.

"Then you do admire the stars and stripes? I admire our flag more than anything in the world, except a beau-tiful face," said he looking down at Ione.

She took no notice of the remark, and asked if he re-membered what the Chinese called it.

"No ; I regret I do not speak Chinese. Is that one of your accomplishments ?"

"No, but a friend of mamma's returned from China not long since, and charmed us all with the force of their words. Our flag, they call a '*flower flag.*' Amer-ica is called ' kaw-kee-kwoh' Flower-flag country, and an American 'Flower-flag-countryman,' more complimentary than that bestowed upon the Dutch ' Red-haired barbarians,' ' Yan-kee-doo-dle ' means ' Flag of the ocean,' ' Sovereign people of the world !' and Washington, ' Wo-shing-tung' ' Rescue and glory at last !' "

"Rather significant, is it not ?" said he thoughtfully.

"Of what?" asked she.

" Of him we all are proud to call our *rescue* and *glory*,
first and last, I fear I worship that name Washington ! "

" What is your name, Lieutenant Saberin ? "

" Ulm."

" Ulm ! Who were you named for ? "

" I do not know, some old German ancestor, I suppose.
I was not at the christening."

" Ulm Saberin,— I like that ! "

" Quite fortunate, since it is at your service."

" O, it is far too pretty to be thrown lightly away."

" I understand ; very nicely done, but I shall not accept
the rejection, Miss Ione ! "

" Rejected, Saberin ? " laughed Lieutenant Burlyton, as
he ran past him up the steps of the hotel.

" Yes, and most elegantly done ! "

Ione found Viola holding a levèe in the north parlor
with Madam Maryglot, the Colonel, Lieutenant Mera, and
two of the Board. Ione and Lieutenant Saberin joined the
circle, and soon Lieutenant Burlyton came in to complete
the mirthful party, and songs, music, and the " lancers,"
closed the evening.

" Right (or left) Dress."

" Guard mounting, breakfast, drill, dinner, parade, tea,
serenade, on the piazza till eleven o'clock with Lieutenant
Saberin." Such was the record of one day in Ione's jour-
nal, nor one day alone, but day after day. At the exami-
nation hall, at riding, on the plain, to witness the wonderful performance of constructing the " pontoon bridge,"
Ione's never failing attendant was Lieutenant Saberin.
She went everywhere.

Mrs. Bobaline was very jealous, and said, " Let him
alone — he is too intellectual not to tire of her ; indeed,
any man will tire of any woman after such a siege, and
then he will be mine more than ever. It is only to be
near me to watch me and see who I am with. It is West
Point *Tactics !* But I will show him what retribution is,

7

when my time comes." In the mean time she was indulging in every variety of "small-sword" exercise that a jealous woman could inflict on the object of her envy, by putting Ione to torture in a thousand trifling ways.

" *To march to the Front.*"

For a long time Ione avoided Lieutenant Saberin, and even told him that he was Viola's friend first, and should not neglect her, as it made them both unhappy. He replied that Ione did very wrong to countenance a married lady in receiving the attentions of a young gentleman in her husband's absence. He would put his wife in a cage if she did not do right. This seemed very correct to her, and she gradually became resigned to her aunt's discomfiture, and came to like the caressing deference shown her by her elegant beau. Lieutenant Mera treated her with dignified coldness when they met, leaving his friend master of the field, and attended Mrs. Bobaline everywhere.

A cold, rainy day imprisoned the ladies in-doors. There was no getting out. Ione wandered from door to window and back to door again, till Miss Celeste Randolph came down and challenged her to a game of chess. In a few moments two of the cadet officers came in to call on Miss Celeste, who introduced Ione. The gayest mirth was already defying the storm without, quite divesting the house of the gloom which pervaded it, when Lieutenant Mera passed the window and glanced in. Presently the bell-boy handed Ione a card with " Lieutenant Mera — In the north parlor," upon it. Why did the blood leave her cheek at receiving a card with that name on it? She would gladly have flown in an opposite direction. She excused herself and went forth feeling like a culprit.

Lieutenant Mera was surprised at the very rosy face that greeted him. " Pardon my intrusion, Miss Ione, but I hoped those young gentlemen were Miss Randolph's friends, and you are so seldom to be seen lately, that this moment seemed precious."

This address sent the blood flying from Ione's face to her heart, and back again to her brow, till it burned painfully.

"I don't understand you," was all she could utter.

"I fear I don't understand myself, lately."

She stood before him as if he had come in on business. She raised her eyes, his were resting on her face with a strange burning light in them. Her cheeks glowed and her heart fluttered.

"Miss Ione, will you give me this?" touching a little blue bow on her hair.

She did not answer, but bowed her head to him.

He tremblingly untied it from her soft curls, letting them fall over her blushing cheek. He carefully retied it saying, "I will keep this till Azrael wings me from earth, — and take it with me if permitted."

Like a devotee before an idol, with folded hands and downcast eyes stood poor Ione.

He drank in the beauty of the perfect being before him, little understanding the terror — undefined even to herself — yet no less terror, of the girl so little versed in the ways of the world. "Is this affectation? she is not so timid," thought he. "Have you seen these fine sketches of the scenery here, Miss Ione?" He unfolded the pictures on the table. She had no alternative but to advance and examine them. While thus engaged he said, "I should suppose you would become a fine linguist in a short time, you are so constantly under the tuition of Madam Maryglot. Does she give you lessons in German?"

"Oh, no! She speaks German to me sometimes, and then translates it for me," she replied quietly.

"Do you not remember any of it?"

"O, yes, I know what liebling means, she says that so often to me," she answered smiling.

"Suppose I be promoted to an assistant professorship, and finish that lesson?"

She glanced at him inquiringly.

He blushed like a girl, and recited "Begin now: liebling, ich liebe dich."

Ione's face and neck were dyed in crimson, showing
that she at least half guessed the meaning of her new lesson.   She bowed her head very low over the picture on
which his hand lay.   The large ring on his finger attracted
her eyes just in time to open an escape from her perilous
situation.   " Lieutenant Mera, what an unique ring you
wear, is it an heir-loom ?   It is very curious."

" This ring?   It is a talisman : pshaw ! a mockery !
Yet I cling to the bauble, as if it were the key to my destiny ! "   He took it off and handed it to Ione.

" Tell me about it, please : — ' J. A.'   Does it belong
to your lady love ? "

Yes, if she likes it ! " and he took her hand to put it
on her finger.

" O, no ! It is too conspicuous — besides, what would
she say ? "

" Who, say ? "

" Miss Arnold — is it not hers ? "

" Miss Arnold !   Miss Ione Smith is the only Miss that
has ever touched this ring — at least since it has been in
my possession."

" Is it so sacred, then ? "

He looked out of the window dreamily, and sighed, " I
don't know why it is — or should be so — still the queer
motto in it binds me to it : ' Have faith in me ! ' "

" What does it mean ? Ione asked, very much interested.

" Well, there is a family story connected with it.   My
mother's only brother was beside himself about a young
lady, but her mamma thought her too young to marry, so
the gentleman fled beyond the seas, and sent back his miniature and this ring to his dulcina, but the vessel convey-
ing them was cast away, and after three years my mother
received them from the mother of my poor uncle's false
love, who had married, and gone to parts unknown.   My
mother gave them to me, thinking — deluded lady, that I
should be his heir.   That is the story of the ring."

" But your uncle,— your uncle, what became of him ? "

" Really, I can hardly tell ; he never married, and I

have heard he died a millionaire, leaving all his money to strangers."

The last words were said a little bitterly.

"GUIDE RIGHT (OR LEFT.")

"3d. March."

Lieutenant Saberin lay stretched on his white robe reading Guy Livingstone, when Lieutenant Storme came in. "Saberin," he began, "wont you go over to Indian Falls with us this afternoon? Alton has backed out, because there is not a black-eyed girl in the party he says, but it is only his indolence. I have brought the doctor to tell you your health demands that you should take this trip. Everybody is so intolerably slow here. We have a grand party to go."

"Who?" asked Lieutenant Saberin, laying down his book.

"I don't know," said the doctor, "I'm not even acquainted with the young lady I'm expected to play the skillful to!"

"Who is it, Storme?" laughed Lieutenant Saberin.

"Miss Ione Smith."

"Yes, Smith is the unique name."

"And who else?" questioned he of Lieutenant Storme.

"Mera is going to take my cousin, Maria Hamilton. Nora Kearney goes with your humble servant, and ma petite sœur has no escort."

"Then I shall be most happy, if you can swear to the petite. When did your sister and cousin come, Storme?"

"Last evening. Be at the hotel at four o'clock and I will introduce the little one to you. He left Lieutenant Saberin and the Doctor together to report progress to the ladies. The doctor lighted a cigar, tipped his chair back, raised his heels on the window-sill, and said.

> "I rather tell thee what is to be feared,
> Than what I fear. For always I am Cæsar."

Lieutenant Saberin retorted,

" I dare assure thee, that no enemy
Shall ever take alive the noble Brutus ! "

" Keep a stout heart doctor ; we may escape unscathed,
and slip the net that's dropped for us ! Have you seen
Storme's sister ? "

" Yes, I saw her this morning, at guard mounting,
where this unfortunate affair was concocted. I invited
her to go with me, but she expected then to go with Alton,
so I was portioned off to Miss Smith. Then Alton begged
to be excused, and you have got the one I prefer, and I
have your choice, if what I hear be true, my only consolation is, they say she is rather brilliant."

" Well now, Oglevie, such being the case, I propose a
compromise. We'll start all fair, you get introduced to
Miss Smith and I will to Miss Storme, we will stay by
them in the boat, but on the other side, we will change off.
How would you like that ? "

" O, very much."

" Who told you Miss Smith was brilliant ? "

" Miss Kearney said when Miss Storme refused my invitation on account of her brother having spoken to Alton, ' Never mind, there's Miss Smith take her ; she has
as much money as a clover has honey.' "

" Well ? how do you make that brilliant ? "

" O, I see, it is not all gold that glitters ! "

" Pshaw ! " replied Lieutenant Saberin, laughing.

" How goes the enemy ? " asked the doctor.

Lieutenant Saberin looked at his watch. " Four o'clock,
I declare ; we shall be late." He arose, soaped his moustache, and they set out. They met the party at the hedge.
Lieutenant Saberin was presented by Lieutenant Storme
to his sister and cousin, and the doctor to Ione ; but Lieutenant Mera was at her side and did not leave her till
they reached the boat. Lieutenant Saberin scrutinized
Miss Storme, and Miss Storme when she got the opportu-

nity scanned Lieutenant Saberin. Their eyes met, and both smiled. "Excuse me Miss Storme, but may I tell you what your thoughts were, then?"

"Certainly, if you can; but I shall not tell you, if you are right."

"I shall know that without your telling. You were thinking, ' I wonder if I shall like him as well as the doctor!'"

"Now the answer, Lieutenant Saber."

"I'm not so sharp, as you think me, Miss Storme, I am only a Saberin!"

Miss Storme laughed merrily, "I shall always call you Lieutenant *Saber*, you were so keen as to divine my thoughts!"

As they arranged themselves in the boat, Lieutenant Saberin blessed the doctor for his adroitness, for he found himself wedged in between Miss Ione and Miss Storme. He had full scope for his fine powers of entertaining, as the doctor seemed perfectly indifferent to all the party. They probably thought the doctor absorbed in some profound problem in his profession, but he was not so much more profound than the rest of mankind; he was studying the diagnosis of the affection of the "brilliant," for Lieutenant Saberin, and said to himself, "She may admire him, but she loves some cadet, I suppose;" so did not put himself out of the way to neglect her, for the sake of Miniehaha, as Lieutenant Storme called his laughing sister; but went in quite a professional manner from one to the other, as if they were sick and needed his most humane attentions. He fulfilled his agreement, to walk up with Miss Lou. But as soon as they reached the foot of the falls, and were finding seats, the doctor said, "Here Miss Smith, this is a pleasant one," and seated himself at her feet. It was a relief to talk to a stranger. In spite of her determination to enjoy herself, she found her head full of unpleasant thoughts. Cadet Smith had just got out of the hospital but avoided her. Lieutenant Mera was all devotion to Miss Hamilton, and apparently unconscious of her

presence, and Lieutenant Saberin's very presence was
enough; and she said "Thank you Doctor Oglevie," lan-
guidly, as if he had given her a potion to cure the heart-
ache.

Accustomed to understand the tones of the voice, he
said, "You are tired, and must have something. What
have you in that basket?" cried he to Lieutenant Storme.

"Some good things generally Doctor Oglevie; what
will you have?"

"Well, let's have some good things generally!"

Lieutenant Saberin arose and opened the basket, and
laying a napkin on the ground, he piled one thing after
another upon it. "Here are sandwiches, tarts, cake, lem-
ons, sugar, tumblers and bottles."

"Ah, I will take a cork-screw, Lieutenant Storme, if
you have one, and now all draw round the festive napkin,"
said Lieutenant Mera.

Lieutenant Storme proposed that the ladies should not
be permitted to taste a drop of the nectar, until each had
sung a song. A glass was filled and held towards Miss
Storme. "A song, a song," called the gentlemen. "Not
one drop until you sing, Miss Storme," holding the brim-
ming little Bohemian glass above her head, threatening to
pour its contents on her. She sang out in a very musical voice, "A great big bar, came out de wilderness, out
de wilderness, way down in Alabam — bam — bam — way
down in Alabam."

Lieutenant Storme joined in the chorus, with a fine
bass.

Lieutenant Saberin, perfectly delighted with the gay
little lady, knelt as he handed her the glass, saying very
sentimentally,

> " It was very wrong
> To say I would deny thee anything,
> Be not angry with me, for though God
> Forgive me, I could ne'er forgive myself,
> If I brought sorrow to thee — could I? "

"False flatterer, cease!" said she waving her glass at
him.

He pressed his hand to his heart, and said,

> " It is my fate
> To love, and make who love me hate."

" O, go on, go on, Miss Sterme, give him the rest!"
said Lieutenant Mera. " Miss Ione, don't you remember
Marian's answer?"

> " No, 'tis to sue — to gain — deceive —
> To tire of — to neglect — to leave ; "

Said Ione, looking most meaningly at Lieutenant Mera.
" I vow, I'll hang myself," said Lieutenant Saberin,
" and never speak to a woman again ! "
" A toast to the ladies from Lieutenant Mera," said
Doctor Oglevie.
" I object," cried Lieutenant Mera, " The doctor must
not select the theme ; his own toast shall be to the la-
dies ! " handing him the glass.
" No," said the doctor, " Mera first ! we'll never let you
off."
Lieutenant Mera turned and bowed to Ione.

> " Here's to beauty's finest flower,
> The maiden of my own birth-land ! "

Ione arose and acknowledged it, formally, with a blush
and a courtesy.
Now was the doctor's turn, and all expected him to say
something very smart or very funny. And so they laughed immoderately, when he gave " Dinah is the gal for
me ! "
" I should think you were of Southern descent," said
Miss Lou."
" O, yes ! Well do I remember the whites of those celestial orbs, and her teeth —

> ' Delicate little pearl-white wedges,
> All transparent at the edges. ' "

7*

He then recounted to her some of his home memories in
the South.   One after another strolled off, some up the
falls, others across the brook and up the hillside, and till
the moon arose, and the time arrived for the boats to come
for them.   The doctor and Miss Lou. had made astonish-
ing headway before the rest returned.   Lieutenant Saberin remained at Ione's side all the afternoon.   Lieutenant
Mera acquitted 'himself in the most faultless manner with
Miss Hamilton, and Lieutenant Storme had a wild flirtation
with Miss Nora.   Once more on the water, they all joined
merrily in fun and song.   As they neared the shore, they
heard the band playing that sweet selection from " The
poet and peasant."   They dipped the oars to listen.   Ione
was charmed.   She had never enjoyed such a vision of
enchantment.   The lull of the water on the little boat;
the glimmer of lights on the hill-side; the delicious notes of
the band stealing down through the summer air; the grand
dark mountains, surrounding them like a curtain of shade,
while the moon's bright crescent formed a fitting tiara for
the brow of " Cro' nest " — all combined to make a scene
of inimitable beauty.   The music ceased, the boat was
moored, and the weary party ascended the hill, each occupied with their own thoughts.   They said adieu, at the
hotel, and the cool breezes fanned to sleep tired ones, as
they stole to their respective couches.

" *Right (or left) Oblique.   2. March.*"

Ione determined she would not rest until she had seen
Cadet Smith, and had an explanation with him.   " Why
should she appear in such a false light to him, when a few
words might make them friends again ? "   This dictated
her early appearance on the piazza the morning after the
excursion to Indian Falls.   She hoped to see some one she
could walk out to " guard-mounting " with, but there was
not one she recognised, and she had fully made up her
mind to go alone, when she saw Mrs. Maryglot coming
through the hall.   " Oh, you good angel ! wont you come
out to see the cadets with me ? " cried Ione rushing at her.

" Yes, my dear; no one likes to go to see the boys more than I, but you don't want the whole battalion! Who do you wish to see?"

" Any of them will do, dear madam, only hurry, or we shall see none at all!"

They were soon surrounded by the handsome young cadets, looking like so many fresh dolls. Ione still did not see Mr. Smith; he was there, but made a complete circuit to avoid her. After a little, Madam, who had felt a deep interest in him, and saw her pet's eyes roving after him, left her and followed him.

" How are you, my friend? Has your accident destroyed your memory, or has absence obliterated the little interest you felt in your friends?"

" O, no!" he answered, bashfully."

" I have not seen you at the hotel; I thought you might at least have come to thank those who did not forget you when you were in the hospital."

" O, Madam! am I indebted to your great kindness for those lovely flowers? they were the only bright things I saw, all the time I was there!"

" No, no! they did not come from me; but if I chose I could disclose the secret; but after such neglect, I think I will keep my own counsel."

" Please, please, Madam! I will show you how grateful I am if you will only tell who I am to thank. Just think how I must appear!"

" Guess, then," she replied.

" Miss Lizzie Arnold!" he said confidently.

" Lizzie Arnold! Indeed, they never came from her!"

" They did not? O, Mrs. Maryglot, I have wasted more sweet words, and divine thoughts, than I shall ever have to spare again! You could not begin to count them."

" I am truly sorry to rob Miss Lizzie of such a garland, but a prettier than she deserves it."

" A prettier? You cannot mean Miss Smith?" said he excitedly, but in a low voice, as if fearing she might hear him.

Madam nodded.

He dropped his head and bit his lips, as if he would make the blood spring from it. " O, madam ! how can I thank her ? Will you help me out of this ? I know you will ! Tell me what to do."

" Leave me frantically ! as if you had just discovered her, and cry you are so glad to see her. Don't mention the flowers, but ask her to walk this evening, and then thank her, but mind, don't tell her any lies ! "

" Splendid, splendid ! shall I go now ? "

" Yes, now ! " At the word *now*, he sprang, as if it had been a command.

Ione suspected Mrs. Maryglot had spoken of her to him, but little thought he was acting under orders. She was content ; she had accomplished what she wished, and treated him in the kindest manner, but when he asked her to walk, she laughed and said, " Do not let us meet at the hedge again, for I fear I shall not find you."

" No ; in the north parlor, and I will not move till you come, if it is a month ! " He walked up to the hedge with them.

Ione went into the parlor, and could not resist giving air to her happiness by sitting down to the piano. She played superbly ; and this morning her lightness of heart seemed to give wings to her fingers. In a few moments the windows and doors were full of listeners ; but she was perfectly unconscious of everything but her music.

Mrs. Bobaline came out of the dining-room, and saw Lieutenant Burlyton standing peeping into the parlor, behind the door. She came slily up and said, " Who is it ? "

Lieutenant Burlyton snapped his fingers and replied, " Crackey ! but don't she play like young David ? as if the very d—l was in her fingers ! I beg your pardon, madam, but I suppose you may have heard of the gentleman before ! "

" Let me see who it is ! " said she, offended at his rudeness. She pushed open the door, " Ione ! " she exclaimed so loud that Ione started, supposing that she was called.

Lieutenant Burlyton ran into the room, on his tip-toes, took hold of the corners of his coat-skirts and made three or four courtesies, in front of her. She now saw eyes to the right of her, eyes to the left of her, eyes in front of her, and eyes all around her. She rose, colored deeply, and making a stage-courtesy to Lieutenant Burlyton, ran into the breakfast room. Lieutenants Saberin and Mera took a long breath as they turned from the window, and as they passed the dining-room windows, they looked in and bowed to Ione.

" Mera, I did not dream she played so finely."

" Nor I; she has played for me often, in Mrs. Boba-line's parlor, but only agreeably."

" Do you know I think she is a consummate actress, Mera! And I am always wondering what she will astonish us with next."

The latter arose, and went to meet Madam Maryglot, whom he saw on the piazza, to see if he could find out a little more about Ione. He had won madam's good opinion by his uniformly well-bred deference to her. She liked to talk to him. " Madam, where have you hidden yourself this long time? " he asked in a most interesting tone.

" O, I have been with Miss Ione to see the cadets, and since then to my breakfast," she replied shortly, for she was so thoroughly a woman of the world that she knew he was not so anxious to ascertain how she spent her time, as to make it an especial errand to her.

" Then you missed the delicious music! "

" No, I heard enough of it. I like better to hear her converse."

" Do you know anything of her history? " for once asking a direct question.

" Yes, her father is dead, and her mother lives in San Francisco, where they removed from South Carolina, when she was a little girl; and that is all I ever heard."

Lieutenant Mera stood turning the signet ring on his finger.

" Is that your class ring, Lieutenant Mera ? '

" No, but a ring that possesses a charm, and yet I am angry whenever I look at it ! It was a gift from my mother ; she gave it to me, as it was all the fortune she had to leave me."

" A ring? how curious, tell me more," and she took the ring and examined it closely.

" There is nothing to tell. It came from her only brother who was immensely rich, and died in the East Indies, leaving all his money to strangers, not a sou to his sister or her son."

" J. A." read Mrs. Maryglot, " what does that stand for ? "

" For Juan Alcantara,— it is my name too, I was named for this uncle. I have his miniature and this ring." He mused long and then said, " Sometimes I think I would sacrifice every thing for the power that wealth gives ! and my very name seems to remind me of what I have lost."

" You can easily marry money ! such a fine looking fellow as you are ought suerly to secure a good market."

He answered in a husky voice, " I will never marry a woman that has more than I have, and that would be too little to ask any woman I could love, to live upon. So you see, madam, my fate," *Single Blessedness*."

" O, don't talk in that fearful way ! I shall think you a grown up boy; any man can take care of himself and a wife, if he has health and your income. Why I know many clergymen in my country who live elegantly on less than you have."

" Yes, but they, live on faith ! I have no hope in this world, or that which is to come."

" Pray, pray ! you talk like a suicide ! "

He smiled sadly. " I'll take your advice, madam."

" To what, to kill yourself ? "

" O no,— to pray ! " and he left her, with a pleasant little nod. She sat and watched him : " I have no one to leave my money to, I could make him my heir, but then the young scamp would only wish me dead, and I should be like the poor old man, who left an empty chest with a hammer in it, and a line saying, ' He who gives his money before he is dead, had better take this hammer and knock himself in the head!' " These sage reflections brought her back to her sober senses, and she prayed devoutly that she might be kept from such an act of insanity.

" *To march to the front in double-quick time.*"

Ione and Miss Storme came out arm in arm, after dinner, and a man with half an eye might have seen there was a precious secret on the tapis.

" Now Ione, I want you to promise me the last week in August, will you not ? "

" Is there anything to transpire of unusual interest." Lou. blushed and she went on. " Tell me now, or I'll not promise ! mamma is wild to have me home before the cold weather."

" O, I'll tell you all, I don't know why I should not. I have " and she lowered her voice, and whispered it in Ione's ear, " I have accepted Dr. Oglevie ; I think he is an angel of a man ! and brother is very fond of him, and when I go home — if papa and mamma are willing — we — will — be married in August ! You looked shocked ! it is not so very soon ; mamma knew papa only eight weeks ! Besides, Dr. O. says he may be ordered off—and then — why we should be all married."

Ione laughed nervously.

" Now I want you my third bridesmaid ; brother and Nora are to serve, and cousin Maria and Lieutenant Mera, and you and Lieutenant Saberin, the very perfection of a party. Is it not funny that it should be the whole Indian Falls-party ! What if all should be matches ! Do tell me, are you affianced to the proud Lieutenant Saberin ? "

Ione turned to whisper to her, and caught a bite of her rosy cheek between her teeth.

She screamed and said, " Guilt, guilt ! " She made Ione promise to serve.

" When do you leave ? " said she sadly.

" Well, brother hopes to get off in three or four days ; he cannot go until the Board leaves ; those horrid '*planks*' as the cadets call them, must be ' fired off,' before any one can move a step."

" And do you know what they call their wives and daughters ? " laughed Ione. " They call them ' shavings' and ' splinters' and 'slivers.' "

Lou. shouted, " O, that's dreadful ; I am glad I'm not a ' sliver.' "

The two girls went to their rooms to prepare for the afternoon's campaign. Miss Lou. was to go from Fort Putnam, serenade with Dr. Oglevie, and Ione to see " Flirtation," through the lens of a cadet's eyes.

Mr. Smith would not permit any unpleasant references to be made, that is against cadet principles. He chatted on as if there had been no break in their agreeable acquaintance ; he culled a bunch of wild flowers and tied them with grass, insisting, that she should give him a hair-pin to arrange them in her hair. A French maid could not have done it better. On their return they inspected Fort Clinton, just reconstructed ; from the bastion they saw cadets coming out on the plain in their fatigue-jackets. There was to be fencing and bayonet exercise, and they went over to see it. They found Madams Bobaline and Maryglot, Lieutenants Mera and Saberin, going through a similar exercise ; tongues for foils. There were peals of laughter from the groups of spectators, at the cadets. All cried well-done, and separated in high glee.

Cadet Smith walked around the plain with Ione, to the hedge, " cutting his tea."

She asked him to come up in the evening.

He regretted he had not put in a permit, but perhaps, he should not be able to see her if he came.

She said she should always be happy to see him, but now he had lost his tea, would he not let her go and get him some cake.

" O, no, I am not late for my tea, and if I am, Everton will save me a piece of bread."

"A piece of bread! that is too hard! Please do not leave the hedge till I come back, or I'll sit down and cry." She flew up the walk to the dining-room, whispered to Mikey to hand her two or three sandwiches and some cake, in a napkin.

Only too glad to execute an order so pleasantly given, Mike was back in a trice, suspecting it was for some favorite cadet.

Ione did not dare to go through the hall, so ran down the north steps, to the hedge. As she passed the path leading to the flag-staff, she saw an officer coming to the hotel, but did not see who it was.

Cadet Smith took the napkin and said it was 'manna in the wilderness,' that she was his ministering spirit, etc. Everton and he would feast.

As she entered the hall she saw an officer standing in the shadow of the door; she could not distinguish him, but light from the hall falling on her face, enabled him to see her plainly enough. She did not like to feel that she was watched, and with an unpleasant sensation around her heart, she entered the supper-room. Viola was not there, but Ione did not give her many thoughts. They had grown very independent of each other. She sat at her tea some time, thinking of the secret that had been confided to her. She rose from the table, and as if led by an invisible hand, made her way through the crowded hall to the north door. The same officer still leaned against the pillar; he had evidently been looking into the dining-room. He stepped towards her. She walked rapidly away and seated herself in an empty arm chair, near a group of ladies and gentlemen, thinking she would be lost sight of by him, and perhaps could see who he was. He soon passed, scanning them closely. Ione saw that he thought her one of the party. He passed a window, the light from which showed it was the Colonel.

She sat wondering whether it could be she he was in quest of, or was he looking for Viola. He reappeared, and this time peered into the ladies' faces, begging pardon each time, saying he supposed it was his friend. When he came to Ione he stopped. " I have been in search of you ever since parade ; have you intentionally evaded me, Miss Ione ? "

" Indeed, Colonel ! I have been conscious that some one was on my track, but could not divine who the dark shadow was."

" Will you walk ? " said he, not noticing what she said about his watching her. She arose and took his offered arm. " Miss Ione, I have good news for you. The Board of Visitors are going to give the graduating class a hop to-morrow evening, and I am in doubt whether to accept it. Have you any friend you would like to meet ? "

She remembered that he saw her come up from the hedge, and replied, " O, yes ! I have a number of friends I should like to see."

" Then I must let them have a hop. To-morrow evening the Board of Visitors will give the first class a hop, nominally, but in fact it will be given to Miss Ione by the Colonel. Will you accept it ? "

" Yes, indeed ! anything to give the poor fellows a little pleasure ! "

" Poor fellows ! I wish we poor officers could manage to awaken a little sympathy."

" You do not need it, and they do," she said, simply.

" What, the whole corps, or only the poor fellow you were playing ministering angel to a few moments ago ? Are not your feet damp ? I must inform your aunt of this little clandestine meeting of yours."

" She will not care. She knows that I am old enough to take care of myself."

" Which I fear Miss Ione is not, on West Point. You little know the snares and wiles practised here. Please let me be your protector ? I know the young men on West Point pretty well, and can warn and advise. Please come to me at any time when you are in doubt as to what is right or proper ! "

Ione was overwhelmed with his condescension,— an officer of his rank to feel any interest in such a friendless young girl! How very kind! She would do as he had requested, and come to him.

He found retired seats for them, and recounted little romances of his "victories and defeats," as he called them, in the art of love. But he was too old now to marry, but not too old to feel an interest in pretty young girls such as she was.

She was beguiled into thinking the Colonel very fascinating, but frightened when she found it was eleven o'clock. She did not seek Viola, for guilt made a coward of her · she knew she had no right to be talking to any of Viola's beaux. The Colonel too had slipped a note into her hand at parting, she laid it on her bureau, and forgot it till just as she was going to sleep. She sprang up and looked at it. It was a bit of poetry.

WHAT THE COLONEL SAID TO HER.

BY GEORGE P. MORRIS.

" All that man should be to woman,
  In his friendship true,
All that Rolla was to Cora,
  I would be to you ;
For you have a noble nature,
  Golden as Peru.

Don Alonzo married Cora,
  Well her heart he knew,
But his friendship was for Rolla,
  Faithful, leal and true —
Feelings he approved in Cora
  I discern in you.

In this strange, romantic story,
  My devotion view ;
Rolla gave his life for Cora
  And Alonzo too —
So I, with the same motive,
  Peril mine for you.

Men their homage pay to women,
  And with love pursue ;

> But long since my heart forever
> Bade to love adieu : —
> All I have on earth is friendship —
> That I give to you.”

She crushed it in her hand, and feared him ; and dreaded to see him on the morrow.

“ *To face about in Marching*.”

Ione came into breakfast late, as she had taken a long walk with Cadet Smith, after “ guard mounting.” Every one she knew had left the table, except Lieutenant Alton.

He brought his plate, and asked to sit by her, as he wished to tell her about all the prospective gaiety for the next four days.

She greeted him with pleasure. “ Tell me what and where ! ”

“ To-night the ‘ Board,’ give a dance to the first class here. To-morrow night, there is to be a party at the Superintendent’s ; and the evening before we leave, which will be, I hope the next again, the officers give one at the ‘ mess.’ ”

“ That *is* delightful ! But what shall we do when you are all gone ? ”

“ O, *you* will have Cadet Smith back, and we expect to return in August. Old Tempest will fugit ! ” Ione laughed at the free translation. Miss Ione, will you give me the pleasure of being your escort to-night ? ”

‘ I shall be most happy to accept your invitation.”

“ Poor Saberin is looking pale, he feels so foolish to be eclipsed by a second class-man. Which is the accepted, Lieutenant Saberin, or Cadet Smith ? ”

She looked quite indignant, and felt deeply, her position. “ Why should you speak so, Lieutenant Alton ? They are both good friends, I hope,” she admired Lieutenant Saberin more than any officer she knew, but felt that “ concealment was a sin ” in matters of such moment, and yet his avoiding a display of attention, seemed delicate, and was in fact a thousand times more charming than the exhibition of an announced engagement. She hastened to join Viola in the parlor, who greeted her haughtily. "Really Ione, I shall soon need an introduction! I suppose you have been invited to the hop, this evening?"

"Yes, Viola; there is to be one to-morrow, and one the next night."

"Where, who told you?"

"At the Superintendent's, and at the officers' 'mess.' Lieutenant Alton just told me."

"I must send to New York for a dress, for the 'mess party,'" she said in a business-like way. "Come up stairs and help me to select what I shall wear to-night." They ascended to Mrs. Bobaline's parlor.

Ione threw herself on the lounge, and taking the comb from her hair, it fell in masses of curls over her shoulders; she glanced in the glass opposite, and thought, "that is becoming, I'll wear it so to-night."

Viola emerged from the bed-room loaded down with green boxes. She opened them and displayed every shade of silk and tarleton, one could imagine. A mazarin blue tarleton festooned with white 'crush-roses,' was decided on. "Now, Ione, select your dress and bring it in for me to see." Ione picked up "Pickwick," and started. Viola cried after her, "Don't take that book, or I'll not see you again."

She promised to return immediately, and sat down on the floor by a large trunk she had only once inspected since she came to West Point — the unhappy evening of Mrs. Colde's party. The crimson silk lay on the top, and she thought of the unmanly way in which Lieutenant Saberin had behaved to her that night, — now she was engaged to him! She wondered when she should again array herself in the gay habit. She was more undecided what to choose than Viola, for her dresses almost frightened her with their gayety and elegance,— she dreaded to expose them to jealous eyes. She lifted one, a pink tarleton; it looked like a rosy foam-wreath, "This will do; it looks more like

what they wear here,"and she ran in to show it to Viola.
She examined it closely, " Ione this is very lovely, have
you any more ? "

" Yes, mamma has put up evening dresses for a campaign ! "

Madam said, " You must show them to me, I had no idea
that you were so fancy, in San Francisco ! "

    " Squad, right about." 2d. March."

Ione arrayed herself early, and sat on the bed, reading
her text book, " Pickwick," it was a great comfort to her,
these days. Mrs. Bobaline sent her maid in for Ione, she
snatched her fan, handkerchief, and gloves, and ran, as
there was no time to lose, if Viola was ready.

As she entered, her aunt exclaimed, " How lovely your
dress is ! and your hair in ringlets, that way ; you look
only five years old ! too much dress for a party given in
the house though." She must say something to take the
wind out of Ione's sails, and draw a shadow over her face.
They descended to the north parlor. Lieutenants Alton
and Saberin soon joined them.

The latter whispered to Ione, " Why have you cut me
to-night ? "

" You did not ask me, and Lieutenant Alton did."

" A glorious redowa, Miss Ione, may I have the pleasure ? " offering her his arm ; Lieutenant Alton bore her
off in triumph. Mrs. Bobaline and Lieutenant Saberin
soon followed.

Lieutenant Mera and Miss Hamilton stood in the door
watching the dancing, — " They are very fine looking, are
they not," said he.

" Who ? " I am not a witch, to know who you are
thinking of," she said.

" The Altons and Saberins ! "

" Yes, but they ought to change partners. Lieutenant
Alton is too light for Miss Ione, and Mrs. Bobaline is too
dark for Lieutenant Saberin."

"Why, must light and darkness blend? that would make a twilight!"

"Always! that softens and blends the two,— don't you see?"

He looked at her eyes and hair, and said "Please make one exception."

She looked at him in a vacant way, and said, "Every one says they are engaged."

Lieutenant Mera. (Mentally.) "Wasted sweetness, 'Desert air.'" (Aloud.) "Miss Hamilton, may I dance the next Lancers with you?"

She accepted with a very sweet smile.

"I'll go and see when it will be." He left her and stationed himself near a window, where he could watch undisturbed, Alton and Saberin, and their beautiful partners. Mrs. Bobaline rested at each turn of the room; but Ione and Alton whirled on, like tops. When Mrs. Bobaline stopped, Lieutenant Mera stepped up behind her and asked for the next dance.

She bowed assent, and they went to promenade in the hall.

Lieutenant Alton set off for the piazza with Ione, and engaged the next three dances, just in time to forestall Lieutenant Saberin, who had come in search of her.

"Miss Ione, I shall claim the next two dances," said he after the manner of one who had authority.

"Indeed, will you?" said Lieutenant Alton, "She has just given these into my custody!"

Lieutenant Saberin looked daggers at the handsome, blue-eyed Alton, who smiled listlessly, and slowly sauntered to the dancing room. Lieutenant Saberin said to himself, "She is a flirt, but she has found her match!"

Ione regretted what she had done, but it was too late; and she could do nothing but finish her dances in a very distracted way, with Lieutenant Alton. At last her "bonny boys in grey" came to her rescue. Cadet Allen rushed up to claim his dance, and asked her to go out on the piazza, as he had something grand to show her. They hastened to the north piazza. There he stepped where the light from the window fell upon him, and stooping, turned up the bottom of his pantoloons, and shewed her his boots. "Real boots, with red kid tops, Miss Ione!" putting his heels together, and rising on his toes, while holding still, on his pantaloons.

Ione clapped her hand over her mouth, to save the assembled people from an electric shock. Redowa, Gallop, Mazurka, and Waltz, were flown through by Ione and her mad partners, and then came the "March" through the hall, around the piazza, in "double-quick-time."

As soon as Lieutenant Alton saw her at liberty, he executed one of "Lord Dundreary's little wuns" to secure her for the Virginia Reel. "Miss Ione, I wish you lived round at the gate, or at Castle Cozzens."

"How so?" she asked.

"That I might have the very great felicity of escorting you home!"

"Ha! ha! wish she lived down at 'Buttermilk,' that would be a longer walk," said Lieutenant Burlyton.

When the dance commenced, Ione found the little Napoleon at the foot of the dance. As she advanced to meet him in the reel, she said, "You have not spoken to me this evening, Lieutenant Mera."

"No, Miss Ione; you have been so surrounded."

When they met again, — "I determined to have one dance with you, so I took this position!"

She acknowledged the compliment by a smile, which she saw was noticed by Lieutenant Saberin. As they left the room, Ione called Lieutenant Saberin to her, and said tremulously, "Will you take me to the party, to-morrow evening?"

"Most certainly, Miss Smith!" said he, very stiffly.

She felt relieved at the prospect of making all straight again, and said "Good night," in her sweetest tones. She ascended the stairs, "wondering why lovers always made each other unhappy."

"TITLE THIRD."

"SCHOOL OF THE COMPANY."

"*Lesson First. To open ranks.*"

The Superintendent's quarters were thronged with the gay and beautiful. Brocades and diamonds; tarleton and pearls; swiss-muslin, and coral; black coats, and white kids; blue coats, scarlet sashes, and epaulettes; grey coats, bell buttons, and chevrons, mingled in one grand melée. But of all the assembled, none were more elegant than the guests we shall escort thither.

The crowd near the door stood aside to admit Madam Bobaline, Ione, the Colonel, and Lieutenant Saberin. Madam in her full bridal-robes, leaned on the arm of the Colonel, as if she were that moment being led to the altar; and Ione the perfection of loveliness, in white, her curls caught up with a pearl comb, looked like a timid young brides-maid. They had some difficulty to find the Superintendent, as the dancing had commenced.

Lieutenant Saberin promenaded leisurely up and down the parlors, much to the discomfiture of the dancers, and admiration of those he made to "stand round." Ione, a belle to-night, received attention from every one she knew, except Lieutenant Alton, who seemed to have forgotten that he had ever seen her. It might have been that he was very much occupied in exercising his ingenuity to keep a young belle, a beautiful dancer, in a window, conversing on matrimony, as the night was too warm for the young gentleman to feel equal to the exertion of dancing, and he showed consummate skill in keeping one of the finest dancers in the room, spell-bound at his side.

At supper Madam Maryglot chanced to be near Ione. As Lieutenant Saberin left her he asked, " What shall I

8

bring you. A kiss?" She smiled and said " Yes."
"' Væ victis,' that's Latin," whispered one over her shoulder, so suddenly it gave her a chill.

"I do not understand!" she retorted back over the same shoulder.

"But why blush, ma petite? c'est une affaire flambée."

"You did not suppose we were in earnest, madam! you are unmerciful."

"No I'm not, ' mais il y a dans cette scene beau-coup de pathetique.'"

"O, madam! what should I say?"

"You are beautiful to-night, but I suppose you know it. Madam Viola regrets you receive so much attention from l'atout, as you will occasion remark."

"Did Viola speak to you of it?" please tell me what she said."

"No, no! jealous; that's what she is, You're a little too young and a shade to pretty! Go ahead, and take all the kisses you can get."

Lieutenant Saberin returned before Ione could reply, and spoke to madam very pleasantly.

"This is the first officer, I have had a speak at this evening! I have been dependent on those ' beams,' as the cadets call them, for all my information. One might as well be at Saratoga or any other stupid place, if one is not to see an officer."

He laughed and said, "Which will you have, madam? I will get the Colonel to detail him for especial duty!"

"Lieutenant Mera," said she,—"where is Ursa Minor, this evening?"

"He is at present among the stars; having given too much attention to the dipper," said he, bitterly.

"Wretch," exclaimed she, "Do you dare to say he is drunk?"

Lieutenant Saberin humbly begged pardon, but he only meant to carry out the astronomical figure.

"Look out that you don't have to be carried out yourself!" responded she indignantly.

As they left the supper-room, Viola, who was leaning on the arm of a senator, stopped Ione, and asked her to accompany her to the dressing-room, under cover of adjusting her apparel, but in reality to get away from her senator, and stand a chance of getting Lieutenant Saberin, as she knew that he would wait for them. She was desperate, and determined that Ione should not take her particular property away from her any more; and she did tell her so while poor Ione was replacing a pin in Viola's dress that she had taken out herself. "Ione, I am shocked at you, for monopolizing Lieutenant Saberin to such a bare-faced extent; it may flatter him, but he is too much a man of the world not to feel contempt for you; he knows that after a certain length of time, a young lady's pride and good taste ought to dictate that she should *leave him* of her own accord! It is not likely he is going to be amused and pleased at being detained at the side of a child. You should be more considerate for me, he has not had a moment to speak to me this evening; he is an old friend of mine, and I expect a certain amount of respect from him in public! the lack of that will cause remark, and your behavior will bring down every tongue on you! Miss Vera Colde was so very impertinent as to open her great eyes on me, and ask *who you were,* that Lieutenant Saberin danced attendance on you so meekly! So you see! and it is only because he did not wish to attract attention to me, in my husband's absence, that he attends you, but I don't intend to give him up to you!" She had run on in such a frantic way that she did not think how loudly she spoke, nor regard Ione's flashing eye, and crimson cheek.

When she finished, Ione said in a low tone, "I have a right to Lieutenant Saberin's attentions!" and ran past Lieutenant Mera in the hall, down the stairs.

If Lieutenant Saberin had not heard one word, her changed appearance would have told the tale. She looked wondrously beautiful; she was the pearl changed to the flashing diamond.

If you have improved madam's appearance as much as she has yours, she should be much obliged to you," said he scornfully.

"Lieutenant Saberin, will you grant me one favor?"

"I am afraid I cannot, Miss Ione."

"How do you know till I tell you? It will make me *happy;* I think that might make you do it."

"Tell it, Ione."

"I wish you never to speak to me in my aunt's presence, or show me any more than the coldest civility."

"Never speak to you! that would be extraordinary incivility, I could not be that to any one, certainly not to my sweet-heart, ma petite fiancée," he replied, tenderly pressing the hand that rested on his arm.

Ione felt a thrill of pleasure and pride in her veins that was a new sensation to her, *she was beloved!* She looked down on his hand, the diamond glittered there.

"What a superb ring!" she observed. And the thought that perhaps it was an engagement ring for herself, flashed before her mind, creating an unusual halo there.

"That? that a very dear friend put on my finger, when we parted, perhaps — forever," said he, with an awkward attempt at a melancholy tone.

"Where have they gone?" asked she innocently, interested by the tone of his voice.

"They live a long way from here! — and — and I am to return it, if I ever see them again."

"Does it belong to two people?" laughed she like a child.

"Yes, it belongs to me now, and my friend when we meet," he replied playfully, as if speaking to a child.

She raised her eyes to his and looked him fully in the face for the first time.

He felt that she was reading his heart, with a woman's intuition, and dropped his eyes.

> "How guilt, once harbor'd in the conscious breast,
> Intimidates the brave, *degrades* the great!"

" Come little one ! I want the ' old Virginnay never tire,' with you," said Lieutenant Burlyton, rushing up. He took Ione's hand, drew it in his arm and started off with her, making a hideous grimace over his shoulder, in return for the brow-beating Lieutenant Saberin was trying to inflict on him.

" You are so funny, Lieutenant Burlyton, I always make ready a laugh when I see you coming ! "

" And you are a beauty, so that just makes it ; we two together, are beauty and the beast ! What was that humbug of a Saberin saying, to make you look so amazed ? Tell me as you would a father, and I may be able to protect you against the wiles of the adversary, as the Colonel says to all the young girls he wants to interest in him."

She looked frightened, " Does he really talk that way to every one ? "

" Ha, ha ! has he been talking so to you, little innocent ? "

" Yes, and did you know I believed him ! "

" That's right, my dear, believe everything everybody says to you."

" I'll not except Lieutenant Burlyton ! "

" O yes, accept him when he proposes, you could not get a finer fellow ! " Right merrily flew the " viewless spirits of lovely sounds," right merrily flew the tiny feet in response.

> " Through every pulse the music stole,
> And held sublime communion with the soul ;
> Wrung from the coyest breast, the imprisoned sigh,
> And kindled rapture in the coldest eye ! "

Lieutenant Burlyton stopt breathless. " This must be the music," said he " of the spears, for I'm blest if each note of it doesn't run through one."

Ione and he danced like wild creatures ; never was the ' Virginia ' entered into with more spirit. The clock in the tower struck two as they left the gate. Lieutenant Saberin whispered, " Good-night ! don't let anything trouble you, I heard all she said to you. ' Sweet be your slumbers,' and dream of me ! "

"2. *Alignments in open Ranks.*"

This day was truly eventful. Ione found the diplomas were to be given in the afternoon, then " the last parade ! " The officers gave " the Board," a hop, and on the morrow — Ione was not happy — this was the last day she should see many pleasant friends she had made. On the morrow the first and furlough classes would leave ; she had friends in both. There were many pleasant ladies she knew, who were going. Miss Storme and Miss Hamilton were going, and would take cheerful Lieutenant Storme and the agreeable doctor with them. Lieutenant Saberin, Alton, and Mera, all going ! She could not define her feelings with regard to Lieutenant Saberin. She certainly was sad, but was it for him ? It was strangely mixed up with the grief she felt at parting with others. Was it just to him ? Did she feel the thrill of anguish she ought to feel at the thought that she might never see him again ? She was sorry Lieutenant Mera was going, yet he had been more distant and indifferent than any of the officers. She must not think of him again, but must look her prettiest for her lover's handsome sake. O, yes ! now for her regal robes, her rarest jewels, daintest gloves, and sweetest smiles. A dip into Pickwick, and laughing and crying by turns — all the morning. Her dear cadets could not come to her, they had to pack their trunks, and try on their *boots*. But after dinner they would be up like so many honey-bees, gathering honey, and golden spoils from all.

Ione dressed early and went to Madam Maryglot's room. As she entered Madam exclaimed, " Lo ! the rajah-pootna bride ! You outshine the lilies in your whiteness."

" Am I too white, madam ? I wished to look my best, and chose this."

" Can a swan be too white, my dear ? No, no ! cela vous va bien : " you are lovely in it."

" O, Madam ! you are the only one who praises me, and I am getting to love it, I fear."

" Because I am the only one who speaks my mind,

dear. Ione sat down on the carpet, at the side of Madam's bed, and said in a sad tone, "Lieutenant Mera is going away to-morrow, Madam."

"What's that to thee, honey? get up off the floor, you will ruin your dress!"

"No, it does not rumple: but oh, my heart aches so!"

"Heart? does it? Have you seen Lieutenant Saberin to-day?" for, despite every other consideration, she loved to see her pet with the finest looking officer on the Post.

"No, madam: I don't know but it is that, but parting makes a fool of me. It don't matter who goes."

"Who takes you to the party, to-night?" she asked in a lawyer-like way.

"No one has asked me yet."

"Did not he speak of taking you, when you were with him, last night?"

"No."

"How strange!"

"Nothing is strange on West Point."

"True, true, child!—we are on West Point."

"I hope a cadet will ask me, if Lieutenant Saberin is so very indifferent. Madam Maryglot, what do you think Lieutenant Saberin cares for me,—'a child, and a poor, unfriended girl,' as Viola says."·

"Did she say that?"

Ione told her all: all the tantalizing comments, &c., for her full heart was ready to burst, with its burden.

Madam assumed a look of overwhelming sorrow for her darling. After a struggle superhuman in its greatness, one "that might have created a soul under the ribs of death," she sat down and gazed on Ione. The girl looked up.

"Do you think he could have heard that I was rich?"

"No matter, whether he has or not!" She spoke low, and in a very desperate way. "You *are* rich!"

"Did Viola tell you?"

"Viola; no! but I will make you rich! be as a daughter to me, and you shall have my property; don't interrupt me. I say, if you will be my daughter, I will make you my heiress, and at my death you shall inherit — a thousand pounds a year.

Ione smiled, a miserable little smile, and hesitated.

" You think that is ' waiting for a dead man's shoes ! ' eh ? but I'll give you a marriage portion now."

" Darling Mrs. Maryglot ! I should have been ingenuous with you before, such a dear, good generous friend as you have been to me. I *am* rich, to the most fabulous desire of my poor unsatisfied heart."

" Mrs. Maryglot sat up and looked at her. " What do you mean ? you unworldly spirit ! "

" O, I mean, that when mamma was very young she was engaged to a sort of person, he in a pet, because her mother would not let her marry so young, sailed away to Pekin. It was long enough after my inconstant mamma was married, that she heard from him again, and then it was to leave all his money to mamma's oldest child. Such a freak ! But I never speak of it. I don't know why ; every one knows it where I live, and only that Viola kept telling me that I must look to getting myself settled in the world to relieve my dear mamma of me, I should have told her I suppose, but when I found she did not know about it, and I did not care what others thought, I was determined not to say a word, but see if some one would not love the poor girl ! Was I foolish ? "

" No, by Jupiter ! " cried the delighted old lady, with tears in her eyes. Was she glad she had played at a romance, and saved her money too ? I don't know. She " rumpled " Ione's hair, throwing her arms around her. *How much colder is worldly pity, than worldly pride ! there is no shyness in the exhibition of the last mentioned.* " What was that man's name?" she asked as soon as her worldly wisdom returned to its citadel.

" A splendid name ; Juan Alcantara. I can never forgive mamma, for not waiting for him. Then I should have been Miss Alcantara, instead of Miss Smith."

Mrs. Maryglot repeated,

"What fates impose, that man must needs abide,
It boots not to resist both wind and tide!"

"Madam I am the victim of circumstances," said Ione in a desponding tone.

"In that your name is not Alcantara?"

"No; in that my name will be Saberin."

"Why don't you wait till you find an Alcantara?" said madam thoughtfully.

"I *will!*" said Ione, starting to her feet with one bound, "An Alcantara knows how to love!"

"Alcantara? Lieutenant Mera —" she started and said "Quelqu 'un a la porte!" Ione opened the door, and was handed a card with the names of three of her cadet friends on it. "I thought you said Lieutenant Mera was at the door, does he call on you?" laughed Ione in childish glee. Shadows fled from her brow like mist before the rising sun! she had untied the heavy load from her shoulders, and it had fallen. She had a friend! And the light had penetrated her soul, that she need not marry till she chose to do so. Viola had intoned so many axioms about the positive necessity of any young lady marrying the first man that offered himself, and saying thank you! particularly a poor widow's daughter, that she began to imagine herself in such a case. But after comparing her own independence with that of Madam Maryglot, she began to think herself somebody; but she shrank from the notoriety that an announcement of this would expose her to, and that Lieutenant Saberin would never release her in the world, she threw the card on the bed, and went at Mrs. Maryglot like a highway-woman: "Mrs. Maryglot, I would give my life, that I had not told you! I beseech you not to divulge it, or I am irretrievably lost! Lieutenant Saberin will never give me up, and I would rather be any servant in this house, than be married for my money!"

Mrs. Maryglot was in too good a state of mind not to promise every thing she demanded. She made her bathe her face in old cologne, and pearl powder it, and promised to follow in a few moments, and guard her secret as an

eagle guards her young. After her departure, the fine
old finasseuse sat down and laid all her plans, like a Napoleon premier.   Mrs. Maryglot was to go to see the diplomas given, with Ione, as Viola was to rest all the afternoon, to look her brightest in the evening.

" 3.   Manual of Arms. "

The cadets proved to be three of Ione's friends, and the
adjutant, her new acquaintance.   Cadet Smith invited her
to go to the library with him, and soon Mrs. Maryglot
joined them, and they hastened to secure seats.   The
Colonel politely designated a seat to Ione and madam, the
young men going to their class.   Ione was delighted.
She had always thought the library grand, but to-day it
was bright with decorations, and crowded with happy
faces.   There was a platform erected, on it sat the dignified and honorable of the Post ; — General Scott, our second Washington ; the martial but urbane Superintendent ;
the Professors, reminding one of the Roman senators ; the
courtly Colonel ; the Board of Visitors, and the graduating
class.   The rest of the room was crowded with the officers' families, and distinguished persons from abroad, the
other classes of cadets in the gallery.   The band, a fine
military-looking body of men, could be seen above the
beautiful portrait of General Scott, draped with flags.
The President of the Board of Visitors addressed the
young men about to receive their diplomas, in the words
of a father.   " A most wise and touching appeal," madam
pronounced it.   The superintendent then in a very felicitous manner, distributed the diplomas they had toiled so
long for, and now prized more than untold wealth.   The
band played the " Star Spangled Banner."   Then followed the greetings — the congratulations ! while each cadet's
eye, glowing with proud feeling, seeks his reward in the
delight and interest pictured on the fair face, or the pa-
rental one he loves best.   Alas for those on whose hearts
those sacred feelings have to be crushed back !   There

were those there, but not to croak at such a time. They each found the young lady they admired most at that particular time, to place in her hand his diploma. This, the proudest moment the young soldier ever sees, makes him an Alexander in his own eyes, and in many other dancing pair brighter than a victory, for it is a victory without a regret,— no remorse, no haunting faces of the slain, nor regrets for their heart-broken dear ones!

Ione had a diploma to read, and thought Smith looked very imposing on parchment. They two excused themselves to Mrs. Maryglot, and went to walk, till parade. That last parade! There are moments when one's nature resembles the ground prepared for the seed, all softened and touched to tears by a breath of perfume, a note of music, an evening sky, — anything that reminds one of the past, or points to the shadowy future! Ione stood entranced, as she heard the sweet notes of " Auld lang syne," great tears filled her eyes. " Home, sweet home!" bursts from that glorious band, and every heart feels the silken cord tightening, the quivering thread that binds to cot or hall. The manly heart beats quicker at the thought of again lifting the latch, and greeting the loved mother and father, brother and sister, after the years of separation and toil, that makes months seem years— and years to the young cadet, a life-time. As they marched into " Barracks," the band played " I see them on their winding way!" The first class cheered, and threw up their hats, and at breaking of ranks, embraced each other with shouts of joy.

" Cadet Smith came back to Ione and walked up to the hotel with her. He asked who she was going to the hop with, that evening.

She said " with my aunt."

He asked if he might escort her.

She accepted gratefully, right glad to be independent of the tardy, indifferent officers.

" O, Miss Ione! your aunt just informed me, that you were quite neglected, not having received an invitation from any of the officers yet, for the hop to-night. Will you oblige me by joining my party ? I have two other ladies under my wing. This was said by the Colonel, all gold lace and plumes, just as the cadet left Ione. She was indignant.

" Thank you Colonel, I have an escort ! " She bowed and ran up the steps. Here she encountered Lieutenant Alton with his very bland smile.

" Miss Ione, Lieutenant Saberin is not at all well and may not attend the hop this evening, sends his apology by me, may I hope for the pleasure of taking you ? "

She replied, " I am very sorry Lieutenant Saberin is ill, and much obliged for your politeness, but I am going with Cadet Smith."

" I regret extremely I have been too late in my invitation, and hope Lieutenant Saberin may be able to attend, as he is almost indispensable to all of us at our parties," and he smiled slyly at her.

As she ascended the stairs, she thought she would stop in Viola's room. She found her under the artistic hands of a new hair-dresser from New York, her head was a chef d'ouvre.

Viola said, " The Colonel has asked me to tell you, if he did not see you, that he would be glad to escort you to the hop."

" Yes, I saw him, but am engaged."

" To whom ? " her aunt said quickly.

" To Cadet Smith, as perfect a gentleman as I have had the good fortune to meet."

" Have you seen Lieutenant Saberin ? "

" No, no, no ! " sang Ione, and left the room, with perhaps an indifference slightly assumed for Viola's benefit, and she was deceived.

"TO CLOSE RANKS."

Tattoo is beating, and the gay groups are gathering to the rooms of the "officers' mess." Brilliant are the gas-lights, brilliant are the jewels, most brilliant are the bright eyes, and inspiring the sweet smiles and sweet sounds, the music echoes through the long rooms, and soon the dainty feet are tripping lightly. Leaning against the window opposite the door, stands an officer, quietly watching the entrance, as if in expectation of an arrival. He looks pale and stern. Who is he looking for, that handsome worldling?

> "Should he not wear a brow of care !
> That with three hearts to trifle dare?"

Is he musing of one he cannot think of leaving on the morrow, even for a few weeks, without this look of sadness? Or dreams he of a dark-browed beauty with eyes like the glittering gem on his finger, that sparkles amid the dark masses of his hair as he passes his hand through his curls. Could she "cast that shadow from his brow, and bid her dark-eyed lover be glad awhile?" or is he haunted by an apparition of other days.

> "Lightened by the softened splendor
> Of a lovely harvest-moon,
> And of saint-like eyes so tender,
> Glowing in the midnight noon,
> Many a song of wondrous sweetness
> Which thy heart can ne'er forget,
> Bearing with their cloud-like fleetness
> Thy most passionate regret ! ''

A party of four enter, — an officer, as fair and ruddy as a boy,

> " He is true and he is bold,
> Full of mirth as he can hold !
> Through the world he'll make his way,
> With jest, and laugh, and lightsome lay ! "

On his arm leans a superb woman, in a gold brocade and diamonds, regal in bearing. All eyes beam admiration or envy, as she passes. Lieutenant Burlyton led her forward as if he had captured Queen Victoria ! A cadet and young girl followed them : he is tall, dark-haired and vigorous ; his physique powerful, his eye keen and penetrating. He leans towards the lady at his side protectingly, as she looks up at him. She evidently deems those broad shoulders no mean fortress. She is very beautiful, a flowing robe of black lace, her hair in rich masses of curls, a single diamond blazing on her fair brow. Yes, indeed, she was very *beautiful!* Why frowns and stares the officer in the window ? Is he jealous of the fine looking cadet? Does he wonder at the loveliness, and uncommon dignity of the young girl ? or — or — what.

The doctor and the Colonel passed without seeing him.

" Which is to be the successful one, Colonel, Saberin or the cadet ? "

" I don't know," said the Colonel, " I should not object myself ! "

" No, she would not be a disagreeable patient ! " the doctor replied.

Ione looked well, and looking well she received attention, and though she danced all the time, she had not seen Lieutenant Saberin to speak to him.

After her entrance he joined Madam Maryglot, and she led him off in search of the Randolph party. She planned as well as he could have done himself, and Miss Celeste had often found him at her side. He was sufficiently indifferent to her to really enjoy the society of the sweet, artless girl, and then she was an aristocrat " of the first water." He avoided Madam Bobaline, only watching her from a distance, and as the evening wore on, and he did not come to her, she grew gayer and more brilliant, indulg-

ing her sarcasm and wit relentlessly, proving to his practised eye her deep feeling, but to the thoughtless woman,
a proof " strong as Holy. Writ," that she was quite indifferent whether he were at her side, or that of the " belle of
the ball." Ione he could not read, she could not read herself. He had yielded to an undefined reluctance to ask
her to go with him that night. Did he feel that a net
was gradually closing around him ? His plan of resigning
in Mera's favor might not work ; some one might turn up
to call him to an account in some of his tacks, and then
was he not a little cruel to delude that sweet innocent into
the belief that he would marry her ? He could not afford
to be honorable in the matter, and it was not his fault if
every foolish little girl ran after him. In fact it was a
quid pro quo, she was under obligation to him for a great
deal of polite attention, and if he fluttered around her, it
attracted others to her, and would probably be the means
of getting her a fine match, and so the sophist pacified his
conscience. He really respected Lieutenant Bobaline, and
perhaps that noble fellow might object to his niece being
one of three dangling on the same hook ! After all it was
only two. He could by no possibility encounter his rural
divinity again. If Ione was only rich, she would be a terrible rival to Pauline. Now the momentous question rested
on which he could give up the easiest, for his own person-
al comfort. While these thoughts were flitting through
his mind, he was carrying on a lively little " passage of
arms," with Miss Randolph, in the refreshment room.

Ione was standing on an elevated platform that ran
round the billiard room where the refreshment table was
laid. Lieutenant Mera and she were entirely oblivious to
the keen glances thrown towards them as they conversed
so earnestly about the affairs of the nation. His dark
eyes said more than words could convey, and she felt herself culpable to enjoy so much, every moment with him.
She saw Lieutenant Saberin was avoiding her, and felt the
slight, and determined not to permit him to spoil her
pleasure as he had on former occasions, she would be

grateful for attention from any one. Lieutenant Mera did not seem to weary of her, but remained at her side to dance, to promenade, to entertain her. Few men have power to bind as with a spell; Lieutenant Mera was one of the few. They dreamed on till Mrs. Bobaline came leaning on the arm of Lieutenant Saberin, resplendent in her triumph. He shaded his eyes from the gas with his hand, and gazed anxiously at Ione. She was looking pensively happy, too dreamily so for his jealous eye not to understand the whole affair at a glance. He spoke as tenderly as if he had been her caro sposo for twenty years. " Good evening Miss Ione, I hope you have enjoyed the evening very much, I have had ocular demonstration of the fact." He advanced to her side, and lowering his voice said, " I have not lost sight of you this evening; and oh, I have been so jealous ! "

Ione grew crimson, and asked, " How is your health, Mr. Saberin ? Lieutenant Alton told me you were ill."

" Not just that ; but wishing very much for the opening of the millenium ; but all this mundane gorgeousness has quite reconciled me to this life as it is."

" Come, Ione, we *must* go ! " Mrs. Bobaline said impatiently.

Ione stepped to Lieutenant Mera, who had moved out of hearing of Lieutenant Saberin's whispered communication — " Will you be so kind as to take me to Cadet Smith ? "

They met him looking for Ione. Madam Maryglot had captured Lieutenant Burlyton, " to convoy her hame," who was only anxious to do his part of the onerous duties of society, and get to his loved pillow. Cadet Smith assured Ione he enjoyed the walk home more than the entertainment, and begged she would meet him at guard-mounting to-morrow.

Lieutenant Saberin left Mrs. Bobaline in time to meet Ione and her friend ; he did not speak, he only lifted his cap as he passed her, but by the moon-light she could discover a stern unloving look, and her heart sank within her.

" 5 Alignments and Manual of Arms in Closed Ranks."

Ione hardly recognized her cadet friends in citizens' dress, at the breakfast table, and they scarcely seemed to know each other, they were so evidently on their good behavior. Some in the very last agonies of dandydom, others looking like young quakers, others still, like very well-to-do farmer boys. Released from the thraldom of a hotel table, however, in one respect Richard was himself again, for they all rushed at Ione like brothers.

" How grand you look in ' citizens, ' " cried she. She meant Cadet, or rather now, Lieutenant Smith.

They all thanked her, and Lieutenant Smith said " When shall we meet again ? "

" Please don't make me any sadder, shall we not see you back here ? "

" I will come back if possible, but the lot always falls upon those who would rather go to jail than to return, while those who wish to come are not permitted."

The hateful omnibus came rumbling to the door, and amid tears and sad faces of girls left behind them, it swallowed them all like so many Jonahs, and scrambled off.

Ione left Mrs. Bobaline conversing with some ladies, and laughed with the real tears in her own eyes, at the doleful look on every face, and wondered if she was such a good illustration of " the girl I left behind me." She went back to the breakfast table and began devouring rolls and chops, to the great amusement of the young waiters, who had already given the unsentimental lady one breakfast. She might have injured the host in a serious manner had not Mrs. Bobaline and Lieutenant Saberin entered. As they passed her he laid a sprig of evergreen at the side of her plate ; she took it quietly and arranged it in her hair.

Lieutenant Saberin began in a loud voice to tell madam that he was to leave at twelve o'clock.

" O don't go to-day, the cadets are going into camp."

"That *will* be something new and interesting; are there no weightier inducements to offer?" He leaned on the table to look at Ione. "Miss Ione, will you not go with me? I am off for Niagara, and Montreal, and will meet some friends at Newport, on my return. Those are all new places to you, are they not?"

"They are indeed, and it would be delightful."

"I will take good care of you, and bring you back in time for Miss Lou.'s wedding."

"If it has come to that," said madam, "I shall have to be consulted, as Ione has no nearer friend here."

"I am nearer, am I not, Miss Ione?"

"Yes, one seat," and she colored deeply.

Madam saw the blush, and heard the unusual softness of her hero's voice, and sickened with apprehended evil. She rose from the table, where Ione sat destroying the bit of roll she could not consume.

He leaned over her chair and whispered, "Meet me at the foot of the steps behind the hotel at eleven o'clock."

She shook her head in a very determined way.

"Do, Miss Ione, I must see you one moment."

She said "No."

He whirled on his heel and followed madam. Ione trembled violently, and mechanically followed them. He said, "Good morning ladies, I must go and pack. I will return to say good bye, at eleven," and he glanced at Ione. She went and got her hat, and walked rapidly down the path to the Laboratory, on her way to "Band-practice," repeating.

> "O, give me music! my soul is sick,
> I pant for music!
> My heart in its thirst is a dying flower!
> As the bruised and wiltering violet,
> Its fragrance breathes for the cheering shower,
> Such shall my heart's deep incense be —
> *Though thirsting yet.*"

She met Lieutenant Mera. "Where are you going, Miss Ione? I was just going up to say farewell, but may I accompany you?"

She accepted his attendance, they climbed half way up the hill, and sat on a large stone, to listen to the music.

He told her that he was about to apply to be relieved from West Point. Where would she be? when was she to return home?

Ione did not know — would like to go home this morning.

"O no, you must not go now! you are to stand at Miss Storme's wedding. We will have a glorious time there!" said he to cheer her, for she looked sick. It did cheer her, it was a door open from despair.

"So we will, and I will try and live for that," she said, with an effort at deceiving him, lest he should think she was miserable on account of the departure of the graduates.

He noticed the evergreen in her hair, and asked her for it. "Ah, give it me, and at the wedding you shall see it."

She thought of Lieutenant Saberin, and thought too, "He does worse things every day. Does he not devote himself to Miss Randolph and unnumbered others, every day in the cruelest way," and she snatched it from her hair. Conscience whispered he is a man, and you are a woman, and must be perfect, smile when he condescends to show you attention, not feel resentment when he neglects or treats you with scorn; — that is being an angel.

He watched her closely, as she looked at it in her fingers, while these thoughts were running through her distracted little head. He took it from her passive hands, and put it in the button-hole of his vest. "There you have worn that in your hair, and it is a precious relic."

She smiled sadly, and they walked to the hotel in silence. Mrs. Maryglot was in the parlor.

"Madam, I am come to say good-bye!" said he in a very measured way. "I regret to leave; you have been very kind, and I have not always deserved it."

She extended her hand to him, for she really liked him more than any of the officers, in as much as he had interested her in his future. "God bless you."

> " Wish me partaker in thy happiness,
>   When thou dost meet good-hap ; and in thy danger,
> If ever danger do environ thee,
> Commend thy grievance to my holy prayers,
> For I will be thy beadsman ! ''

" I thank you ! '' he replied. " I shall not forget your blessing, nor your promise. " He took Ione's hand, " May I count upon your prayers? ''

A great tear upon his hand was her only answer. She stood in the window and watched him as he walked rapidly across the plain. Mrs. Maryglot left the room, and still she stood buried in thought. She felt the presence of some one, and turning her head saw Lieutenant Saberin standing by the table.

" Ah, Miss Ione, I hope I have not disturbed any pleasing dream. I have been waiting an age, for you to speak to me.

It flashed on her mind that he had seen her looking after Lieutenant Mera. " You should have spoken to me, I *was* in a reverie," she said modestly.

Of what were you thinking, Ione ; was the little Lieutenant carrying your thoughts captive to-day as well as last night?

" Yes, I was thinking of Lieutenant Mera, he has just bid me farewell," she replied, with a little defiance in the tone.

" After I am gone will you be as unconscious of the presence of others, as you were just now, of mine ? ''

" I presume so, it makes a fool of me to part with anyone, yet I think you could easily have arrested my attention, if you had made any noise."

" I fear I am growing jealous, Miss Ione, for the first time in my life ; you must forgive me."

" O, you make a lovely penitent ! but as you have not the same right to be jealous of me, that I have of you, I will not forgive you ! He is as perfectly indifferent to me, as I am to — ''

" Stop, stop, Miss Ione ! don't tell a story, besides he is my most intimate friend."

"Yes, I have a faint recollection of getting that impression, before I knew either of you very well," she answered with a little scorn on her pretty lips.

"Ha! ha! yes, I have a sickening recollection of a chastisement I received on an occasion I shall never forget. Never mind, lady fair, you have had your revenge! you have the triumph all to yourself."

"Let by-gones be by-gones," she answered playfully.

Madam Maryglot entered accompanied by Miss Randolph, to all appearance as unconscious as a child that she was interrupting a tête-a-tête.

He frowned very becomingly, as if in deep sorrow. "I fear I shall not see all my friends to say good bye."

Ione rang the bell, and sent for Mrs. Bobaline, who requested him to come to her parlor; he asked Ione to go with him. She went to the door but refused to go in. He took her hand and put his class-ring on it, and kissed it saying, "This, Ione, is dearer than anything I possess, it is sacred!"

"Then please do not give it me, I fear I may lose it. It is too heavy for my finger."

Mrs. Bobaline hearing voices outside her door, opened it; Ione blushed and went to her room, and the Lieutenant entered Mrs. Bobaline's.

"LESSON SECOND."

"*To Load in Four Times and at Will.*"

Ione had engaged to go down to parade with Mrs. Maryglot and Celeste Randolph. She stood hesitating like one in a dream, carefully drawing on her gloves, that Mrs. Viola should not see the ring. "If she sees it, she will never speak to me again," she murmured, and sighed as if she were a second Atlas and had the world on her shoulders.

Madam Maryglot called her, and they took their way down the cavalry road to the old Academic building, and stood under the trees. The miniature army were standing in battle array, a fine spectacle. The officers, superbly mounted, fine-looking men, rode to and fro, directing their movements. There were baggage-wagons, with all the appointments belonging to camp-life, drawn by oxen. The newly appointed cadets, designated from the older, or more advanced ones, by the name of " Plebes," were running in every direction across the plain, carrying brooms, pails, looking-glasses etc., and wheeling wheel-barrows, with all sorts of somethings in them. At length the cavalcade moved forward — a very imposing sight, the band in full force, the glittering swords and bayonets, the array of young princes in their handsome, showy uniforms, and their " soldierly bearing; " the dragoons on their fiery steeds, " champing their reins," and prancing about to the great terror of the .hundreds of ladies lining the roads, paths, side-walks' and steps to the different edifices, with every hue and shade of costly array. The locale is altogether unsurpassed,

" As those who have been there, know,
And those who have not, had better go,"

and see it for themselves, as it will repay them for a short journey. The plain, surrounded by an amphitheatre of nature's " mountain fastnesses and retreats," the lovely homes and massive structures at their base, the grand old trees, and tempting paths beneath ; the glorious Hudson, rejoicing in its beauty and strength, flowing proudly to the sea, toying with its chatelaine of tiny ships, and emerald islets. The beautiful town of Newburg in the distance, with-its soft vail of haze floating between the sunset sky and the glowing mirror beneath, like a city in a dream ; the charming residences dotting the mountains sides, and filling the breasts of the denizens of cities with envy — ah, 'tis an Eden ! But a grand march from the Band of bands brings us into line, and the hundreds follow to the camp-ground. The floors of the tents are laid the canvas lies beside them, preparatory to an attack from the " Plebes " initiated for the first time into the occupation of tent-makers, and now it becomes " confusion doubly confound-ed," but soon one white tent after another rises, till all stand in beauty and order. The spectators wonder where that small army has disappeared to, " surely not into those tiny tents ! " A very unmusical, but welcome sound booms over the plain, and the hungry multitude take their way to the hotel. Omnibus after omnibus, with their sad, or eager crowds, are running away like unrelenting time, after the boats and cars, while those that remain, look into each oth-er's faces, as if each expected he would soon be left alone to tell the tale.

" 2. *To fire by company.*"

This lull was just what Ione needed to collect her flushed senses ; she walked, and talked to Cadet Allen, listened to the music, attended guard-mounting and parade, and mu-sic in the evenings, until the fourth of July ; then the re-lentless omnibus seemed determined to make amends for their former cruelty, and came from every boat and train, with what a New Yorker would consider a pretty fair number inside and out.

Lieutenant Smith returned and begged Ione to permit him to see that she lost none of the pleasures of the sea-son, and to begin by allowing him to accompany her to the hop, on the evening of the fourth. This was a very brilliant affair, and the beaux and belles of a few weeks ago were no more missed than if they had never been, ex-cept in a few hearts. At drum beat, such a rush for the dressing room, one who has never witnessed the perform-ance could scarcely imagine, and all found themselves on the plain in an incredibly short space of time, where wheels and Roman candles, and the rocket's red glare, were already making the heavens bright with the meteoric show-er, while patriotic sentences and devices, written in letters of flame, added to the grandeur and brilliancy of the scene. Through all, and above all, rose the music of the band playing national airs, that fired the breast with patriotism.

Ione had fallen into the hands of a clergyman, to whom Miss Randolph had introduced her.

He offered her his arm to go out on the plain. As he was a gray-haired man, she dared not refuse ; and Lieutenant Smith followed, making warlike demonstrations at the head of the old gentleman, whenever he could catch Ione's eye. Every rocket that went up he followed with his spectacles, but when he expected the returns, he seized Ione by the hand and ran for dear life, dragging her invariably directly toward the falling baton, intending however to keep from under it, and supposing he was going in just the opposite direction.

Lieutenant Smith kept near her, endeavoring to gain possession, but this only aroused her new friend's ire.

" You will have to come to me one of these days, to take care of her for you when you go to fight the Indians, and I am not going to give her up to you."

" I shall have to shoot you ! " replied the fierce young soldier, in a laughing way.

" Shoot! I am bullet proof, and could not die in a better cause."

" Bullet proof, ha! ha !" shouted the youth, trespassing a little on the good man's indulgence.

His Reverence eyed him from head to foot, and in a fine histrionic style addressed him.

> " Hence
> Horrible villian ! or I'll spurn thine eyes
> Like balls before me ; I'll unchain thy head ;
> Thou shalt be whipped with wire, and stewed in brine,
> Smarting in lingering pickle."

Smith clapped his hands in delight, and Ione joined him. At length the inevitable drum beat, and all wound their way to the hotel. Ione was getting to be herself again. Viola had no one to persecute her about, and was quite agreeable, with the exception of being " out of all patience with Ione for letting Lieutenant Mera slip through her fingers that way." " Miss Storme had done well for herself, took the first offer she had."

Poor Ione looked at the noble class-ring, but that was a heavy link between two hearts that did not beat in unison.

" 3.   *To Fire by File.*"

Ione, here is a letter for you from Miss Storme ! " said Mrs. Bobaline entering Ione's room. She took the letter and Viola sat down to hear her read it.

" STORME TOWER, ———

Dearest Ione :

I write to tell you to be ready to come to me in two or three days at farthest. My brother Harry will come down for you. He says " Tell Miss Ione that I will stop one night and take her to the hop, if she will look at an officer in citizen's dress, on West Point." Maria is here and sends love.

Your friend,

LOU. STORME.

" How charming that will be ! " Ione exclaimed. " Viola I do wish you could go, and not be left here alone ! "

" O, I shall be at the wedding, and that is all I care for."

Ione was like a bird in her joyful mood, while preparing for her trip. It was a perfect dream of delight to her. Shortly after, as she was sitting on the piazza with Madam Maryglot, the omnibus drove to the door, and Lieutenant Storme sprang out. Seeing Ione he ran up the steps and greeted her warmly. " Well, Miss Ione, all ready ? "

" Yes, for the hop to night ? "

He sat down in his own natural way, told her all the little interesting et cetera going on at home. He had just returned from visiting Miss Nora Kearney, with whom he was more deeply in love than ever. All who heard him,

9

admired, and wished him success in his manly, honorable
love.

Ione was a belle that evening, and with her lively companion attracted a great deal of attention, and was envied
by not a few.

"4.   *To Fire by Rank*."

The fine steamer bound up the Hudson, landed at West
Point the next day, the passengers gathering in a black
mass, to look at the fine buildings, and stare at those coming on board. "That handsome officer, papa ! Is he a
general ? "   " Yes, I think he is ! "   " O, no ! he is one
of the cadets.   They say they are terrible fellows among
the girls ! "   This was a conversation overheard by Ione
and Lieutenant Storme ; the general was a dragoon senti-
nel, at the ferry house.   As they neared the pier, a few
miles up the river, among the crowd Ione discovered Lou.
and her young brother, awaiting their arrival.   When
they went on shore she found two arms were around her
neck, and Lou.'s musical voice reiterating, " I'm so glad
to see you !   This is my brother Johnny, Ione."

The brother Johnny was dark-eyed, broad-shouldered,
and finely moulded, with a face browned by exposure.
His manners were elegant, with an air of well-bred modesty, charming in a young man of twenty-two.   He shook
hands with Ione, and his hands were hard and brown as
any farmer's, he boasting himself captain of a yacht.
Ione was hurried from the crowd into an elegant carriage,
drawn by two superb chestnut horses.   Young John
mounted the box, handling the rains like Plato's " Grecian
youth."   A delightful drive along the river-bank for several miles, with desirable homes on every side, brought
them to a gate, with a bird-cage of a lodge beside it.
Johnny shouted " Gate ! " and a curly-headed urchin
ran out all smiles, to open it for them.   A serpentine
carriage road on the margin of the river, gave her a fine
view of the expanse of lawn, and of the home-like man-

sions, with its verandas and pillars draped with roses and honey-suckles, the arm-chairs so temptingly arranged, the fine glass adjusted to look at the vessels on the river, the pretty fountain, with its murmuring music, made a fairy land to Ione. Maria Hamilton was reading on the piazza, and ran down to meet them. Mrs. Storme came too, and greeted the new arrival like a mother.

She was not disappointed in anticipating a pleasant visit. The days flew like moments. Johnny took her to sail every day, or to gallop over the fine roads, or out in his little trotting-wagon, and even the day the wedding party arrived, found Ione and John up the river the entire morning. As she came up from the beach on her return, all drenched with waves they had shipped, Maria met her on the steps, and said, "Ione, you naughty girl! go right to your room and dress. Lieutenant Saberin and Lieutenant Mera, and the Doctor have come, and Nora Kearney is up stairs waiting to see you; hurry, or you will not be ready for dinner."

Ione rushed up stairs, arrayed herself in her favorite blue silk, in "double-quick time," and entered the parlor after every one had assembled. Lieutenant Storme offered his arm and introduced her to the guests as the second mate of the fast-sailing yacht, "Speed." John did not happen to be present or perhaps the joke would not have been so vociferously received. There were many warm greetings, and each made his way to take the distinguished " tar " by the hand.

Ere long, Lieutenant Saberin was ensconced in a cosy window, behind the curtains, whispering sweet things to Ione. The Doctor and Lou. had betaken themselves to one piazza, Miss Hamilton and Lieutenant Mera to the other, and Harry Storme and Miss Nora were walking around the empty conservatory, as if it had been the lost site of Eden they had just discovered. Robert was sent in search of the young people, and being an expert in this sort of thing, he soon brought them in. They bore Doctor Storme's merciless jokes in a very shamefaced way. At dinner there was a good deal of "by-play," among the young people, and the health of the Doctor and Lou. was drank by each one calling out to pledge them in his turn, as if he had been the first to propose it. After dinner they adjourned to the grounds.

John offered Lieutenant Saberin the use of his fast horse and buggy for a drive, which he accepted, and invited Ione to accompany him; they whirled down the road, amid cries of caution not to run away, and not to disable themselves for their onerous duties for the morrow. Lieutenant Saberin was perfectly lovely, admired the scenery, asked what she had been doing at West Point, and said " What would I *not* give if we were in the Dr's. and Miss Lou's place to-morrow; but oh, that dream of happiness may not be fulfilled in long years."

Ione did not look as desparing as he anticipated. If he had been sure that Ione had such a home as Miss Storme, would he have postponed his dream of happiness so long? On their return they found Lieutenant Mera entertaining Mrs. and Dr. Storme, Maria and John. Lieutenant Saberin went wild over their country, its roads, its fences, — in short, everything. Robert came to say tea would be served, and the lovers came from caves and grottoes, and condescended to sip a little nectar, and take a dainty bit of cake.

Lieutenant Mera and Mr. John suddenly disappeared, and the moon having risen, not to mention a fine breeze, the "perfect brick," as Lieutenant Mera called him, proposed a sail. " Who shall I take ? " asked Lieutenant Mera.

" If I were to choose, I should say Miss Ione. She is not afraid of anything."

" But she belongs to Lieutenant Saberin."

" I guess not, soul and body ! " said John, confidently. " I'll manage that."

And he did manage. He walked into the parlor, and stood in front of the window, until he attracted Ione's attention, and then left the room. She knew well enough who he wanted, and in a few moments went after him.

" Would you like to take a sail by moonlight? " said he,
as she went up to him.

" O, yes indeed ! But what will they all say ? "

" I don't know," replied he laughing, " But Lieutenant
Mera wishes to go, and I proposed you ; he understands
boating, so I will stay, and no one will miss you but Lieutenant Saberin ! " added he slily.

Ione said, " Hush," and turning, saw Lieutenant Mera
buried in an immense arm-chair.

He rose and said, " Will you go ? "

Ione nodded smilingly in reply, and ran down the steps.

Mr. John suggested the propriety of not shipping
many waves in that blue silk.

They sailed down the river, tacking from side to side,
now in the deep shade of high rocks, then running in a
sunny little cove, next out in the bright moon-light, as if
they were sailing in liquid silver.

> " Night on the waves, and the moon is on high
>   Hung like a gem on the brow of the sky —
> Treading its depths, in the power of her might,
>   And turning the clouds, as they pass her, to light."

Lieutenant Mera told her one or two incidents connected with his own history, commencing with commenting on
the family they were visiting, and the happiness Dr. Storme
must feel in his old age, to have a home of elegance for his
children, with no anxiety to shorten his days. " I shall
never know that pleasure — my father an officer, was
killed in Florida when I was an infant, leaving my mother,
a beautiful, gay young woman, an independence. She went
to Paris and mingled in the beau-monde, but her slight fortune soon melted away, and she married a French gentleman and returned to New Orleans, where he owned an immense estate. I was sent to my father's brother, when I
was four years of age, and have never seen my mother
since. She had a brother in the East Indies, that was very
fond of me as a baby, who she thought would leave me
his fortune ; but a number of years ago I heard of his

death, and that he had left it to some one there. However,
I shall never dispute it, but carve my way to fortune with
my sword, and be wedded to my profession. I enjoy ladies'
society as a gleam of sunshine, which may not linger with
me. Being more than usually interested considering our
short acquaintance, and as I would wish an honorable
man to do by my sister, I speak to you now. I have told
you this about myself to show you that I am not selfish in
what I am going to say; though I am speaking of a friend,
I hope I am speaking to one. You are, or may be, interested in Lieutenant Saberin, if you have any dear friend in
whom you can place implicit trust, on whose judgment
you can rely, tell him or her everything, lay open your
heart to him, and all that Lieutenant Saberin says and
does, and be guided by that friend, if you know such an
one; there can be no harm in that. I should not suggest
Mrs. Bobaline, as she is young and inexperienced, I — wish
your uncle were with you, he is a noble man."

Ione did not speak till he had finished, she then said,
"I thank you a thousand times, Lieutenant Mera, and shall
take your advice. Do you approve of Madam Maryglot?"

He answered "Yes, in her truth, but her judgment I
know nothing of. She has never known a mother's anxiety,
and may not decide so nicely, but you will know Miss
Ione."

She saw they were running past the bay that they
should enter, and spoke quickly, "In here!"

He turned the boat in short, the lower side struck a
rock, the wind blowing strongly at the time, she immediately capsized. Ione rose and clung to the boat, but soon lost
her hold, and fell into the water. Lieutenant Mera plunged
after her, as she disappeared in the shadow of a great rock,
but he missed her; she rose again, he clasped his fingers in
her hair, and drawing her up, put one strong arm around
her, and swam to the beach; when reached he found her
almost lifeless. Seizing her in his arms he set off for the
house.

John was watching for them, and as they came in sight

he ran forward with an undefinable dread. Seeing the almost lifeless form of Ione he snatched her in his arms, and carrying her to his sister's room, called his mother.

In a few moments the whole household knew what had happened.

Lieutenant Mera went to his room to change his clothes, but soon returned to answer the thousand and one questions always asked on such occasions.

When Lieutenant Saberin bid him good-night, he said, " I hope you will not suffer from it, Mera, but you came near losing my wife!"

Lieutenant Mera looked ghastly, and replied, " You could not have lost more. Thank God, she is safe!" There was very little sleep in the house that night. Poor Mr. Mera walked the floor all night, scarcely knowing which he felt worst about, Ione's engagement, or the ducking he had given her.

"LESSON THIRD."

"1st. To March in line of Battle."

The day was perfect as all wedding-days should be. Ione arose looking very pale and interesting, but not injured in the least by the dive she made to the caves of the Naiads. Lieutenant Mera looked worse than she did, as promenading all night with a mind ill at ease, is not likely to tinge the cheek with vermilion. Many times during the morning, when he looked at Ione, he almost wished they had never risen from the waves, but had slept peacefully there until the last day; while she avoided or looked shyly at him.

The wedding party had assembled in the upper halls and piazzas, and the train from down the river having brought crowds of guests, the grounds and parlors were filled with cheerful friends. Twelve o'clock arrived. All are assembled. Lieutenant Saberin and Ione descended first; Miss Hamilton and Lieutenant Mera; Miss Nora Kearney and Lieutenant Storme; then the bride and groom. The Doctor, radiant with happiness, seemed to say,

> "She is mine own !
> And I as rich in having such a jewel,
> As twenty seas, if all their sands were pearl,
> The water nectar, and the rocks pure gold."

The bridesmaids represented all the colors of the National flag — Nora in red, Maria in white, and Ione in blue. The officers in full uniform.

The greetings of Louisa's father and mother and brothers over, joy took the reins. The family well knew she would not have to brave any of the hardships of army life, but the thought was touching, that she might be stationed where she would have no gas ; hence their sadness. That over, joy took the reins, as I said before.

At five o'clock, the bridal party and guests took the trains, the former to spend the night at West Point, and attend the twenty-eighth ball.

" 2. *To halt the company marching in line of battle, and to align it.*"

The crowd at Roe's hotel, were " fast and furious," but the host " polite with candor, elegant with ease," seemed a wizard in accommodating his dear five hundred. The mats and blankets were laid in parlor and hall, while the " citizen-kings," were grateful for a peg to hang their crowns upon. The wedding-party arrived.

Lieutenant Saberin immediately consulted the pages of what seemed to him the " book of fate," lo, there in very legible characters, stood, " Lieutenant Ambert, and lady, Miss De Saye, New Orleans." He sent his card to their room, grasped Lieutenant Alton by the arm and said, " Let me introduce you to a dear friend of mine, rich and beautiful ! I have one lady too many to attend to, to-night ; will you be so very kind as to take her to the hop if you are disengaged ? "

" Certainly, I am always disengaged when there is an heiress to escort ! "

Mrs. Ambert and Pauline came down.

Lieutenant Saberin said he was wild with delight at their coming, introduced Lieutenant Alton, asked after his friend Ambert. He had gone to Lieutenant Burlyton's tent, he would go and find him. He left Alton and Pauline in a lively conversation, and " with contending emotions."

Lieutenant Alton invited her to attend the hop with him.

She said she could not accept, as Lieutenant Saberin had invited her, last spring.

" Ah ! " said he, " I may be able to persuade him to re-

sign in my favor, may I make the audacious attempt ?   He
has just returned with a wedding party and has a bride's-
maid to take care of.''

" In such a case, I will accept your invitation now."

Lieutenant Alton bowed and left the parlor, to report to
his friend.

" But Saberin, I should think you would rather give up
Miss Smith ! Miss De Saye is queenly."

She is ! but I cannot break up the wedding-party ; it is
only the matter of walking over and back."

"The deuce, I imagine you will find it more of a matter than that, if I take her ! " and he walked off highly indignant.

" 3. *Oblique march in line of battle.*"

The thousands of yards of tarleton, tulle, and organdy,
crowded into the hotel hall at eight o'clock, would have
astonished Stewart or Lord & Taylor.   As one puff
after another descended and was carried off on the arm of
cadet or officer, another came to fill the place.

The wedding party stood waiting in the hall, when
Lieutenant Alton and Pauline swept by. " Who the dick-
ins has Alton got ? " said Lieutenant Storme, " O, ye
gods, but is'nt she superb ? " Nora trembled in her silk
stockings, and Ione glanced as indifferently at her, as one
lies down, when he hears the sounding of the fire-bells,
and finds his own walls cold.

" *Assemble on the Battalion.*"

80 = ♩ *Andante.*

Pauline verified the description given by Lieutenant Ambert in his letter to Saberin, she moved through the gay assemblage, truly reminding one of an Indian Princess. She wore a white satin dress, entirely covered with a golden tissue, the dark waves of her hair were wound with chains of gold, and lay in rich coils round her graceful head. Lieutenant Alton thought her "superb," and said to lui-même, "every man must paddle his own canoe," he pointed out the "young bride's-maid in blue as Lieutenant Saberin's bride elect." She was shocked, but chose not to believe it.

He asked if she was going to Washington.

Yes, Mrs. Ambert had promised some friends there, that she should return before going south."

He asked to be permitted to join their company as he was just going on there.

She was very glad, as it would be agreeable to have a larger party.

Lieutenant Alton was quite captivated, trembled, fearing Saberin would come and claim her.

Presently Lieutenant Mera came to his side, and signified a wish to be introduced to Miss De Saye.

Lieutenant Alton presented him with a grand flourish, as "Lieutenant Mera of the United States army."

Mera crimsoned, and invited her to dance. She accepted, and as he bore her off in triumph, his friend whispered "Bring her back to me." He smiled an assent, but as soon as the dance was ended, invited her to promenade. New Orleans was discussed, as she boasted that magnificent city as her home.

"I think Mrs. Ambert called you Pauline, when speaking to you in the dance?" said Lieutenant Mera.

"Yes, that is my name."

"Pauline De Saye!" repeated he.

"That was my mother's name too," said Pauline. "I am all French. I was born in Paris, and all my father's family live there!"

"And your mother's family, do they live in New Orleans?" asked he.

" O, no. She was a South Carolinian. She had but one brother,—all her family are dead," she replied.

" Was she the widow of an officer who was killed in Florida, before she married your father ? "

" Yes, she was wedded to her first husband but one year when he was killed."

A chill crept over Lieutenant Mera as she finished the sentence. Just then Mr. Alton came to take her for a dance. Mera went to Lieutenant Ambert. " Who is the young lady attached to your party ? "

" Miss De Saye ? She is one of the richest girls in New Orleans. But you may keep your heart closely buttoned in, as she is engaged to a mutual friend of ours ! " he answered laughing.

" To whom, Alton ? "

" No, indeed ! yet not to his superior, I must confess ; but one the ladies all admire more."

" You cannot mean Lieutenant Saberin ? " said he, turning pale.

" Why not ? I do mean Mr. Ulm Saberin," he replied, with a shrewd smile, as if he saw the demons jealousy and doubt, peeping through Mera's inquiries.

" Do you know this ? " asked Mera, measuring his words as if they were so many yards of his heart-strings.

" Yes, sir, I know it ! " he rejoined haughtily.

" Villain ! " was all that Ambert caught, through the savage growl, as Mera rushed from the hall.

Ambert became uneasy, not knowing what to fear. He sought his wife, but she was dancing with the Colonel, and Pauline looked so happy with Alton, that he gave her no more thought.

Lieutenant Mera sought to cool his throbbing brow in the night air, but was unable to stop away from a scene of so much interest to him. Returning, he met Alton and Miss De Saye coming out on the balcony. He had been meditating challenging " the miscreant," as he denominated his most loved class-mate. He thought with tears " I will not sleep till I have killed poor Saberin."

Lieutenant Alton stopped him saying, " Mera, Miss De Saye did not hear your name when introduced, and imagines she has known you before.

Lieutenant Mera bowed and begged to converse a few moments with the lady. As soon as they were alone, he asked her to take a seat on the guard-stone.

She began, " Lieutenant Mera, I am persuaded you are a relative of mine, my mother was a widow Mera, before she married my father."

" Indeed ! then I am happy to say there is no doubt of it."

He buried his face in his hands, and

> " Eyes that mocked at tears before,
>   With bitter drops were running o'er."

Pauline sat looking at him, afraid to speak. Visions of his infancy were floating before him. A child-mother, with starry eyes, looking love into his baby face. His soul sickened and he nearly swooned, with terrible and contending emotions. The faces of Ione ; his mother ; of the now hated Saberin ; of his new fonnd sister ; danced before his reeling brain. The cool night winds restored him. He essayed to speak, but was afraid the very tones of his voice would terrify the excited girl. He rose, saying as quietly as possible, yet as one would imagine Joseph to have spoken when he said, " The old man,— is he yet alive ? " — " Your mother — is she living ? "

The light from the door fell on her face, she gave him a woman's glance, her eyes softened ; " My mother ? I hope so. What should I do, if she were not ? Is *your* mother living ? " she asked tenderly.

He drew her hand in his arm, without replying.

She exclaimed, " There is something you will not tell me — are you ill ? "

" Have you never heard your mother speak of a little boy she left, when she went to France ? " he enquired in a low, melancholy tone.

" O yes ! she often, *often* speaks of her baby boy, and weeps bitterly. He died before I was born."

" He did not die, would to God he had ! " he said, un
able to control himself.

She grasped his arm, unconscious of what she was doing.
" Do you know him ? where, Oh, where is he ? "

" Would you care to know him ? " he asked proudly.

" Care to know him ? How can you speak so ! I have
always longed for a brother ; the pure light of a sister's love
has ever burned before the altar where my little brother
is enshrined in my heart ! " She trembled with emotion.

Lieutenant Mera was softened. " Pauline, you have
found a brother, when perhaps you needed one most. I am
your brother." They walked to the edge of the balcony,
and clasping each other's hands, wept in silence. Pauline,
Lieutenant Ambert tells me you are betrothed to Lieutenant Saberin," said he with a sorrowful voice.

" Yes," she answered " with the proviso that mamma
likes him."

" My darling, you have fallen into the hands of an un-
principled man ! The lady he has in his care to-night, is
also his betrothed."

" Lieutenant Alton told me so, but I could not believe
it. Do you know it to be true ? " she spoke in a very
humble tone.

" He told me so this week himself," he replied and she
heard the words choking him, as if he were dying, and
became greatly alarmed.

She was brought up in a city where duels were every
day affairs. She clung to his arm, and murmured " What
shall I do ? "

" Leave him to me ; " he said sternly. She burst
into tears. " Pauline, do you love him ? "

" O, no indeed ! I only fear to lose you now."

Lieutenant Mera plead with her to control herself, if she
valued his life, while she plead that he would leave Saberin to her to punish him.

After reflecting and much persuasion, he consented.
She was so happy now, that she thanked God for her escape and for the protection He had raised up. Little thought the gay butterflies about them, of the tender

scene passing so near them. There was a charm to the romantic girl in the thought of having a brother in disguise in this handsome young officer, which greatly soothed the sting that the infidelity of her lover had inflicted; while Lieutenant Mera could scarcely deny himself the proud gratification of standing forth before the multitude, an acknowledged brother to this beautiful girl. One consideration held him like bands of steel, — the humbling thought, that his young mother had deserted him when a little helpless child, and eloped with a young foreigner of a distinguished family. She had no property, but thought a rich bachelor brother and her widow mother, would take care of her child. She suspended her brother's likeness, and a remarkable ring he had sent her from India, on a gold chain around his neck for toys, these he still had. Her mother dying and giving her child to his father's relatives, a proud austere family of Spanish descent, she never returned to her native state. He had just begun to rehearse the incidents of his life to Pauline, when they were interrupted by Lieutenant Alton, who keeping his eye on Saberin, saw him at liberty and loooking for Pauline, and came to secure her. Entering the hall they met him.

"Miss De Saye, I have come to say that I have at last succeeded in disengaging myself from my bride's-maid, will you honor me with this dance?"

Lieutenant Mera stalked past him, and ground his teeth.

Pauline's eyes glittered, as she said, "Possible! have you succeeded in entirely disengaging yourself from her? You have attained great skill in that art, and accomplish those things in double quick time here!"

Saberin glanced at Alton, but that gentleman not noticing him, said, "You know, Miss De Saye, that is an important part of our education here, to make quick matches."

"Yes, I've been told,

> ' You saucy Huzzars
> Only care for love-letters to light your cigars;
> And 'tis said — I must tell you — 'tis such a good joke,
> That with soldiers, engagements end always in smoke!'

replied she, with a toss of her queenly head and a scornful laugh.

" Miss Pauline, you wont refuse me one dance this evening ? " plead Lieutenant Saberin.

" Most unfortunately my list is full."

" But I must see you, if only a moment to explain."

" O, I assure you the case will admit of no explanation," said she haughtily.

Lieutenant Alton moved on with her, and Saberin reached the dancing room just in time to see Lieutenant Mera and Ione set off in a frantic redowa.

" 4. To mark time, to march in double-quick time, and the back step."

Were you ever at a cadet hop ? No ? Then don't talk of your grand parties, of your balls, sociables, stiffables and quadrilliones ! They, compared to a *live* cadet hop, are " bosh, all bosh ! " in surgical parlance. There is no waiting for the spirit to move, at one of them. There are no solemn quadrille-marches without a word to say for one's-self, but in the appropriate and poetical words of

" A SURVIVER."

" Round the room, round the room,
Round the room, onward
Like a tee-totum,
Revolved the one hundred ;
For all were in order,
And no one had blundered.
' Onward the bright brigade !
' All around ! ' Palfrey said ;
So round and round the room
Spun the one hundred.
Round then the bright brigade,
No one the least dismayed —
None — for the ladies knew
They never blundered ;
Not theirs to make reply,
Not theirs to seem too shy,
Theirs but fast round to fly,
So round and round the room
Whirled the one hundred.

Rose all their arms so bare,
Flew all their skirts in air,
Sweeping those sitting there
Whirling and spinning, while
Lookers-on wondered ;
Trod on and pushed along,
Some looking quite forlorn,
Some of their drapery shorn,
Till they had reached their chairs
Spun the one hundred.
Gas lights to right of them,
Gas lights to left of them,
Gas lights above them,
By glass pendants sundered
Laughing and blushing so,
At seats all rushing so,
Heated and out , f breath.
And from the figure there,
Now all have reached a chair,
All that are really left
Of that one hundred.
When will the next begin ?
Oh, that enchanting spin !
How old folks wondered,
How can they labor so,
Is that true pleasure, oh,
Lovely one hundred ! "

" 5. *To march in line of battle, in retreat.*"

When Lieutenant Saberin arose the next morning, the first thing his eyes alighted on was the following delicate little billet.

" Lieutenant Saberin : —
            Hearing from my brother, of your engagement to another, it gives me great pleasure to say you are most cheerfully released from your engagement to me.
            With sentiments, &c.
                        PAULINE DE SAYE."

He read the note,— — a carte blanche for those who are adepts in these matters to fill at their leisure. " Who — is her brother ? that — Alton has done this ! Heavens,

what shall I do?"   "Send her her ring," said Pride, and
he followed her advice.

At breakfast Miss Randolph came and told Ione that
her father, who had arrived late the night before, was
going to take her to Professor Weir's studio.   Would she
accompany them at eleven o'clock?

Ione accepted with delight.

Mr. Randolph was a true type of a Virginian gentleman of the Washington school, and charmed them with
stories of his travels.   He was disappointed at not finding
his friend at home, but his son received them.   They
stood before the " Veiled Nun," in silent rapture ; the
white haired man was dumb before the inspiration of Genius, and felt himself in the presence of a divinity.   He
begged permission of the young artist to read a piece of
poetry he had found while in Europe, years ago.   It was
taken from a number of Blackwood.   He would like to
read it to the young ladies in this room.   He stood where
the light fell on his silver locks, and read to the beautiful
group,

AN ARTIST'S STUDIO.

FROM BLACKWOOD OF JAN. 1851.

" I well remember how the light, the pale, pure north light, fell
   On all within that lofty room, and clothed with mystic spell
   A massive oaken cabinet, and many a curious chair —
   Bright armor of the olden time, and relics quaint and rare.

" I marked them well,— the gathered books, the painter's treasures all:
   Here was the resting place of day, whatever might befall ;
   The inner shrine of one whose brow the stamp of genius bore,
   And who the laurels of his fame with childlike meekness wore.

" I touched his easel and his brush ; I saw his colors laid —
   Those simple implements of art, they made me half afraid ;
   For with such trifling means alone, to bid their visions glow,
   APELLES, ZEUXIS, RAPHAEL, wrought wonders long ago !

" Oh, many a slowly-waning hour this silent room alone
   Had seen the dreaming artist sit, like statue carved in stone ;
   Absorbed in patient watchfulness of all that Fancy brought,
   Gleanings of gladness or of gloom from out the fields of thought.

" With steady gazing eye upraised, he heeded not at all
  The light and shade of shimmering leaves upon his study wall ;
  The light that o'er his poet soul its lovely radiance threw,
  Was shadowless and pure as stars, when all the heavens are blue.

" The breeze that through the window came, to fan his lifted brow,
  Fold of sweet perfumes all abroad, of blossoms on each bough .
  He heeded not its fluttering, nor listened to its sigh,
  As sadly it stole back again, along the wave to die.

" He recked not that the golden eve on old Fort PUTNAM glowed,
  Or that the tiwlight in the vale enveloped his abode ;
  Or that the river glided by, majestic, calm and free,
  While on its bosom snowy sails were flowing tranquilly.

" For bright unto his soul there came, while wrapped in revery,
  A noble theme of other days, and lands beyond the sea ;
  Of men who strove in vain to break the stern oppressor's rod,
  And boldly sought in other climes the right to worship GOD !

" Firm on its heavy rollers hung a canvas broad and high,
  Dusky at first, but glowing soon with vivid imagery ;
  Life-like beneath the painter's touch, the little 'Speedwell' rose,
  Frail hopes of beating, trembling hearts, escaping from their foes !

" And kneeling on the open deck, beneath the o'erarching sky, .
  A Bible in his hand enclasped, and heaven-ward, holy eye,
  The pastor prayed — a thrilling prayer — that GOD would guide and bless
  The pilgrims and their tossing ship, in night and loneliness.

" That He who with a word can calm the wind and wave at will,
  To the wild sea of Galilee who whispered ' Peace, be still ! '
  Would guard them with a Father's care, on billows white with foam,
  And grant them on a foreign shore, a haven and a home !

" Around him bent a reverent group : — a bridegroom and a bride,
  To whom all places were alike, so they were side by side.
  A mother and her pallid boy, with look of patient woe —
  Strong was the faith, high-hearted one ! that prompted thee to go !

" Miles Standish, with his stalwart form, and soul of manly might,
  Ready to don his armor there, and battle for the right ;
  While on his shoulder fondly leaned his wife, so fair and true —
  Sweet Rose ! how love and sorrow strove within thine eye of blue !

" CARVER, and WHITE, and BRADFORD too, strong men and stern were these;
  They stayed not for the unknown wastes of trackless, stormy seas ;
  The hope of safety and of peace their every doubt beguiled :
  Here, dark Oppression lower'd in gloom — there genial FREEDOM smiled

" Childhood was there, and youth, with eye keen-looking far away,
  Longing to ride the lifting crest of ocean steeds at play ;
  Naught cared he for the coming night, for visions new and strange ;
  Joy dwelt for him in stirring life, in scenes of chance and change.

' And timid women tearless stood, with courage firm and rare,
  Waiting to hear the deep ' Amen ' of that most fervent prayer,
  And then to see the white sails set to catch a favoring wind,
  And know each early home and friend forever left behind !

" Borne from his studio's silent walls, to meet a nation's gaze,
  The painter's vision hath received its meed of fitting praise ;
  But dearer to his thoughtful soul, of far more solid worth,
  The noble lesson he would teach, than all the fame of earth.

" Tell ye, O mute, yet speaking forms, — creations of his skill,
  How trust in GOD and lofty hope, and firm, unconquered will,
  Sustained and soothed each aching heart among that little band
  Who bore with them across the sea, the freedom of our land !

" Thank GOD, my country, that the seed in doubt and meekness sown,
  To such a spreading, lordly tree in later times hath grown ;
  A pilgrim sire's beloved name a noble boast should be ;
  A pilgrim's grave a holy trust, Oh, children of the Free ! ''

" LESSON SIXTH."

3. *To march in column, in route, and to execute the movements thereto.*"

As our little party left the studio, the young artist accompanied them to see the tents struck. He told them
it was a beautiful sight, the tents falling in an instant.
The crowds were hastening to the spot, regardless of the
burning rays of the sun. The band was in attendance, and
the cadets were swinging their mallets about their heads
like so many young Vulcans, dealing blows on the tent-
pins.

On the ground Lieutenant Mera introduced Miss De
Saye, whom he had brought with him, to Ione and her
party. She asked many questions about West Point. She
said, " Do you know I always thought there was some
thing magical in the falling of the tents, but I should call this
taking down the tents ! " As she said the word tents, she

glanced over her shoulder an instant, and on looking back to see the cause of the huzzas, she was so startled at the collapsed appearances of the camp-ground, she fairly shrieked. Every one laughed that heard the " O ! " and saw the affright depicted on her face.

Unhappy Lieutenant Saberin stood off near the Colonel, not daring to approach either of his flames, lest he should be rolled up like a scroll.

Lieutenant Alton came up, " looking lovely," in his travelling suit; — " All ready for the omnibus Miss De Saye ? "

" Yes, I need not return to the hotel." She bid Ione a tender good-bye, wishing they might meet again.

Lieutenant Mera scarcely touched Ione's hand, saying, " Remember what I said the night I came near drowning you ! "

Ione looked up, her eyes welled over, and she said, " I will, Lieutenant Mera ; I promise you I will not act unadvisedly."

The omnibus stopped in front of camp, and the many that were to leave, bade adieu again and again, to their friends. Lieutenant Alton ran back twice to shake hands with Ione. Lieutenant Mera returned to linger a moment near, and gave one look of agony that Ione never forgot. " Well, I should not wonder if he should change his mind about marrying a rich girl, for he looks at Miss De Saye very lovingly," thought she. She walked off the camp-ground perfectly unconscious that she had come there with any one, till she found the polished young artist had kept near her and was now at her side. He walked to the hotel with her, and bade her adieu in a very graceful manner. She met Lieutenant Burlyton, who faced about, and offered her his arm, stepping as if he were walking over dogs and cats. A bleak smile played coldly over her face. He sighed like a blacksmith's bellows, and repeated in the saddest, and sweetest way —

" Alas, for my weary and care-haunted bosom !
　　The spells of the spring-time arouse it no more,

> The songs in the wild-wood, the sheen in the blossom,
> The fresh swelling fountain — their magic is o'er !
> When I list to the stream, when I look to the flowers,
> They tell of the past with so mournful a tone,
> That I call up the throngs of my long vanished hours,
> And sigh that their transports are over and gone."
>   Singing " Ri tu, di nu, di na ? "

" You are a host of joy in yourself, Lieutenant Burly-ton. I cannot be very miserable, while you are left ; I wish every body was just like you, and then this world would not be such a " weary, stale, flat and unprofitable, unweed-ed garden."

He answered in a half bitter, half sentimental way,

> " Don't you know that the people wont employ
> A man who wrongs his manliness, by laughing like a boy ?
> And suspects the azure blossom that unfolds upon the shoot,
> As if wisdom's old potato could not flourish at its root."

Ione laughed heartily. They went into the parlor and she sung, " Robin Adair," for him. He was much affect-ed, said it was his lullaby when he was a baby, that she must stop or she would have him boo-hoo-ing right out. But he was ha-ha-ing a few moments after, and begging her " To take him for her lover, and let all those incon-stant swains glide, they were not worth one of those invalu-able pearls he saw in her eyes, when he met her."

At parade Mrs. Bobaline was startled by hearing the order read that Lieutenant Bobaline was ordered to Wash-ington immediately. She clung to Ione's arm, and looked into her face aghast. She could not tell whether she was glad or sorry. After she had regained her composure, she said, " I wonder if Lieutenant B. has applied to be relieved. In his last letter, he said he would be at home soon, but dreaded the duties of West Point more than ever." The ladies gathered round her to express their sincere sorrow at the prospect of losing one who had been the life of the post. The officers stood off in front of the " officers' quarters," making their own comments. Lieu-tenant Saberin left them and walked after Mrs. Bobaline as she left the parade ground. He politely expressed his

regret that she was going, and said the winter would be un-
endurable; but if this political excitement continued,
they would probably *all* meet at Washington.

"Yes," cried Lieutenant Burlyton, "as the beavers do
at the hatter's. That's fur enough from — from —"

"From one head!" laughed Ione. "I fear you'll need
a scratch after that."

"I think you have given me one, 'free gratis.'"

"If we have war, I hope Lieutenant B. will resign!
If he does not, I shall go home to Florida."

"Don't 'secesh,' while under orders, Mrs. Bobaline;
that would not be honorable, you know!" said Lieutenant
Burlyton.

"I think things are coming to a pretty pass, if there is
to be a war because Southerners will not free their slaves,
and work their plantations themselves, like your great
northern men do. I presume that at home, this President
of yours was no better than any slave in the South! ac-
tually digging in his own farm! Just think of putting
such a man to rule over gentlemen.

Lieutenant Saberin glanced scornfully at her, while
Lieutenant Burlyton called a dragoon to haul down those
stars and stripes and run up a palm-leaf fan, which threw
Mrs. Bobaline and Mrs. Maryglot into spasms of laughter.
Mrs. Bobaline turned away angry at herself for counte-
nancing him in his ridicule of her dear, sacred South.

Lieutenant Saberin walked between her and Ione to the
hotel, and took seats on the piazza.

Lieutenant Burlyton offered Madam Maryglot his arm,
and conversed quite intelligibly till they arrived at the
foot of the steps. He said, "Let's go and make friends
with poor Mrs. Bobaline," and rushed along the piazza,
dragging the old lady by the arm, until he confronted Mrs.
Bobaline. He bowed to the floor. "Madam, 'horresco
referens!' what I heard at parade, entre nous; this is a
faux coup! When you leave, I will turn down my chap-
eau de bras, and make a monachus of myself, mais quand
on empriente' on ne choisit pas! on dit, poco a poco, post

nubila jubila! moi vous oublier? non jamais! honi soit,
qui mal y pense! Ich dien, E pluribus unum!" at
the last word he put his hand on his heart, threw back his
head, and waved it to and fro, as if he were executing a
trill in an opera; then turning abruptly to Madam Maryglot, who stood holding her sides, " Sprachen sie deutsch?"
said he in a most polished and graceful manner, " Quid
vides?" he exclaimed saucily to the other ladies.

" Ha! ha! ha! O, you fool!" screamed the amiable old
lady, in great distress.

" ARTICLE FIRST."

" *To break the company into platoons.*"

Lieutenant Bobaline returned in a few days, and insisted that Ione should spend the winter in Washington, with
them. Viola was heart-broken at leaving Lieutenant
Saberin and her cadet friends, but Washington contained
many to interest a beautiful woman, and she consoled herself with the thoughts of what a Phillipa she would be
there. Lieutenant Saberin made himself perfectly fascinating now that Lieutenant Mera was gone, and with his beauty and sweetness of manner and disposition, a woman must
be adamant not to do as our heroines did, fall in love anew
with him. He was kind and considerate with Ione, never allowing the slightest change, or shade of change of his tenderness toward her, gave her no opportunity to find fault
with him. She could scarcely recognize him as the same
man. Mrs. Bobaline was occupied in making preparations
for her winter's campaign, and overseeing her packing; but
when she did appear, Lieutenant Saberin was her ever
ready and willing attendant. On the morning of her departure, Ione said farewell to West Point with deep regret. She was to leave Madam Maryglot, who however
promised to go after them as soon as the cold weather commenced. She must say good-bye to jolly Lieutenant Burlyton. What should she do for some one to make her laugh

when she was sad, and say touching things when she was laughing? But he said he should apply to be stationed near her, and resign if Mr. Secretary did not comply. Cadet Smith would come to see her as soon as he graduated, and Lieutenant Saberin accompanied them as far as New York, and whispered to Ione that if he was not ordered to Washington before spring, he should get a leave to spend a week with her. These asurances robbed her several partings of their sting.

" *To re-form the company.*"

Arrived in Washington, the first persons Mrs. Bobaline and Ione met, were Lieutenants Alton and Mera; now bosom friends. They greeted the party as if they were relatives. The first question Lieutenant Mera asked Lieutenant Bobaline, was, "*Are you going to stand firm?*" Lieutenant Bobaline grasped his hand, saying, "I can't give up the old stars and stripes! I cannot fight under any thing else! How are you?"

"Firm as a rock!" said Mera. Lieutenant Alton waved his cap above their heads, repeating,

> "O'er the proud heads of freemen, our star-banner waves,
> Men firm as their mountains and still as their graves!"

"You know Ambert has gone over?" said Lieutenant Mera.

"Gone under, you mean!" Lieutenant Bobaline replied.

"The night before he left," said Alton "we gave him a supper, and embraced all round at parting, — possibly to meet next on the battle-field, ugh!"

10

ARTICLE EIGHTEENTH.

Time flew to Ione, in sight-seeing, with Viola from day to day. Viola was constantly meeting old army acquaintances, and attended by half a dozen distinguished gentlemen, her ladyship became quite reconciled to the change, and as "soft as the dawn."

Madam Maryglot came on in haste, the first rebuff she received from "Storm King," who holds undisputed sway over "all he surveys," quite half the year. Her very caps and ribbons brought up charming, lovely, enchanting West Point *now*. She told Ione all the news, brought her a love-letter from Lieutenant Saberin, and a bouquet of autumn leaves, from Lieutenant Smith, which she wore in her hair to the President's levee, then pressed them on Bristol board, and framed them to hang in her room.

Lieutenant Mera had introduced to her a lovely young girl, the daughter of an M. C., —Miss Mary Greenleaf. He had been very attentive to this lady, so much so, that Ione was jealous for Miss De Saye, who had been spirited away almost immediately after her arrival in Washington, by Lieutenant Ambert and lady, seeming to feel worse at parting with Lieutenant Alton than with Lieutenant Mera. Ione began to suspect an engagement between her new friend and her old beau, Lieutenant Mera. He was strangely variable in his treatment of Ione, sometimes with the affectionate familiarity of a brother, and at others cold and distant, as if he was deeply offended. Madam Maryglot, the repository for all her sorrows, would be duly informed, and then she would forget it all till the next time. Mrs. Bobaline was attending a party every night, and sleeping all day. After the first month, Ione became so weary of society, with a mind ill at ease, that only on especial occasions would she accompany her aunt and uncle. Lieutenants Smith and Corridor she saw whenever they came in from camp. Her weariness of everything in Washington was not abated by the reception of a letter from her sister younger than herself. It had gone thousands of miles out of its way, came to West Point after her departure from that post, and was forwarded to her.

"SAN FRANCISCO March 25, 1861.

Darling Isie.

You wish me to write, to atone for all mamma's omissions by telling you every thing we do every day! Well, you know the old routine, studies, rides, sails, etc. There are some charming young officers here now. Our lovely Dr. H. brings them to spend the evenings with us, and Edestina often comes in, and then we wish for you, and Gertrude is called upon for the sweet songs she warbles so like a bird; her favorite she always sings, "Farewell! — but whenever you welcome the hour," and when she murmurs, "I wish she were here!" we all join in but mamma,— I'll not tell you what she does. The spring and summer has been very gay, but as I have not "come out" yet, I see but little of it. Now "I'll wager," as mamma says, that you have not been written a word about our holidays, and all our presents. Yours were bought the same as if you were here! You wrote about the deckings of churches, etc. with evergreens. "The sweet spring comes to deck our lovely land!" For three days before Christmas, mamma, Dr. H., and Lieutenant De See, and us four girls, attended the sales and auction at Blank and Flash Halls, and the Dr. said that the scene rivalled Paris. He said, that we saw enough Japanese cabinets sold, to "furnish one to every house here, and then supply Washington with a new one every week for the next four years!" There were nine festivals in the city Christmas eve; we attended one. There were five hundred children gathered around loaded tables, and an immense evergreen, forty feet high, which bore gifts on every twig. There was delightful music, and the children played and danced, and Grace had her arms full of gifts, and a stocking full the next morning. New Year's eve a terrible shower set in, and we feared we should have a rainy day for our calls. Gertrude and Edestina came in all the rain, and we were all to sleep in your room. It stormed till nearly twelve o'clock, and then we sat in the open window, not a breath of wind stirring, and the moon shone like day on the bay, turning the crest of the waves all to snow. O, it was glorious! Gertrude sang, and Edestina too. We were saluted at twelve with the booming of cannon. At seven o'clock the next morning we threw open our windows, and it was June! The warm rain had brought out all your delicious flowers in full bloom; the warm sunshine turned everything to gold, and across the bay, the ridge three thousand feet high, you know the snow on its top looked like a vast opal, with the rays of the sun, while the warm ravines at its base in their green freshness was like an emerald setting. The birds were flitting about and the humming bird clinging to the legumes of the locust trees, made it all look like fairy-land. We dressed as quickly as possible, and went into the garden to cull flowers to deck our tables and parlors. The Jeddo urn on the side-board, we filled with gilly flowers, verbenas, red and white roses, fuchias, veronica, abutilons, mignionette and heliotropes, and locusts and acacias, all out of our own garden, and all the Japanese vases were filled with flowers. Your Lamarque roses, and Australian pea, made a lovely bouquet. We dressed our hair a la Japanese, and drank our coffee from the Japanese cups; sliced Oregon apples, weighing two pounds each, on the Japanese plates; had bananas and melons in Japanese dishes; received cards on the Japanese platter; arranged the Josses, or Japanese gods, on the mantle piece, and displayed all the trays and work baskets and, (this is a secret) we "showed off," three new Japanese cabinets, *all presents*, yours the largest and most beautiful, and a *surprise* for you on your return ! — not from mamma, — from the good Dr. H., don't dare to mention it, or I will freeze you into ice cream ! We had two hundred calls from gentlemen without overcoats, in parlors without fires ; and at dark sat down to dinner, and all cried a tear or two about you. Here is the bill of fare : " Radishes straight from the ground, and cauliflowers fresh and tender. Isn't that anything to make a fuss about ? well, we had lettuce not raised under glass. Are you still stoical ? we had new potatoes, and splendid ones too ; and a heaping dish of green peas, genuine marrowfats, large and sweet. Now you begin to open your eyes, I see, if not your mouth. I don't speak of the fresh salmon, that is a drug with us all the time. But wait for the climax — strawberries ! do you hear that ? grown within city limits, in the open air, without any stimulant or coaxing, and we had a large box of them, and their average size was that of a big walnut,— I shan't tell you what they cost." Why don't you speak of coming home ? The Dashers often speak of you, and how much they enjoyed your society on the voyage, Mrs. Dasher says she loves you from head to foot. We all send you a sweet kiss, mamma and all ; and our best love to our beautiful new aunty, she must bring you home to us and stay as long with us as you have with her. But uncle ! how we would like to see him Just think of he and mamma not knowing each other. Do make him come to see us. I cannot bear to stop writing, but here I am with pages checkered over and over, and no more place to write ! Dear, dear, dear Isie, all send kisses and love more than tongue can tell.

YOUR OWN DAISY.

Ione sat in her room and wept herself nearly sick over this letter.

Mrs. Bobaline and Mrs. Maryglot were out, and went to seek the recluse as soon as they came in. They supposed she had heard the death of her dearest friend, her cheeks were so blistered with tears. She read them the letter.

Mrs. Bobaline was wild over it. She would go home with Ione : — " Let us go immediately, and you, Mrs. Maryglot, with us ! "

" Thank you, I should prefer not being snapped up and taken to Barbadoes or Barbary, by your enterprising privateers," she replied grufly.

Oh, sure enough ! we can't go out of our own country, or stay in it in *safety!* " said Mrs. Bobaline, for the first moment tasting some of the bitter fruits of secession. They went to their parlor.

Lieutenant Saberin came in, and Mrs. Bobaline must read him " the letter from Paradise." He was charmed, and told Ione he thought he would wait till he saw " Daisy." He knew Dr. H. very well — had been with him in Mexico. They made Ione describe her home, and the bay, and the golden gate and Fort, and the entrance into the city at night, so like the scenes depicted in the " Arabian Nights," and Mrs. Viola was justly indignant that she had been permitted to remain in ignorance of such a wonderful place till this time.

" *Position of the Sword or Sabre, under Arms.*"

Cards were issued to the bon ton of Washington, for a grand reception at the mansion of the Secretary of State, Mr. Seward. The elegant saloons were ablaze, every person of distinction was present, and the assemblage had more the appearance of a foreign court, than of a democratic party. " Our Chief," the Lieutenant General of the American army, was present, moving among the throng, with the majesty of a sovereign by " Divine right." Many a line of care is added to his brow. What wonder? His gigantic mind grasps the terrible responsibilities resting on every freeman, high and low, in all their magnitude, realizing that they are sufficient to crush an archangel, unassisted by the Almighty hand. May God direct him! On all sides one can see the wise and sage of our land — the paddlers of our canoe of state. Not inappropriate is the motto we see inscribed on the service of blue and gold, — " esse quam videri." Near the door stand a group of United States army officers, surveying the gorgeous scene. " Our young engineer officers," I presume, or they would not be *surveying* at such a time.

At length one of them directs the attention of the rest to a foreigner, — a distinguished looking young man, with a lady leaning on his arm. " Who are those? She is the most beautiful woman I have seen to night," he said.

The gentlemen stared and admired, but did not know.

The eldest of the party questioned some one standing near, and found the gentleman to be a young attaché, but could not learn who the lady was, — surmised her to be his wife.

The first officer that spoke, vowed he must know who she was, and with this view set off after them to ascertain who their acquaintances might be, but they appeared to know only each other, as they looked " neither here nor there," but into each other's faces. He said " they are not married, but may be engaged," and tried to distinguish how they addressed each other, but they spoke so low, he could only hear that they were conversing in French. The more he watched the girl's beautiful face and graceful play of features, the more interested he became, and the fact that she was a foreigner, and evidently the young man's betrothed, only added to his flame. Late in the evening found him still her shadow, yet not once had the heavenly blue eyes rested on him, so entirely were they engrossed by the pair of dark hazel ones at her side.

> " She gazed upon a world she scarcely knew —
> As seeking not to know it,
> And kept her heart serene, within its zone ;
> There was an awe in the homage which she drew
> Her spirit seemed as seated on a throne,
> Apart from the surrounding world, and strong
> In its own strength, — most strange in one so young."

Still lingering near the unconscious pair, he was startled by a hand laid on his shoulder, and a familiar voice. " O Saberin, you here ? " He started as if he had been shot when he saw Lieutenant Bobaline. They shook hands and went in search of the ladies. He found Ione not at all inferior to the belles of Washington in her San Franciscan ball dress, and Indian jewels, and took, what he supposed was his place beside her, but she was lost to the world for the hour, in listening to the wiling voice of a fascinating little R. N. to whom she introduced her inevitable inheritor; but the R. N. stood his ground, without the slightest idea of giving up the ship, and stood by her till the last man left, in search of Madam Bobaline, who showed too plainly her delight at the addition of this brilliant to her crown.

" Where are you stopping ? you must come to us! "

" Beyond a question, what would be more charming than to re-form our West Point circle, complete in Washington ! " It was farthest from his thoughts at that moment to change his hotel, at least not till he had accomplished an object, and that was to find out his incognita. He could not at once give up his habit of going on from " conquering to conquer."

Lieutenant Bobaline came to say, they must go home to breakfast.

Lieutenant Saberin attended Ione to the carriage, whispering a tender little speech about his happiness being complete, as they drove away !

" Manual."

" *For relieving Sentinels.*"

At the fashionable hour for calling, Lieutenant Saberin dressed in all the " pride and pomp of glorious war," thought he would see the buildings of interest, and then call on Ione. He accordingly took himself to see the home of the Russian minister. There were many more abroad on the same errand, that is, reviewing the public buildings.

> " There were foreigners of much renown,
> Of various nations, and all Volunteers ;
> Not fighting for the country or its crown,
> But wishing to be one day brigadiers ;
> Also to have the sacking of a town ;
> A pleasant thing to young men of their years,
> 'Mongst them were several Englishmen of pith,
> Sixteen called Russell, and nineteen named Smith ! "

Lieutenant Saberin promenaded past Russian Place, after a very troubadourish fashion, gazing as a miner would for glittering ore, but no soft blue eyes looked forth from the casement, or golden locks gleamed from the doorway, and too late, for his call, he hurried to his hotel, lest he should lose his dinner. At a most unheard-of hour, when all ladies of taste, are " snoozing ! " Lieutenant Saberin sent his card up to Miss Smith. She was alone in the parlor, Viola was permitting

> " Sleep to kill those pretty eyes,
> And give as soft attachment to her senses
> As infants — empty of all thought."

As he entered, Ione arose saying, " I feel the breezes of West Point fanning my cheek, when I see you, Lieutenant Saberin ! "

" Yes, and they sent their regards to you and a kiss," said he laughing. " But ah, West Point is sadly changed."

" Changed ? West Point cannot change. Her beauties changeless, her hills everlasting, her Hudson exhaustless, and her sunsets to eternity,

> " Fairest of all that earth beholds, the hues,
> That live among the clouds, and flush the air
> Lingering and deepening at the hour of dews."

" Oh, Miss Ione, you make it a heaven, when without the presence of those we love, it is the reverse, while

'Heaven would be hell, if loved ones were not there,
　And any spot a heaven, if we could save
From every stain of earth, and thither bear,
　　The hearts that are to us our hope and care ;
The soil whereon our purest pleasures grow,
　Around the quiet hearth, we often share,
From the quick change of thought, the tender flow
　Of fondness waked by smiles, the world we love below ! ' "

Ione said, " Really, you should have an audience, you recite so well ! "

" I wish no more appreciative audience, than I have at present."

She asked if he had seen many he knew since he came. He replied, no — he had spent the morning looking at the buildings.

She asked in surprise, if he had never been in Washington before.

" O yes, many times ! but there are sights of beauty we cannot see too often ! " He could not appear himself, was restless, at last plead an engagement, and promised to call soon again.

A few moments after he left, Mary Greenleaf entered to tell Ione she was going to ride on horseback.

" Why did you not come in sooner ? I would have introduced you to such a handsome young officer ! "

" I am always a ' day after the fair,' why didn't you send for me ? "

" I will when he comes again." The girls chatted on till it was time for the ride. Ione stood in the window, and watched her out of sight. She felt a little sad about Lieutenant Saberin's call, — it had left an unpleasant impression on her heart, and she intuitively attacked the book-case, for Pickwick, which she had not seen since she left West Point. She took the old volume down, with a very solemn face, but before long forgot her own griefs, to be happy "with Samivel." When Viola came down, she told her of Lieutenant Saberin's call, and gave his pleasant messages ; but she received them very ungraciously, was indignant that she was not sent for, while poor Ione would gladly have exchanged places with her, and given her the calf and taken in its place her painless sleep. Some one knocked. Mrs. Bobaline called " Come ! "-

Lieutenant Alton entered and said a la Phœnixiana " how are the 94 young, and 100 beautiful ladies this 90 fine day ? "

Ione shouted, " Thank you, I feel like 60."

" I am 150 ! " he replied. "I have just heard from N. O. A gentleman direct from there, saw our 74 friend, and she is as 1000 beautiful as ever."

" O, dreadful ! New Orleans, why don't you stand 99 true by 100 firm for our country's flag of 34 stars ? "

Mrs. Bobaline entered the lists, for his resigning at once. " They will make you a Brig ! "

" I would rather be shot a Lieutenant under my flag, than resign and be a Napoleon ! "

" Well, they'll beat you any way, and take you prisoner ? " she replied, sneering.

" ' The flag of our Union forever.' Is Washington safe ? " said Ione.

" Not quite if they attack us now, I fear ; but it soon will be," he replied thoughtfully.

" Now that the 7th have arrived," said Mrs. Bobaline.

War, war, war ! was the only topic discussed by small and great, and Washington was one " tented field," and ladies drove to the camps to see parades, and drills, and meet their friends.

Lieutenant Saberin daily gave hours of toil, and inches of sole, to the pursuit of beauty " under difficulties."

"ARTICLE SIXTEENTH."

" *Rules for manœuvering by the rear rank.*"

Lieutenant Saberin's only hope is to meet his incognita in the street, and follow her home. This decision leads him up the Avenue early one afternoon, fearing that he should not meet her, yet hoping against hope. A lady and gentleman dash by him on horseback. 'Tis she, and the young foreigner! He follows them at a rapid pace, but he is soon distanced, and they have turned off the Avenue, and are out of sight. Disappointment clouds his brow. But they must return! He will while away the time by sitting in Madam Bobaline's windows, and watching for the only woman in whom he *now* feels any interest. He accordingly repaired to their hotel, sends up his card, and waits for the ladies. On a chair in the window stands a bijou,— a lady's work basket. Supposing it to be Ione's, he takes it up, and showing a very gentlemanly curiosity, examines its contents. He finds a tiny book, formed of a sheet of note paper, folded till it was but two inches square. He opened it and was surprised at the date, written in a very familiar hand, but dated years before he had seen Ione. He looks again; the writing is not Ione's, nor is it Mrs. Bobaline's, but more familiar than either. Then the date,— why should that recall memories of the past? He reads—

Oct. 27, 1856.

I wait for thee, as morning waits
　　With dewy eye, the coming sun,
My soul sits trembling at her gates,
　　To greet her best beloved one !

I wait for thee as waits the flower—
  I droop for thee as droops the flower,
Beneath the noon-tide's fervor deep—
  Ere pitying stars at twilight hour,
Put on their snowy veils to weep.

He turns the leaf, and reads

March, 1859.

I waited for thee — ah, how long !
  You came — but ah, how changed !
Your self-conceit was — ah, how strong !
  Self, in the shade at 90 ranged !

Both dates came up before him like apparitions. He was as much surprised as he would have been in his cadet days, by the appearance of the " great highankadank," on his post at dead of night. What a strange magic there is about dates ! How they thrill one, as they are seen on the letter or page, the figures that have brought to us some joy or sorrow, and how strangely near, becomes the inscriber of those figures ! The rest of the tiny book is a blank, and he begins again to read its contents. He has just finished as Mrs. Bobaline and Ione enter. He quickly put the little record in his breast pocket. He sat conversing for a long time, often glancing out of the window, but the fair equestrian did not make her appearance. Impatient and weary he was about to excuse himself and seek her through the streets again, when a low tap, tap, tap ! said some one was coming, and Mary Greenleaf entered. When she saw a strange gentleman, she hesitated and said, " I came to get my work-basket ! " She approached the chair, took the basket and changing color painfully, excused herself and retired. Lieutenant Saberin moved away to the window, shocked to find his long neglected blue-eyed one, and the beautiful foreigner he had been pursuing so untiringly, were one and the same person ! This at once solved the enigma of the little blank-book, its dates, and familiar hand-writing. What had changed her so ? — Had a few years wrought such a transformation ? With a profound sigh, he turned to the ladies, trying to look wonderfully indifferent. "Who is the young lady?"

Ione answered, "She is the daughter of the Hon. Mr. Greenleaf. They are stopping here, isn't she lovely?"

"Yes! Is she engaged to the young foreigner with whom she rides?" he asked as deliberately as if each word was the last he could utter.

"O, he is wild about her, but she,— I am not her confidant — I cannot say." Ione showed in her manner that there was something she would like to say, but did not. She was thinking about Lieutenant Mera.

Lieutenant Saberin bade her good day, saying he would see her often as possible, as in these times, they knew not what a day would bring forth.

She shuddered, for she had seen all the terrible preparations with an aching heart, fully realizing that they were more than a gay parade, or an idle pageant on West Point. Had not Sumter borne testimony to the stern reality, the wild forgetfulness of all that we hold sacred? the lives of our precious ones there — our hero-martyrs, was it a dream to them in their prison of flame — their fiery furnace, from which they came, pure gold, to shine forever in our crown of Freedom? Noble men! When forsaken by men, God delivered, to show how He could save! May the God of battles be their shield in like manner, in every hour of trial. Ione sat in the window, till the gray twilight deepened round her, realizing in all its terrors the dark cloud that hung over our beloved land. Every hour brought nearer the fearful struggle. Hearts must know anguish, deeper than death, and "men must work, and women must weep." O, why? Will the "by and by" tell us?

> "O, wonderful visions of long ago!
>   Lighting so the warm young brain,
> You've lost your aura of golden glow,
>   You are tarnished now, by the touch of pain.
> Can Love retint what rust hath lain?
>   Can it kindle again for the eager eye?
> O, beautiful dreams, will you live again,
>   Will you live again, in the by-and by.

"They who began life's race with me,
    The amber-haired, and dewey-eyed,
Who made life sweeter than dream can be ;
    Alas ! how many of them have died !
The *old, old* story — beside the way,
    In low cold houses, mute they lie !
When all shall come forth, to immortal day,
    Shall we love again in the by-and-by?

"The tangled web of mortal life,
    Will Jesus' pitying hand untie ?
That error and evil mingle strife,
    Despite His love — Will He tell us why ?
Why glorious promises stranded lie ;
    Why hearts are wrecked on this lower coast,
Why heirs of a God-born destiny
    Reel into chaos, rayless, lost ?

"Many who love in silence here,
    Walk as strangers, far apart,
Never naming the name most dear,
    The being born their twin in heart ;
In God's after-day will it all be clear —
    The story of Fate and its sorrowful " Why ? "
The loved and longed-for, waiting here,—
    Will they know and love in the by-and-by ? "

                  Saturday, 16th June, 1860.

Twilight deepened into darkness, still Ione sat dreaming on of the future.

Mrs. Bobaline came in with a letter from Colonel Bobaline, in Western Virginia. The gas was lighted and the letter read. Lieutenant Mera entered, and they were eagerly discussing the news it contained, — the victory under their glorious young General. "Colonel Burlyton is with us," it said, "the same brave, noble fellow he was at West Point. He is idolized by his men." I knew he would be !" exclaimed Lieutenant Mera warmly.

"He is too pleasant and lovely for a warrior, I wish he were here ! " said Ione.

Tap, tap, and the gentle Mary Greenleaf opened the door. Lieutenant Mera shook her hand kindly, and told her about the letter and Colonel Burlyton, what Ione just said, and how he envied him.

" Dear old West Point! " cried Ione, and they began re-
calling reminiscences of that enchanting spot.   One said
" Do you remember ? " and then another, till a perfect
picture gallery was established, whose bright colors and familiar scenes brought back words and smiles long forgotten,
whose reflected light brightened the faces gathered round
the table.

" Miss Ione, you remember one morning playing the
'officer's call,' and all of us rushing in, to see who was
calling us ? " asked Lieutenant Mera, in a livelier humor
than Ione had seen him in since her early acquaintance
with him.

" Yes, indeed ! and the scolding Viola gave me for being
so improper ! But do you remember that you tried to
make me promise to play it when I wished to see you, and
you would come directly ?"

The partings came. Colonel Burlyton fresh from, and flushed with victory, came with his great heart and sonorous voice to cheer on our troops. Captains Alton and Saberin brought him to see the ladies. He sang for them, "The soldier's dream," and "Ah, doth not a meeting like this make amends," drawing tears from every eye. Captain Alton looking like a young David, with his gentle blue eyes and beautiful hair, came to say "good night, until the morrow." It was all he would say; his hopes were high. He commanded a battery. Captain Mera came not. What! gone without one word? Ay, so true love should do; it cannot speak. Captain Saberin came last of all, determined to bid them good bye cheerily, as Alton had done, but was petrified to find Ione and Mary Greenleaf sobbing in each other's arms! Ione bowed her cold brow for him to kiss. He shook hands with Mrs. Bobaline who was nearly in hysterics, and flinging one glance to Mary, who had retreated to the sofa, he fled from the room. Poor Mary! "Through the lashes of her darting eyes she shot her soul at every glance!" inwardly saying, "I part with thee, as wretches that are doubtful of hereafter, part with their lives — trembling at Futurity." She left the room, fearing she should die, if she did not hasten to give way to her great agony. She threw herself on her bed alone, exclaiming,

> "Oh! had he ever loved, he would have thought
> The worst of tortures bliss, to silent parting!"

{ CENTERVILLE 20th *July*, 1861.
Saturday night, 10 o'clock.

> "Centerville! centre of 'uncertainty, fell demon of our fears
> The human soul that can support despair,
> Supports not thee.'"

Our glorious land, thy great hopes center here to-night. Will they be dashed to the ground? The arteries of

every great heart in our beloved country, center here,
shall the life blood of Freedom redden Liberty's soil?
God knows! This is one of the most beautiful nights the
imagination can conceive. The sky is perfectly clear, and
the air as serene and still as that of Eden. The bright
moon cast the woods which bound the field into deep shadows, through which the camp-fires shed a clear and brilliant
glow. From the crest of the hill, the scene is a picture
of enchantment. On the extreme right, in the neighbor-
hood of the Fire Zouaves, a party were singing the " Star
Spangled Banner;" and from the left rose the sweet strains
of a magnificent band, intermingling opera airs, like the
beautiful serenade of Don Pasquale, with the patriotic
bursts of " Hail Columbia," and " Yankee Doodle."
From far beyond the woods came the hum of the hosts
encamped in the extreme rear. How many to-night either
in their heart's deep silence, or in converse with friends—
new found, or mayhap " grappled together with hooks of
steel," quoted More's touching lines.

> " Sweet moon ! if like Crotona's sage
>   By any spell, my hand could dare
> To make thy disc its ample page,
>   And write my thoughts, my wishes there ;
> How many a friend whose carelsss eye
>   Now wanders o'er that starry sky,
> Should smile upon thine orb to meet
>   The recollection kind and sweet
> The reveries of fond regret,
>   The promise never to forget,
> And all my heart and soul would send,
>   To many a dear loved distant friend."

" FORWARD."

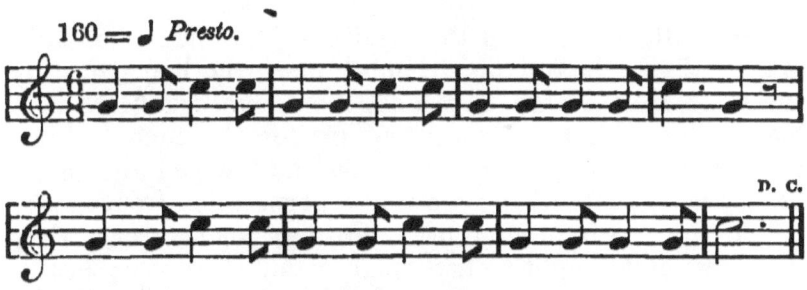

"By the hope within us springing.
   Herald of to-morrow's strife ;
By that sun whose light is bringing,
   Chains or Freedom ; death or life ;
Oh ! remember life can be
   No charm for him, who lives not free !
Like the day-star in the wave,
   Sinks a hero in his grave ;
Midst the dew-fall of a nation's tears ! "

The terrible word, "Forward," had gone forth, and all the household gods taken from their altars to be placed in the van, to lead on our brave soldiers, and to "shield them in the fight." Sanguine of success, all panted for the sanguine combat. Forward in the moon light of the stillest hour of night. Forward, thirty six thousand freemen, through the hazy valleys and o'er the hill slopes, past the burning fires at which forty regiments had prepared their midnight meal ; miles apart in the vistas, opening along a dozen lines of view. Forward, our artillery, hope of the conflict, whose black mouthed republicans shall awake the country to what will be the order of the day, whose detonating arguments shall shake the distant hills.

" And thunder in their ears, their country's cause ! '

Forward, white army wagons, with their hearse-like am-
bulances, draped like the hearts of the American people
with

> " Black images
> Of stern agony, and shroud and pall,
> And breathless darkness, and a nation's woe ! "

Forward, not to meet the armies of the aliens, but fathers, brothers, class-mates, friends ! men who had sworn by
the same Holy Name, to protect their country's flag ! who
had fought side by side contending for the sacred rights
now trampled upon, who had knelt and wiped the death
damps from each other's brow, and borne them from scenes
of carnage, to light and life.   Fathers against sons, they
had blest and taught to lisp their evening prayer ; brothers who had slept, clasped in each other's arms, in the
same little crib, under the same roof-tree.   Class-mates,
whose hands have pressed the sacred volume, when
they swore by the Almighty God, to be true to their country and the constitution.   Friends that have stood the
test in hours of trial, and deep woe !   Such must " Forward ! " in the moon's tender light, with the soft rustle of
our idolized stars and stripes above them, for which who
would not die ? through the grey of dawn, and white
morning twilight — on under the splendor of such a sun
as rose on Austerlitz !   It was Sunday morning. Even
in the wilderness the sacred day seems purer and more
hushed than any other.   It was ours first to break the sacred spell of the god of silence as he sits ever thus — his
only song to earth and heaven, " Hush, all hush ! "   To
becloud the clearness of that serene atmosphere with the
rude clangor of the avant messenger, that heralded our
challenge to a disloyal foe.   The fortunes of the day rose
and fell like the waves of a mighty ocean ; we heard
continuous tidings of heroism and victory ; we could catch
glimpses of the advances and retreats, could hear occasionally the guns of a battery before undiscovered, could guess

how terribly all this accumulation of death upon death must tell upon those undaunted men, but could also see — and our cheers continually followed the knowledge — that our forces were gradually driving the right of the enemy around the second quarter of a circle, until by ten o'clock the main battle was raging directly opposite where it had commenced six hours before !   We heard of the intrepidity of Burnside and Sprague ; how the devoted and daring young governor led the regiment he had so munificently equipped, again and again to victorious charges, and at last spiked with his own hands the guns he could not carry away !   The victory seemed ours.   It was an hour sublime in unselfishness, and apparently glorious in its results.   The question was quickly to be decided for us.   " The issue of this hard fought battle, in which certainly our troops lost no credit, in their conflict on the field with an enemy ably commanded, superior in numbers, who had but a short distance to march, and who acted on his own ground on the defensive, and always under cover, whilst our men were of necessity on the open field, should not prevent full credit being given to those officers and corps whose services merited success if they did not attain it."   Such is the history of a day.   Why hid not the sun his face from such a scene ?

" Give me the death of those
Who for their country die ;
And oh ! be mine like their repose
When cold and low they lie !
Their loveliest mother earth
Enshrines the fallen brave ;
In her sweet lap, who gave them birth,
They find their tranquil grave."

" The prayers of fair women, like legions of angels,
Watch over our soldiers by day and by night ;
And the King of all glory, the chief of all armies,
Shall love them and lead them, who dare to be right.
As each column sweeps by,
Hear their hearts' battle-cry,—
It was Warren's,—' Tis sweet for our country to die ! ' "

The parlor, the hall, and the respective rooms were traversed with unsteady steps, by Mrs. Bobaline, Ione, and Mary, unable to sit quietly at their patriotic employment of making every needful article for the army, from a havelock to an embroidered flag. They followed each other, or sought their chambers alone, weeping and praying by turns.

Madam Maryglot gave way to her own great heart, by denouncing the demagogues and politicians in good healthy English, forgetting her accomplishments in her honest ire, at the sorrow and terror of those she saw weeping around her. Occasionally she would break forth into sneers, that there was no head to our affairs; that of we only had a king, he could send at once and take the miscreants, and hang them as high as Haman. " Shame on the American people, for their sleepiness, allowing traitors to disarm the government, and then bully them or destroy their country ! If they had the spirit to hang every traitor they get hold of, the trouble would soon be put an end to. They should have hurled Davis from his seat in the senate, and Floyd from the cabinet, as the old disloyal and ambitious nobles of England were ; taken and decapitated them at once, and there would have been an end to a thing ! " This was strong meat for the broken and crushed spirits she was haranguing, and she received no reply. Then she would tell them stories of heroic women, who freed their country by their super-feminine bravery. Joan of Arc, and Charlotte Corday were introduced, but her " words were as idle tales " to those whose bowed heads were humbled, whose hearts were bleeding. Again she would endeavor to read to them, but finally gave it up and entered into the grief and anxiety of those most vehement in their great agony for their absent ones. She ran through the house for news, till one would have thought her own sons were on that awful field. Whenever she heard a regiment or battery named she cried, " Is there any one I know in that battery or regiment ? " Her mind was in the wildest confusion as to the whereabouts of her favorites. She had them numbered on her fingers, and before reading the papers would count them over as if she were saying avas for their souls :—" Colonel Bobaline in Western Virginia ; Colonel Burlyton, Fairfax court-house ; Captain Alton in command of a battery, Captain Saberin, Assistant Adjutant General ; Captain Mera, Aid de camp ; Lieutenant Smith, Griffin's battery ; Lieutenant Corridor, Sherman's battery." Long before she could finish her drolly numbered list, every one present was smiling through their tears.

Mrs. Bobaline was sadly tried by receiving little missives from the rebel colonel, begging for one word, that she had no interest at stake at Washington, she was a Southerner ; her husband was a rebel against his own land. She answered one or two of them, but gave no very important information, till she became alarmed lest she should be arrested, when she wrote to him not to dare to write to her again.

Madam Maryglot suspected her of disloyalty, and improved all occasions to rant at wolves in sheep-skins, and pretended friends, till they came to be open enemies. In the darkest moment of suspense, she would taunt her with being sorry that we were triumphant, or glad that we were beaten, when really the poor lady was nearer dead than alive, fearing to hear that some one she loved was killed. Madam M. was better than any news-boy of the city ; she would make her appearance and astonish a group of listeners with, " Our army is outflanked. General Lee is threatening Washington ! McDowell is encircled with bayonets, had nothing else to do but surrender at discretion." She would stand and watch the effect of this piece of intelligence upon her listeners, as one administering laughing-gas to an audience would do, in a highly scientific manner. When they were a little come to themselves, she would leave them for new supplies. " We took Bull's Run batteries in the morning, but they were retaken in the evening. Johnson, Beauregard, or Mr. General Fine-to-see, and Lee, are concentrated at Manassas with 80,000 men, and as God is on the side of the big batteries, we are most likely to be whipped in the contest." It is twelve o'clock at night, and the doors of private houses are open, groups of sleepless ones are on the steps and on the side walks, hearing and telling the latest news in undertones. Afar the faint rolling of the drum of the different regiments hastening towards General McDowell's head quarters is heard, the city is awake but silent, as if the last trump had brought the inhabitants of a " city of silence," from their dark beds and houses. Toward morning the rumbling on the pavements of wagons going to the camps, the trampling of the courier's horse galloping in the avenue, and the conversation in the streets are all that is heard. At one o'clock a regiment passes Willard's. Three cheers are exchanged between the citizens and the soldiers, and they take their run down the avenue. Colonel Burnside came into town on Monday evening, and after an interview of a quarter of an hour with General Mansfield, returned to join his brigade. His hat and coat were riddled with balls, and his face grimed with dust. He did not say a word to the persons who obstructed his passage in the lobby of Willard's. Colonel Burnside, you are not alone in your speechless agony, America, the world is dumb with grief !

THE BATTLE FIELD.

" Here you might see
Barons and peasants on the embattled field,
Slain or half dead, in one huge ghastly heap,
Promiscuously amassed. With dismal groans
And ejaculation in the pangs of death,
Some call for aid neglected ; some o'erturned
In the fierce shock, lie gasping, and expire,
Trampled by fiery coursers : Horror thus
And wild uproar, and desolation reigned
Unrespited."

A young rebel officer moves cautiously among the wounded and dying and dead, on the scene of the late bloody encounter. His large eyes are dilated, his lips compressed ; his breath comes quick and hard like that of a

dying man, as he motions to his men rather than give
them orders, to execute his wishes. He fears each ghastly face will reveal the well remembered features of a relative, a class-mate, or bosom friend. A low moan call-
him to the side of an officer, lying on his face. He carefully
raises him, wipes the black dust away, and lo! a cherished
friend! He lays his hand on the heart. It still beats. He
calls for water, bathes the face and raises him in his arms.
A groan very low and faint comes from the parted lips,
tears rain on the pale face, and an outburst of manly
grief causes the dying man to open his eyes. He sees a
loved class-mate. A sad smile plays like the light of a win-
try sun, for an instant around the purple mouth, and he is
insensible again. "Alton, Alton, my friend, ' Would to
God I had died for thee!'" cried Lieutenant Ambert. The
men gathered around him, and the great hearts leaped to
the eyes, and ran in big drops over the rough faces stained
with powder and blood. He is no longer a foe, they no
longer thirst for his blood. He is raised tenderly in strong
arms, and borne to the hospital. Lieutenant Ambert
watches him night and day. Weeks of suffering and the
loving care of two lovely women, Mrs. Lieutenant Ambert
and Pauline DeSaye, brought him to a state warranting a
careful removal to New Orleans, to the home of Mrs.
Ambert. A relapse was the consequence, and a fever ensued. The physician gave him up to die, a clergyman
was called, and at Lieutenant Alton's request united him
and his frantic Pauline, in the holy bonds of marriage,
in the presence of Madam De Saye, who already loved him
with a mother's fondness; indeed, it was impossible to look
into his sunny blue eyes, and ingenuous face, and not become attached to him,—so Pauline thought. As the crisis
of the fever approached, she hung over him, unwilling to
be relieved for a moment, as if calmly resolved to die with
him. The crisis came. The morning broke gray and chilly, the mist creeping through the open casements like spirits from a "city of silence," throwing a death dew on the
faces of Pauline and him she would have died to save

11

The physician returning after but two hours' absence, was shocked to find his patient gone, as he supposed, and the young wife fallen, apparently as lifeless, forward on his bosom. Pauline had listened to the last sigh of her lover, and throwing herself on his pillow, swooned.

> " Alas, the love of woman ! it is known
>   To be a lovely and a fearful thing ;
> For all of theirs upon that die is thrown,
>   And if 'tis lost, life has no more to bring
>   To them, but mockeries of the past alone ! "

Pauline had seen her mother looking exhausted and worn-out, and persuaded her to retire for a little rest. Half an hour after, Lieutenant Alton rose in the bed, a faint sigh only escaping him, the terrified Pauline threw herself on the pillow beside him, and swooned. The whole house was like a church yard, so noiseless and still. The physician rang the bell, took up Pauline and bore her into the open air. The servants came, but at the sight of their loved young mistress, fled through the house crying " Miss'es Lena dead ! " The household gathered round her, making every effort to restore her to consciousness. At last the light of life came to the staring eyeballs, but seeing the anxious faces hanging over her, she appeared to comprehend it all, and swooned again. She was borne to her chamber, and a brain fever supervening, she lay in blessed unconsciousness of her sorrows for ten days ; and when God in his mercy restored her reason, the first eyes she looked into were those of an angel ! ay those of one dearer to her than all the angels in heaven — her husband's ! As time sped on, our dead restored to life, lived but for each other. Every ray of intelligence respecting the war was kept from Lieutenant Alton, but there were times when he seemed to realize his position — an officer of the Government — a captive, doubly indebted to his captors for life — and a — husband ! Long hours he would sit and ponder, thinking of that terrible day, — of his comrades in arms, — of his noble friend Ambert, of his gentle and loving nurses — and last though not least, of his distracted country ; and he would bow his sick and weak head on his hand and sob like an infant, as if his heart was broken ! Pauline would get her guitar and accompanying it with her delicious voice, soothe his melancholy, causing him to feel as he looked upon her, that he would almost forfeit heaven itself to gaze on the heaven of her face !

In the list of the brave among the reports culled from the national papers, Pauline discovered her husband's name among many of his class-mates and friends. She knew they would be precious to him, and kept them sacredly for him. She surprised him one morning with her treasures in his hand, eagerly devouring their contents while the tears rapidly followed each other over his emaciated face. "In conclusion, it gives me great satisfaction to state that the conduct of the officers and enlisted men of the several batteries was most exemplary. Exposed throughout the day to a galling fire of artillery and small arms, several times charged by cavalry, and more than once abandoned by their infantry supports, both officers and enlisted men manfully stood by their guns with a courage and devotion worthy of the highest commendation. Where all did so well it would be invidious to make distinction, I therefore simply give the names of all the officers engaged. viz. Major Hunt, Captains Carlisle, Ayers, Griffin, Tidball and Arnold. Lieutenants Plat, Ransom, Thompson, Webb, Green, Edwards, Dresser, Wilson, Throckmorton, Cushing, Harris, Butler, Fuller, Lyford, Well, Benjamin, Babbit, Haines, Ames, Hasbrouck, Kensell, Harrison, Reed, Barlow, Noyes, Kirby, and Elderkin." She tenderly took the paper, and led him to the — cigar holder.

"AFTER THE BATTLE."

" Night closed around the conqueror's way,
    And lightnings showed the distant hill,
Where those who lost, that dreadful day —
    Stood few and faint, — but fearless still,
The soldier's hope, the patriot's zeal
    Forever dimmed, forever crossed,
O, who shall say what heroes feel,
    When all but life, and honor 's lost ? "

The last sad hour of Freedom's dream,
    And valor's task, moved slowly by;
While mute they watched till morning's beam,
    Should rise and give them light to die !
There 's yet a world where souls are free,
    Where tyrants taint not nature's bliss ; —
If death that world's bright portal be,
    O, who would live a slave in this ? "

Ione stood with the crowd, in the parlor, to hear the
latest news from the dead and dying ! At length, among
a number of officers that entered the hall, she thought she
saw Lieutenant Mera.   How could she be sure it was he ?
How see him ? She walked the hall rapidly, now leaning
on the balustrade, now going to the window, fearing she
should see him go away. As she turned she saw the piano
open.   Like a flash she thought of his promise to come if
she played the officers' call. She touched the keys softly,
fearing the people would think her wild. She listened, but
he did not come. She thought herself foolish to think he
would remember such a thing at such a time, but she
would try once more, and from very weakness she sat
down on the piano stool, leaned her head on the piano,
and struck the notes, one after another, as firmly and as
distinctly as she could.

"What if he is not there, but is lying on the battle field!" A hand rests on her head. She starts and sees Lieutenant Mera at her side. She lays her hand in his and thanks God that he is safe! she tries to speak, but cannot.

"I am safe; but poor Saberin is in the hospital, badly wounded!"

"She looks in his eyes with a wild stare, and drops her head again on the piano. He bends over her and whispers that she shall go to see him; he will take her now. She rises mechanically and goes to her room. Deeply veiled she returns to him. They thread the thronged streets filled with the terrified residents, and the half-crazed, blood stained and terrible soldiers. They reach the hospital, and stand beside the pallet on which he lies. His eye has no intelligence, but wanders as if in search of some one. His lips are drawn, as if his agonies were more than mortal could bear. His dark curls lay in masses on his pallid brow. Ione trembling violently, leans over him, her eyes set, and lips apart, ready to faint. His eye rests on her a moment, and he raises his hand toward her, but it falls again, and he closes his eyes and murmurs "Mary! Mary!"

Ione grasps Lieutenant Mera's arm, to prevent herself from falling on the couch. He supports her, saying "My poor Ione! How much more must you suffer?" The surgeon came.

Lieutenant Mera asked what he thought, giving him to understand they were very near friends of the wounded officer.

He gave Ione a look of pity, and said, "I imagine he is not dangerously wounded, but his life hangs upon the discretion of his friends," which gentle hint Lieutenant Mera took, and led her away. They entered the carriage, and Ione leaned back and closed her eyes, the fountain was stirred and tears came to her relief. Lieutenant Mera raised her veil and said, "Ione I did wrong to take you to him, he was only raving." The tones of his voice came over her like a dream, reminding her of her first Saturday night

on West Point, when he offered her a chair, and said,
" Rest, Miss Ione ! "

> " Her every sense
> Had been o'erstrung by pangs intense ;
> And each frail fibre of her brain,
> (As bow strings when relaxed by rain,
> The erring arrows launch aside,)
> Sent forth her thoughts all wild and wide."

" No, he was not raving ! I thank God you took me,
that I might know, for a certainty, all I suspected so long.
Why did I ever come where none are true ? Lieutenant
Mera, I told you, I would not act, but who was there to
feel an interest in me, except — — indifferent friends ? "

" Ah, Miss Ione, I an indifferent friend ? My heart is
all your own, and God knows what I have suffered since I
knew you — — because I am poor ! " he muttered bitterly.
He leaned back in the carriage. " Juan Alcantara ! un-
natural man ! "

" Juan Alcantara ! The truest man that ever lived ! I
love that name ! "

" What mean you, Ione ? Juan Alcantara was my un-
natural uncle, for whom I was named."

Ione hid her face in her hands. Her unhappiness seemed to have culminated. Lieutenant Mera forgot all his
own wrongs and griefs to comfort her.

He took her hand and for the second time essayed to put
the mysterious ring on her finger. " Have faith in me,
dearest Ione."

She raised the ring to her lips and the tears flowed un-
restrainedly.

" Ione ! dear Ione ! Why do you weep ? "

" Juan ! you spoke prophetically when you called this
ring the key to your destiny. Your uncle's fortune can be
secured to you by it — but — " she added smiling a love-
smile through her tears, " you must take it with this en-
cumbrance ! " and she put her own little hand in his.

"ARTICLE FOURTEENTH."

"The Column march in Retreat, to march it to the Front."

> " O, Death ! all eloquent, you only prove
> What dust we doat on, when 'tis man we love."

" O, father ! I *must* go to the hospital, if I do not I shall die ! " The eyes of Mr. Greenleaf rested tenderly on his daughter ; great tears stood in his eyes.

" My darling child, it will kill you if you go ! and I fear we cannot see him."

" I *must*, I *must !* " she said, throwing her arms around his neck.

He loosened her hand, to go for the carriage. She rushed to her room and tied a thick veil over her bonnet, that none might recognize the tear-stained face beneath. As they entered the room the surgeon was ordering the nurse to keep him very quiet — and he *might* live.

" O, may I not speak one word to him, doctor ? " Mary cried passionately. " May I not hear his voice once more ! "

" Please be quiet, madam," the surgeon answered. " He is very weak, and does not recognize any one."

Mary threw back her veil, and regardless of everything, knelt at the side of him she loved, and whispered " Ulm ! " At the familiar sound, he opened his eyes a moment with a glad look on his death-like face — but the look faded away into one of anguish, and he murmured as before, " Mary, Mary ! " She shrieked aloud for God to spare him to her, in tones that might have reached the ear of Death, and covered his face with kisses that might have warmed to life the marble statue.

She was gently removed to the carriage, the surgeon telling her that everything should be done to save him; that he would not die.

A few hours after, Mr. Greenleaf came to Ione's room to ask her to go to Mary, she was ill and calling for her.

She ran at once. When she entered the room, Mary was lying with her face covered with her hands. Ione forgot her own sorrow while contemplating the despair of her friend. She stepped softly to her side and whispered, "Mary — dear Mary! do you want me?" The sympathizing voice, so full of tenderness, like Moses' rod, opened the sealed fountain — and an agony of tears came like mercy-drops to relieve her burdened heart. Ione wept in silence — held and caressed the small white hand. When wearied with weeping, Mary looked up and kissed Ione fervently, saying, "I do not blame you, Mary! nor — him for loving you — he could not help it."

Ione saw that Mary's eyes were fixed on Lieutenant Saberin's class-ring, adorning her own fair hand. Their eyes met — Mary covered hers with her hand, Ione slipped off the ring from her finger and attempted to put it on that of her friend.

"No, no! dearest Ione, it was placed on your hand by one who had a right to place it there."

"Mary, said Ione, solemnly, "He had no right to place on my finger any ring when his heart was *yours*. You were engaged to him, were you not?"

"Oh, yes!" sobbed Mary, "Years ago, but he has ceased to love me!"

"Do not deceive yourself wilfully, Mary," and Ione persuaded her to lay her aching temples on the pillow, while she rehearsed the short and simple story of her acquaintance with and betrothal to Lieutenant Saberin, ending with the scene at the hospital. "So you see dearest Mary, your hold on his heart, was the one ruling 'strong in death.'"

"Oh, say not that! God forbid that he should die now! He will not restore him to me, only to tear him away again!"

Ione soothed her as best she could, and promised to go every day to the hospital with her, which she faithfully performed.

"ABOUT FACE."

Before the threatening storms that settled darkly over our proud Capital, Madam Maryglot decamped to the city of brotherly love, Philadelphia. Ione wrote to her every week, and such letters! Pauline had sent her brother word by the safest conveyance, assuring him of the health and safety of "her prisoner," and as Mary Greenleaf was gradually restored to light and life, all her secrets were duly forwarded to the grand safety fund — the capacious heart of that good lady! From her we learn that Ione and Captain Mera, Mary Greenleaf and Captain Saberin, — captivating as a penitent as he had been killing as a beau — and being fearfully stung by his irate conscience, as all Captain Saberins, I presume are — and quite cured of his jealousy of "sublime salad oil," as he persisted in calling Mary's foreign lover, (who turned out to be a Turk instead of a Russian) — had enticed the chaplain of the house to prevent further mishaps by bow-stringing all parties with the silken bands of Hymen — a temporary arrangement however — as when peace, the Heavenly dove with the olive branch in her beak, shall again brood over our beloved land, they are to order cards regularly from Gimbrides, and inundate the whole country with them. Madam Maryglot fell back exhausted in a fit of laughter, mingled with tears, tears of thanksgiving that the sorrows of her young favorites were turned to joy — laughter — for she began the Latin quotation, " Quod Deus bene vertat." "May God direct it to a good end " — translating it from habit — when Lieutenant Colonel Burlyton came up before her mind's eye, as she remembered him bowing before Mrs. Bobaline, repeating like a raving maniac, quotations from every language he had ever seen or heard. The recollection came near strangling her. Be-

11*

coming a little composed she adjusted her spectacles, three pairs of them, to take a survey of the Future. Shall we, my patient reader, borrow her spectacles to see what she sees? *Spectacles* 1*st.* The most refreshing of country villages, everything new and fresh as the picture of a village. *The mansion* of the place, in a park of forest trees facing the Fifth Avenue of the town. Lieutenant Saber-in crowning himself, a la Napoleon I. or in the parlance of the rural districts, jumping over the broom-stick. There was happiness worth looking at. *Spectacles* 2*d.* A quiet commotion in the streets of San Francisco, on account of the arrival of a military cortege. A huge San Franciscan full-dress party preparatory to a voyage to China to look af-ter the chop-sticks, in English " the spoons." *Spectacles* 3*d.* New Orleans at night. Paris boiled down! Pauline De Saye Alton wrapped in a misty dream of the past, re-gards her lord reclining on the eider-down couch, in that dolce far niente so peculiarly his own, and so very becom-ing to him. He is enveloping his fine head in a saturnian halo, whiffed lazily through his glittering teeth, and the brown curls of his idolized mustache.

None of my heroes have " lumbered the army down with poor wives ! "

DIXI.

NEW BOOKS

And New Editions Recently Issued by

CARLETON, PUBLISHER,

(Late RUDD & CARLETON,)

413 *BROADWAY, NEW YORK.*

———————

———————

Les Miserables.

Victor Hugo's great novel—the only complete unabridged translation. Library Edition. Five vols. 12mo. cloth, each, $1.00.

The same, five vols. 8vo. cloth, $1.00. · Paper covers, 50 cts.

The same, (cheap ed.) 1 vol. 8vo. cloth, $1.50. paper, $1.00.

Les Miserables—Illustrations.

26 photographic illustrations, by Brion. Elegant quarto, $3.00.

Among the Pines,

or, Down South in Secession Time. Cloth, $1.00, paper, 75 cts.

My Southern Friends.

By author of "Among the Pines." Cloth, $1.00. paper, 75 cts.

Rutledge.

A powerful American novel, by an unknown author, $1.50.

The Sutherlands.

The new novel by the popular author of "Rutledge," $1.50.

The Habits of Good Society.

A hand-book for ladies and gentlemen. Best, wittiest, most entertaining work on taste and good manners ever printed, $1.50.

The Cloister and the Hearth.

A magnificent new historical novel, by Charles Reade, author of "Peg Woffington," etc., cloth, $1.50, paper covers, $1.25.

Beulah.

A novel of remarkable power, by Miss A. J. Evans. $1.50.

Artemus Ward, His Book.
The racy writings of this humorous author. Illustrated, $1.25.

The Old Merchants of New York.
Entertaining reminiscences of ancient mercantile New York City, by " Walter Barrett, clerk."   First Series. $1.50 each.

Like and Unlike.
Novel by A. S. Roe, author of "I've been thinking," &c. $1.50.

Orpheus C. Kerr Papers.
Second series of letters by this comic military authority. $1.25.

Marian Grey.
New domestic novel, by the author of "Lena Rivers," etc. $1.50.

Lena Rivers.
A popular American novel, by Mrs. Mary J. Holmes, $1.50.

A Book about Doctors.
An entertaining volume about the medical profession. $1.50.

The Adventures of Verdant Green.
Humorous novel of English College life.   Illustrated. $1.25.

The Culprit Fay.
Joseph Rodman Drake's faery poem, elegantly printed, 50 cts.

Doctor Antonio.
A charming love-tale of Italian life, by G. Ruffini, $1.50.

Lavinia.
A new love-story, by the author of " Doctor Antonio," $1.50.

Dear Experience.
An amusing Parisian novel, by author " Doctor Antonio," $1.00.

The Life of Alexander Von Humboldt.
A new and popular biography of this *savant*, including his travels and labors, with introduction by Bayard Taylor, $1.50.

Love (L'Amour.)
A remarkable volume, from the French of Michelet. $1.25.

Woman (La Femme.)
A continuation of " Love (L'Amour)," by same author, $1.25.

The Sea (La Mer.)
New work by Michelet, author " Love" and " Woman," $1.25.

The Moral History of Woman.
Companion to Michelet's " L'Amour," from the French, $1.25

Mother Goose for Grown Folks.
Humorous and satirical rhymes for grown people,   75 cts

The Kelly's and the O'Kelly's.
Novel by Anthony Trollope, author of " Doctor Thorne," $1.50